THE COLD DAUGHTER

THOMAS FINCHAM

The Cold Daughter
Thomas Fincham

Copyright © 2017
All Rights Reserved.

AUTHOR'S NOTE
This book is a work of fiction. Names, characters, places and incidents are products of the author's imagination or are used fictitiously. Any resemblance to actual events or locales or persons, living or dead, is entirely coincidental.

The scanning, uploading and distribution of this book via the internet or any other means without the permission of the publisher is illegal and punishable by law. Please purchase only authorized electronic editions, and do not participate in or encourage electronic piracy of copyrighted materials. Your support of the author's rights is appreciated.

Visit the author's website:
www.finchambooks.com

Contact:
contact@finchambooks.com

Join my Facebook page:
https://www.facebook.com/finchambooks/

LEE CALLAWAY SERIES

1) The Cold Daughter
2) The Gone Sister
3) The Falling Girl
4) The Invisible Wife
5) The Missing Mistress
6) The Broken Mother
7) The Guilty Spouse
8) The Unknown Woman
9) The Lost Twins
10) The Lonely Widow

ONE

Sharon Gardener woke up with a splitting headache. She shut her eyes and hoped the pain would go away, but it didn't. She squinted at the alarm clock on the side table. The time was well past nine in the morning.

Next to the clock was a half-empty glass of water, and next to it was a bottle of prescribed sleeping medication. She must have taken one too many. She had to be careful, though. She once made the mistake of mixing alcohol with the pills. Had it not been for her husband, she probably would not have woken up that time.

She looked over at the other side of the bed. Her husband was not there. She was not expecting him to be, either. They had been going through a rough patch. They had fought many times before, but somehow, they always managed to get back together. But this time was different. She knew her marriage was over, and it was her fault.

She could not completely blame herself for its ending, though. There was not much love in the relationship to begin with. Hers was a marriage of necessity. Paul was a kind and caring man, and he loved and doted on their daughter.

She got up from the bed and moved to the bathroom. She turned on the light switch. The light nearly blinded her. She waited a few seconds and opened her eyes.

She stared at herself in the mirror.

She had shoulder-length hair that was dyed red. Her skin was smooth without a single wrinkle to be seen anywhere. This was not due to her age but to the work of a highly-skilled plastic surgeon. Her lips were plump and full, but recently, they were looking a bit thinner. She would need to get them injected again.

She turned her body to the side and examined her stomach. She was still in great shape. She used to be a cheerleader in high school. All the cool boys and jocks were after her. She knew the power her body had on men, which was why she still watched what she ate. Her shapely figure also benefited from her regular trips to the gym and yoga classes.

She smiled at the last thought.

She took a long shower. She normally took one before going to bed, but last night, she lacked the time.

The hot steam reinvigorated her mind and her body, and her headache dissolved in an instant.

She dried herself and dressed in a jumpsuit before she made her way downstairs. She half-expected her husband to be in the kitchen. He was an early riser, and he always put the coffee on to brew. But after their last argument, he was sleeping in the guesthouse.

She walked over to the living room and peeked out the window.

Odd, Paul's car is still in the driveway, she thought. *He's normally at work by now.*

She walked back to the kitchen and proceeded to make breakfast.

As she sat down to eat, a thought came to her mind: *Where's Kyla?*

Their daughter was a junior at the local university. She was majoring in Classical Studies. Paul was dead set against it. He wasn't sure how learning about Greek and Roman history would help her get a job. Sharon agreed with him, but that did not mean she would go against her daughter's wishes. If Kyla wanted to study something with low employment potential, then so be it. The only thing that mattered was that her daughter was happy.

Sharon walked down the hall and checked the home office. It used to be Paul's, but ever since Kyla began going to college, she had made it her study room.

Her backpack and books were still on the table.

Sharon returned to the kitchen and examined Kyla's semester schedule, which was stuck to the refrigerator door by a magnet. She had put her schedule there to remind herself of Kyla's class times.

Sharon ran her finger over the dates. Kyla had Greek Literature this morning. She shook her head. Kyla must have been out late last night with her friends. She was likely still in bed.

On any other day, Sharon would have let her sleep, but her next class was only an hour away. If Sharon woke her up now, Kyla could definitely make it to class.

She went upstairs and knocked on the bedroom door. "Kyla, darling. It's morning, and you're late for class." She waited, and when there was no response, she knocked again. "Kyla, you're late for class," she said.

She turned the door handle and found her door was unlocked.

"Darling, I'm coming in," she warned, in case her daughter got mad at her for barging in.

The room was dark, but Sharon could see an outline on the bed.

"Kyla," she whispered. "It's time to get up."

She flipped the light switch.

Her hand instantly went over her mouth to stifle a scream.

Kyla Gardener lay on the bed with her eyes closed. The front of her dress was soaked in red, and so was the pillow and bedsheet.

Sharon ran out into the hall, fell to her knees, and began to wail in agony.

TWO

Detective Gregory Holt had thick arms, thick hands, and a thick neck. His head was shaved clean, and the skin on his head was wrinkled. His eyes were small and black, and they darted from one spot to another as if taking everything in.

His shirt collar was tight around his neck, but he made no effort to loosen the button. Holt was six-four and weighed close to two hundred and fifty pounds.

He rubbed the wedding ring on his finger three times. He did this before every new investigation. The gesture reminded him of why he chose to be a detective. He wanted to protect his loved ones, and to do that he had to put criminals behind bars.

Holt graduated from the police academy first in his class. He rose through the ranks, starting as a patrol officer, then making detective, and rising all the way to staff sergeant. He missed being a detective, however, and to the dismay of his wife, he requested a demotion.

He felt he could do more good on the streets than behind a desk.

He made his way up to the house. There was a black Audi and a silver Lexus parked in the driveway. They looked shinier than his ten-year-old Toyota Camry. His wife had been bugging him to upgrade to a newer model, but he knew it would be tight on his detective's salary. Maybe he could have considered it when he was a staff sergeant, but that was behind him.

His wife enjoyed driving her two-year-old Prius, which he paid for. Her happiness meant more to him than anything else in the world. So what if he owned a decade-old car? It didn't bother him, so why should it bother anyone else?

He knew he would have to make sacrifices when he gave up the extra pay and the corner office. Detective work involved long hours and a ton of grunt work. The rewards only came when he solved a case. And most cases ended up turning cold.

Greg Holt loved every minute as a detective, though. The rush of adrenaline when he chased a lead. The satisfaction when he put a perpetrator in jail. There was nothing that compared.

He turned and took a look back. A strand of yellow police tape circled the front of the property. *Good*, he thought. *I don't want anyone messing up my crime scene.*

He went inside the house. He was approached by a uniformed police officer. The officer recognized him and eased up.

"Where is it?" Holt demanded.

"Upstairs. The second bedroom on the right," the officer replied.

Holt took each step deliberately. He was never in a hurry for anything. There was no point in rushing. He would eventually get there.

He entered the room and found a woman leaning over a body on the bed.

Detective Dana Fisher was five-five, one hundred and ten pounds, with dark shoulder-length hair. Her green eyes were large and expressive. Her nose was thin and pointed upward, and it moved whenever she opened her mouth.

Fisher had moved up the ranks like Holt, but she made it known to those around her that she would not stop until she became captain. Holt admired her ambition, but he felt she was better suited for detective work. That did not mean he would not support her if an opportunity for promotion ever arose. Plus, he liked working with her. She was as determined to solve a case as he was.

"You wanna fill me in?" he asked her.

THREE

"Victim is Caucasian, age twenty, around five-foot-three by my estimate," Fisher replied, "and from a cursory examination, it looks like she was stabbed to death."

Holt leaned over and saw thick blood spread across the victim's chest. Her eyes were closed, but it was easy to see she was young. She had long blonde hair that fell across the pillow. Her lips were thin and parted, exposing two of her front teeth. Her face was round and had started to turn puffy. Holt knew from experience when the organs stopped functioning, the body started to retain water.

Fisher said, "I don't see any lacerations on any part of her body except the chest."

"You think she was stabbed while asleep?" he asked.

"That would be my guess, what with the amount of blood around her."

"Looks like she was still dressed from the night before," Holt said. The victim was wearing a light blue dress that went down to her knees, and she still had on matching high heels.

"So she comes home after a party and goes straight to bed," Holt said. "Then someone enters her room and stabs her?"

Fisher looked at him. "Do you think it was an intruder?"

"We can check the locks to see if it was a break and enter."

Holt thought of something. "Who found the body?"

"The mother."

"Where was she last night?"

"I haven't had a chance to speak to her yet."

It was Fisher's turn to think of something. "What if the victim dressed for the party but never left?"

"That's plausible."

There was a commotion out in the hall. They heard voices. They turned when a man came racing into the room.

"Where is she? Let me see her!" he yelled.

Holt stuck his massive arm out to stop the man from getting near the body. The last thing he wanted was for the bereaved to contaminate the crime scene.

The same police officer from downstairs came into the room. "I tried to stop him, but he got through," he said.

Holt glared at him. The officer's incompetence nearly destroyed evidence that might be in the room.

Holt gently but forcibly escorted the man back out into the hall.

"That's my daughter," the man said, pointing into the room.

"Your name, sir?" Holt asked.

"Paul Gardener," he replied between heavy breaths.

Paul Gardener was slim with thinning hair. He had stubble on his cheeks from the night before. He looked to be five-seven and close to a hundred and fifty pounds. He wore round spectacles, and his eyes were glassy and moist.

"Mr. Gardener, I need you to calm down."

"How is Kyla?" Paul asked. "Is she okay?"

"I'm afraid not," Holt replied.

"What happened to her?"

"If you let us do our job, we might have answers for you."

Hot tears began to stream down Gardener's face. Holt suddenly felt sorry for him. No parent deserved to see their child this way. It was beyond cruel.

Holt turned to the officer standing next to Gardener. "Please escort Mr. Gardener back downstairs and make sure he stays there until we are done."

"Yes, sir," the officer said, eager to make up for his earlier mistake.

The officer placed his hand on Gardener's elbow, turned him around, and led him down the hall.

Fisher said, "Look."

Holt turned to her.

She nodded toward Gardener. Holt was still confused.

"His shirt," Fisher said.

Holt looked, and his eyes widened. There was a red stain on the back of Gardener's golf shirt.

"Wait!" Holt said.

He moved toward Gardener. He got closer, and he knew instantly what the stain was.

Blood.

"Were you in the room earlier?" Holt asked.

Gardener looked confused. "No."

Holt pointed at the bloodstain. "Can you explain how you got that on your clothing?"

Gardener blinked. "I have no idea."

Holt looked over at Fisher. He could tell she was thinking the same thing. "Mr. Gardener," Holt said. "Do you mind going to the Milton PD to answer a few questions?"

"Why?"

"It would help us get a better understanding of what's going on."

"Am I under arrest?" Gardener asked, looking a little bewildered.

"No, but it would be better if you did so voluntarily."

Gardener stared at Holt. He then glanced over at Fisher and then at the officer.

"Please, Mr. Gardener," Holt said, his voice steely and commanding. "It is in your best interest to cooperate with us. We are here to help."

Gardener swallowed. He then nodded.

Holt turned back to the officer. "Have someone drive Mr. Gardener to the station."

"I'll do it myself," the officer said. He wanted Holt to know he could be relied upon.

"Good," Holt said.

FOUR

Strong winds forced the water onto the sandy beach. The sounds were both peaceful and violent at the same time.

Lee Callaway lay on his stomach with his mouth wide open. His left leg hung over the bed while his right arm was underneath his chin. Drool had accumulated over his hand as he snored in unison with the crashing waves.

The house was a stone's throw from the water. The home was worth close to two million dollars, and it came with its own private beach.

Callaway did not have the money to afford such a place. He was broke, and had been for some time. The only reason he was allowed to stay in such an exclusive property was because of a client.

The soon-to-be-divorced Marla Westerhause was in line to receive her husband's one-hundred-million-dollar real estate empire. Claude Westerhause was a savvy investor, a brilliant businessman, and a world-class philanderer. Claude prided himself for having a keen eye for investment properties, and for being a ladies' man. In some circles, he was nicknamed "Casanova Claude."

Claude relished this title bestowed upon him. His wife, however, loathed that nickname with a vengeance. Claude was not even discreet in his affairs. He took his girlfriends and mistresses to the same restaurants he took his wife to.

The first time Marla laid eyes on Claude was when he was sweeping floors at a French bistro. He had strong arms and a wide chest. He had a prominent nose and a well-defined chin. His hairline was receding, but that did not deter him from chatting up the ladies.

Marla had known for a long time their marriage was over. She stayed with Claude because she loved him and kept believing he would change. She also knew how vindictive he could be. The divorce would be anything but amicable.

Claude already had money hidden in offshore accounts, under numbered companies, behind layers and layers of corporate structures. If Claude wanted the money to disappear, he could do it with the snap of a finger. His numerous lawyers, accountants, and loyal employees would make sure not a trace of that money led to Claude. Marla would not see a penny once the assets were divided up.

Marla never cared for the money, even though she enjoyed a comfortable life. Who did not? But what she valued more was respect. As his wife, Claude embarrassed her by sleeping around with multiple women. Even her friends had begun to pity her for the way she had been tossed aside. She was older than him by a good five years, and as such, she sometimes looked like his mother. She spent money on makeup and minor cosmetic enhancements, but she knew she would never be able to compete with the younger girls.

What irked her most was the fact she had believed in Claude before anyone else did. She used to work at a bank as an investment consultant. She knew the value of saving money, and she also knew where to invest that saved money. She preferred stocks and bonds. She avoided mutual funds as she deemed them too risky. But when the housing market began to appreciate during the nineties (well before the crash), she got involved in a construction project. To protect her investment, Claude volunteered to keep an eye on it. If the project failed to meet certain deadlines, they would pull their money out. He quickly realized he enjoyed overseeing the construction from start to finish. To top it off, they made a good return on their investment.

Marla pulled all her savings, cashed in her 401k, and begged her friends and family for loans in order to fund Claude's very first project, which then led to many bigger projects. Had she not taught him what she knew, he would still be sweeping floors at the French bistro.

Marla was determined to divorce Claude, and she was determined to teach him a lesson for all the pain she had endured.

She was searching for a private investigator when she stumbled upon Callaway's website. She hired him to follow her cheating husband as he went about his many rendezvous. Callaway caught Claude with multiple women. Some were models who had not caught their big break yet, some were students looking to pay their way through school, and some were even high-priced escorts who enjoyed the lifestyle the profession afforded them.

None of them gave Marla enough leverage on Claude. If she confronted him, he would not deny the affairs. He would rub them in her face to show he was still virile after all these years. He would then goad her to divorce him, knowing she would be left with nothing.

Callaway was persistent. He never gave up on finding something on Claude. He hit the jackpot one night when he caught Claude with an attractive blonde woman. He later found out this woman was married to a Russian oligarch who was rumored to be linked to the KGB.

With this information in hand, Marla confronted Claude. He tried to deny this affair, but the photos were irrefutable. They caught him in various compromising positions. Claude was smart enough to know what would happen to him if these photos were to reach the oligarch. He tried to buy the photographs off Callaway. The sum was far more than what Marla paid him. Callaway refused. He always completed his contract, and he never betrayed a client.

Marla took Claude to the cleaners. She got the real estate business and investment properties. She left Claude with enough money to start another business, but this time, he could do so without her encouragement and support.

As a thank-you, she let Callaway stay at her beach house however long he wanted. She was in Switzerland at the time, enjoying the life of a single woman.

Callaway got up and off the bed. He was tall, tanned, and had strands of silver around his temples. He yawned and stretched his body. He glanced out the window and saw the waves crashing onto the beach.

He grinned.

Maybe after I make my coffee, I'll go down and relax on the sand, he thought.

FIVE

Fisher said, "How do you suppose Paul Gardener got blood on his shirt?"

Holt was wondering the exact same thing, but the man's emotion was genuine. Gardener was in anguish when he saw his daughter. Holt had investigated many murders, and he knew enough by now to know who was suffering and who was faking it. Even then, there was no denying the fact that Gardener might have evidence on his clothing.

Holt never liked to jump to conclusions, especially this early in the case. He knew it could derail the entire investigation. Instead of focusing on multiple suspects, the search would become myopic, diverting the police from catching the real killer.

But Holt knew what he saw. It was blood. There was no doubt about it.

"Let's search the house," he said. "We still need to find the murder weapon."

"I'll check downstairs," she said.

He nodded and moved to the master bedroom. It was spacious with bay windows and a fireplace. Holt never understood the point of having a fireplace in the bedroom. Fireplaces used to serve a purpose; they were a place where families would gather to stay warm. Now with HVAC systems, the entire house could be heated with the switch of a button. A king-size bed was in the middle of the room, and across from it was a dresser and a mirror. Nightstands flanked the bed. Holt walked over to one and grabbed a small prescription bottle. They were sleeping pills, and the prescription was made out to Sharon Gardener.

He did a quick walk-through of the other rooms before he made his way downstairs. There he found the medical examiner and her team entering the premises.

"It's the bedroom on the right," he said, pointing up.

The medical examiner gave Holt a nod. "You're not joining me, Detective Holt?" she asked.

"I'll be there in a minute."

He watched her go up the stairs. He moved to the kitchen, and through the glass sliding doors, he saw Fisher in the back yard.

He stepped out, walked around a patio set and a small garden, and made his way to her.

"It's the guesthouse," she said, pointing to a structure the size of a two-car garage. It had a brick exterior, a window, and a front door.

"Apparently, Paul Gardener was sleeping here last night," she said.

"How'd you find that out?"

"The wife."

He nodded and went inside. The space was open but cozy. A futon was in the corner. *Gardener must have slept there*, Holt thought. Next to the futon was a recliner, which faced a flat-screen TV.

There was another window and door on the other side of the guesthouse.

"It's the bathroom," Fisher said, catching him staring at the door. "I'm surprised it doesn't have a kitchen. Most guesthouses I've seen do."

"How many guesthouses have you seen?" Holt asked.

She shrugged. "Okay, fine. I've never been in a guesthouse, but I've seen enough on TV."

Holt knew Fisher lived in a cramped one-bedroom apartment. She talked about buying a house or a condo, but with the sudden rise in home prices, she was always finding herself priced out of the market. At the rate housing prices were escalating, she would be lucky to find a fixer-upper. That was another reason she wanted to move up in the force. The extra pay would go a long way in helping her become a homeowner.

There was a coffee table in the middle of the room. Sitting on the table was a bottle of scotch and a half-empty glass. Holt walked over to the table, and with gloved hands, he picked up the bottle and glass.

"It might be better if we bagged these," he said.

SIX

The medical examiner's name was Andrea Wakefield. She was petite with short, cropped hair and round prescription glasses. Her eyes darted inquisitively over the victim's body as if she was recording and storing all pertinent information in the back of her mind.

"I can confirm the victim suffered external as well as internal wounds. The punctures in the upper chest are indicative that she was stabbed. The amount of blood loss further supports this conclusion. I counted four puncture wounds, but after an autopsy I can give you a more definitive number. However, I don't think she died from these wounds."

Holt blinked. "Then how did she die?"

"The victim was choked."

Holt's eyelids rapidly twitched. "What?"

Wakefield pointed to the neck. "The bruising around the victim's throat leads me to believe that she was strangled, possibly by bare hands. The marks aren't straight or aligned. The pressure applied by the hand is never consistent. This tells me a rope or cord was not used. I will further confirm this during the autopsy, of course."

"But how do you know she died from strangulation?"

Wakefield looked at Holt like he asked a stupid question. Maybe he had, but he would have to wait for her answer to find out. She paused to better articulate her response. "It doesn't make sense for someone to stab her and *then* choke her. It would serve no purpose. It would make more sense if the opposite occurred. The perpetrator choked her, and then, just to be safe, he stabbed her."

"Who could do such a thing?" Holt asked. An image of a suspect was forming in his head, but he wanted her opinion. Wakefield came across as introverted, shy, and even aloof. But she was fiercely intelligent and took her job seriously. Over the years, Holt had come to rely on her expertise. It was born out of necessity. A medical examiner's professional opinion mattered greatly in a court of law. If the ME's findings were flawed or without merit, the entire case could be thrown out. Right then, if Wakefield said the victim died of natural causes regardless of the condition of her body, Holt would have to give her conclusion serious consideration. If they did not work in unity, they had no chance of getting a conviction.

Wakefield paused again, considering all scenarios. "This could be a crime of passion. The person responsible may have become enraged, at which time he or she—more likely he, as men exert more brute force—decided to lash out at the victim. Once he realized what he had done, he then stabbed her to 'finish the job,' as they say."

Holt pondered Wakefield's words. They made sense.

"What happened there?" Holt asked, pointing to the victim's mouth. There was swelling on the right side of her upper lip.

"The victim suffered a cut. Most likely, during the altercation leading to her death." Wakefield pulled back the upper lip, exposing a deep red gash. "When the victim was struck, the lip split open when it came in contact with one of the front teeth."

Holt nodded.

He moved away from the body as if to distance himself from the crime itself. He wanted to let the information sink in before he came to any further conclusions.

He did a quick scan of the room. The bed was in the middle, and it had a dresser across from it. Next to the bed was the closet, and on the other side of the wall was a bookshelf. Holt moved his fingers across the books' spines. They were mostly romance novels, with a few erotica mixed in. The only reason Holt knew the genres was because his wife was an avid reader. She could read a book a day. He had even seen her go through ten books in a single week. He never understood her fascination with the written word. The last time he read a book cover to cover was when he was in high school, and that was only for his English class. His life was already filled with so much excitement he did not need stories to keep him entertained.

But the books did tell him something about the victim: she could have been a romantic at heart.

Could her murder be the result of a relationship gone wrong? he thought.

"Are you done?"

The medical examiner's voice snapped him out of his reverie.

He turned to her and blinked.

"Do you want to take another look, or can I take it away?" she asked.

He stared at Kyla Gardener's lifeless body. She looked almost peaceful in her current state.

"No, I'm done," he replied.

SEVEN

Holt went back downstairs. He found Fisher in the home office. She was seated in front of a laptop.

"The property is surrounded by security cameras," she said, her eyes transfixed on the screen.

"Did any of them capture anything useful?" he asked.

"All the images are stored on the laptop's hard drive. Hopefully it has what we are looking for."

He positioned himself behind her so as to get a better view of the monitor. The images were separated into four squares taking up the entire screen. They were black and white, in high-resolution. The top left image showed the driveway. Holt could see the family's cars parked there. The top right camera was aimed at the front door. Members of the crime scene unit were going in and out of the house. The camera on the bottom left showed the back of the house. Holt could see the sliding doors that led from the kitchen to the backyard. The bottom right camera faced the guesthouse. There was no movement there at the moment.

"Let's see how this works," Fisher said, fiddling with the keys and the mouse. She pressed a button, and the images began to move in reverse. She pressed the button again. People and cars zoomed in and out of the frames at higher speeds. She pressed the button once more, and the images slowed to their regular pace. "We should start from when the family got home," she said.

Holt watched as a Lexus pulled into the driveway. The time on the clock read *8:42 PM*. A woman got out of the Lexus. She was carrying shopping bags. Holt could only assume it was Mrs. Gardener. He still had not spoken to her.

In the video, she walked up to the front door and disappeared from view.

They watched as the time ticked by on the screen. Close to an hour later, an Audi pulled up next to the Lexus. Paul Gardener emerged from the driver's side door. He was wearing the same golf shirt that later got a red stain. Holt squinted and leaned closer to the monitor.

Gardener looked casual as he removed a briefcase from the back seat, closed the door, and pressed a button on his car key. The Audi's headlights blinked as the doors automatically locked. He then flipped through his key ring, found the right one, and made his way up to the front door. He then disappeared from view.

Holt's eyes focused. Gardener did not look like someone who would be responsible for a horrific crime later that night. But then again, the medical examiner believed it was a crime of passion, so anything was possible.

A couple of minutes later, Gardener appeared at the back of the house. He was still carrying the briefcase in one hand, but he was holding a bottle in the other. Most likely, the same bottle of scotch found on the coffee table in the guesthouse.

Could alcohol have played a factor in what happened? Holt wondered. Alcohol had the power to change people, often for the worse. The quiet became loud. The meek became bold. The peaceful became violent.

Gardener walked up to the guesthouse and went inside.

Holt and Fisher waited for something to happen. When nothing did, Fisher clicked on the button to speed up the images. They watched as the clock ticked at the bottom of the screen.

Suddenly, all four screens went blank, and just as suddenly, they came back up.

"Stop," Holt said. "Go back."

The screen went blank, and then the images reappeared. "Let it play," Holt said.

They watched as the seconds ticked by.

At precisely 11:34 PM, the screen went blank. When it reappeared, the clock read *2:38 AM*.

"What happened to the three hours in between?" Holt asked, confused.

"I have no idea," Fisher replied. "It looks like someone turned off the cameras."

Holt's face darkened.

EIGHT

Sharon Gardener tightly hugged herself. Even though she had a shawl over her shoulders, she still shivered. Her eyes were red and raw, and every so often, she would break down in tears.

Holt and Fisher sat across from her on the living room sofa. Holt let her grieve. Nothing compared to the loss of a child. He believed in the old saying *Time heals all wounds,* but only up to a point. Time would not heal Sharon's wounds over losing Kyla when she was so young. Each year, she would be reminded of what could've been had Kyla been alive. She would carry this weight for the rest of her life.

Fisher took the lead, and Holt was grateful she did. Talking with grieving people was never easy. She said, "Mrs. Gardener, can you tell us what happened last night?"

"Call me, Sharon."

Fisher gave her a smile. "Okay."

Sharon grabbed a tissue, wiped her nose, and said, "I came home from shopping last night. I had a headache, so I took my sleeping medication, and I went straight to bed."

That explains the glass of water and the pills, Holt thought.

"What about your daughter?" Fisher asked.

"What about her?"

"Was she home when you got back from shopping?"

Sharon looked away, thinking. "I'm not sure. I never went to her room to check. Maybe I should have." She bit her bottom lip to control her emotions. "Kyla's an adult, so I've stopped monitoring where she goes and when she comes back. I wanted her to have as much independence as possible. My husband, on the other hand, thought we should pay more attention to who she hung around with. He was worried something bad could happen to her."

Fisher jumped right in. "Speaking of your husband, are you and he going through a separation? We noticed his belongings in the guesthouse."

Holt understood why Fisher asked such a question. Sometimes during a nasty divorce or separation, one parent may lash out at the children out of spite to hurt the other parent. This resulted in many cases of murder-suicide.

"We didn't want our family and friends to know just yet, but Paul and I are separated. We just haven't filed the divorce paperwork yet."

"And how was your daughter dealing with this situation?"

"I thought she was handling it better than we were. Paul and I have been married from the time Kyla was born. There have been many good years in the marriage, but also many bad years. Kyla saw how unhappy we were, and she encouraged us to split. We never did it before because Paul and I are both children of divorced parents. We know how it impacted us growing up, and we didn't want Kyla to go through that."

"And how was your husband handling the separation?" Fisher asked.

"Paul's a quiet and reserved person. He doesn't let out his emotions easily. I'm the opposite. I can be loud and erratic when I'm worked up. Maybe that's why our marriage didn't last. But to answer your question, I don't know how Paul's dealing with the situation. Maybe you can ask him yourself. Do you know where he is? I haven't seen him since I woke him up this morning."

So, she doesn't know her husband is at the police station, Holt thought.

Holt said, "Did you notice anything unusual about your husband when you woke him up?"

"Like what?" Sharon asked, confused.

"Was he acting… suspiciously?"

She looked away again. "I don't know… I don't know anything…"

She put her hands over her face.

Holt let silence fill the room for a moment. "Mrs. Gardener—Sharon, can you remember anything from your interaction with your husband?" he asked.

She sighed. "After I called 9-1-1, I ran straight to the guesthouse. I found him sleeping on the recliner. I called out his name, but he did not wake up. I yelled, and still, he did not stir. For a second, I thought he was… *dead*."

"Dead?" Holt said.

She nodded. "Paul's not a deep sleeper, but this morning, I couldn't get him to open his eyes. When the officer arrived at the house, I explained to him what was going on, and he had to physically shake Paul awake. When I told Paul about Kyla, he ran out of the guesthouse and into the house."

By then, we were at the scene, examining the body, Holt thought.

Sharon said, "After that, I don't know where Paul went."

Holt thought of something. "When we were going through your security cameras, we noticed that for a couple of hours, the cameras were turned off. Do you know why?"

She stared at them. "I'm not sure. They are always on during the night and even the day, when we are not home."

"Are they automatically turned on, or do you have to do it manually?" Fisher asked.

"Manually. They are linked to our home alarm."

"Who knows the passwords?"

"I do, and Paul and Kyla, too."

Holt said, "Would your husband have a reason to turn them off?"

"I don't know, but why would he?"

That's something we will ask him, he thought.

A member of the crime scene unit entered the room. "You guys need to see this," he said.

They followed him outside. He led them to the Audi and pointed to the glove compartment. Fisher grabbed a pair of latex gloves and leaned in.

She pulled out what looked like a kitchen knife. The blade was stained with blood.

Holt turned to Sharon. "Whose car is this?" He already knew the answer, but he wanted to see Sharon's reaction.

Her eyes were full of disbelief.

"It's my husband's car," she replied.

NINE

The Callaway Private Investigation Office was located above a soup and noodle restaurant. To get to his office, you had to go behind the building, take the narrow metal stairs up, and knock on a black metal door.

There were no signs outside informing patrons such an office existed. There were two reasons for that. One: there was no space to put a sign. Two: Callaway didn't want unexpected visitors.

Over the years, his reckless behavior had gotten him in trouble more times than he could count. There were wives whose husbands were looking for him because he got involved with them. There were unsavory people he borrowed money from that he never paid back. There were even old landlords to whom he neglected to pay rent before he up and left.

Callaway resented his actions. He never imagined he would become one of those people who were always taking advantage of others. He firmly believed he was not.

The wives he slept with? Their husbands were doing the same thing. In fact, the wives were mostly his clients. They hired him to dig up dirt on their cheating husbands. These women had been ignored, disrespected, and even abused in some cases. He made them feel beautiful and worthy again. He always vowed to stop mixing business with pleasure, but it was far harder than it seemed.

The money he owed was mostly to criminals and lowlifes. They had not gotten their money the right way, and as such, Callaway did not feel too guilty for keeping some of it. He had also vowed to stop associating with such people. They were known to get physically violent when they did not get their money back.

As far as the landlords were concerned, most of them barely took care of their property, and a lot of their properties were not even up to code. The first landlord Callaway refused to pay was because the roof was so badly leaking there was a strong possibility it would cave in. The second landlord would shut off the heat during the winter to save money, and the last landlord did little about the rat infestation.

His current landlord was not any better. His unit had no air conditioning, and during the winter months, the heating barely warmed the small room. Worse still, the room was cramped and windowless. Even if Callaway wanted to install an air conditioner on his own dime, there was no window to set one up in.

During the summer months, though, Callaway would leave the front door open and place a running fan in front of it, allowing cool air to circulate through the room. When the room turned chilly in the winter, Callaway would run a small heater, which he hid behind a Bankers Box underneath his desk. If his landlord ever paid him a surprise visit, she would never know he had one. She repeatedly complained about how high her electricity bill had become ever since he moved in. He could tell her off if he wanted to, but he was not a tenant who paid his rent on time. It was better to keep his grievances to himself.

In short, he had become the clichéd private investigator from the pulp mysteries he read as a kid. He drank, he gambled, he womanized, and most times, he did not have two pennies to rub together. He also had an ex-wife and daughter he barely saw. His life was anything but desirable, and he had no one to blame but himself.

Callaway was once a deputy sheriff in a small town. He had a house, a wife, and a small child. The money was stable, and the crime rate was close to nonexistent. It was a quiet and peaceful existence. It should have been enough for any sensible man. But Callaway was anything but sensible. He wanted excitement and adventure, and when he moved to Milton, he got that and more. There was even danger to contend with.

When confronted with the truth, a few cheating husbands had resorted to pulling a gun on him. If it were not for his quick thinking, he would not still be alive.

He shut the door to his office and took a seat behind a small desk. There was a sofa in the corner, which Callaway had come to use as a bed. He was glad he did not need it at the moment. The beach house was far more comfortable than the springy sofa.

He removed a laptop from his bag and placed it on his desk. While the computer loaded, he grabbed the remote and turned on the flat-screen TV, which hung on the wall. The TV was the only expensive item in the office. A client had gifted it to him a couple of months ago, right after Callaway had been kicked out of his apartment.

The TV was always tuned to the 24-hour news channel. Callaway wanted to know what was happening in the city. This allowed him to seek out potential clients.

He pulled out his cell phone and checked his messages. That was another reason Callaway did not need a sign outside his office. If people wanted to get in touch with him, they could always call him.

He knew word of mouth was the best advertisement. Old clients were always referring new clients to him. Every once in a while, he would drop a business card where he thought someone could use his services. His website had his contact information, and a telephone number was taped on his office door. If someone ever called, they did not need to meet him at his office either. His motto was: *Don't come to me. I'll come to you.*

TEN

Paul Gardener was still dressed in the clothes he was wearing when he first met the detectives, including the bloodstained golf shirt. A police officer had not left Gardener's side at any time, even when he went to the bathroom. There was no telling what Gardener could do to the evidence if he was left alone.

Holt stared at him across the table. Gardener looked dazed and confused. He asked every so often why he was at the police station and not at home with his family. He complained of a headache and asked for painkillers. He was provided a cup of coffee instead. The department was not about to provide medication to a suspect unless it was on the advice of a medical professional.

Holt now believed Gardener was the sole suspect in this case. It was just a matter of how long it took for him to confess.

"Can you tell me what's going on?" Gardener asked, almost pleading.

Fisher, who was sitting next to Holt, said, "Mr. Gardener, your daughter was found dead in her bedroom. Do you know how that could have happened?"

"How would I know? And why are you asking me this?" Gardener shot back.

Fisher ignored Gardener's question. "Do you know how you got blood on your shirt?"

Holt wanted to seize the golf shirt as evidence, but he could not do that until they arrested Gardener. There should be no doubt to a judge or jury that the evidence was found on Gardener, not planted by the police after the fact.

"I have no idea how it got on me," Gardener said. "Do I need a lawyer?"

"You're entitled to one, but you are not under arrest. We are just having a conversation."

"It feels like I'm being interrogated."

Holt moved forward, his elbows on the table. "We are just trying to find out how your daughter ended up dead."

Gardener stared at him and nodded.

Fisher said, "Can you go over what happened last night? And please, don't spare any details. It could be vital."

"Where do you want me to start?" Gardener asked.

"From the time you got home."

Gardener took a deep breath. "Okay. Um… let me see… I came back from work, and I went straight to the guesthouse."

"What happened next?" Fisher asked.

"I had a glass of scotch and watched some TV."

"Do you drink every night?"

"No, I'm not a big drinker, but yesterday I had a tough day at work."

"What do you do?"

"I'm president and CEO of a small software company. We create apps for mobile devices."

"So you went to the guesthouse and had a drink, then what?" Fisher asked.

"I watched a basketball game."

"Who was playing?"

Gardener closed his eyes a moment. "Cleveland and Golden State."

"Who won?"

"I'm not sure. It was a late game. I fell asleep before the start of the fourth quarter."

"What time was it?"

"What time was what?"

"What time did you fall asleep?"

Gardener licked his lips. "I don't know, eleven or eleven-thirty, maybe."

Holt placed his palm on the table. "Do you know why anyone would turn off the security cameras?"

"What?" Gardener replied, surprised. "We leave them on all night."

"They weren't on last night."

"How could that be? I didn't disable them. I was in the guesthouse all night."

"You said your company makes apps for mobile devices, is that correct?" Holt asked.

"Yes."

"What kind of apps?"

"We're a boutique software company; we make products based on customer demands. If a restaurant owner wants to know how much money is going in and out of his cash register in real-time, we can create an app that links the software in the register to the app."

"Can you link your home security system to an app?" Holt asked.

"Of course, it's now become standard with all security devices."

"Do you have such an app on your phone?"

Gardener opened his mouth but then stopped. After a brief pause, he said, "I do."

An awkward silence filled the interrogation room.

Fisher said, "What's your relationship with your daughter?"

"I love Kyla. She's my little girl." Gardener's eyes turned moist, but he quickly controlled his emotions. He looked Holt and Fisher directly in the eye. "I know what you guys are thinking, but I did not hurt my daughter. I can't imagine anyone doing that to their own child."

Fisher changed the subject. "What's your relationship with your wife?"

Gardener sat back in his chair and crossed his arms. "You can tell from the way we are sleeping in separate beds that it's not great."

"Why is that?"

"Are you married?" Gardener asked.

Fisher shook her head, "But Detective Holt's been married for twenty-three years," she said.

Gardener turned to Holt. "Then you know the problems married couples go through."

Holt did. Marriage was not just about two people vowing to stay together through good times and bad times. Marriage was about giving up a lot of yourself for the other person. Holt had sacrificed so much for the sake of the union, but he did not regret anything he had given up. He could not imagine his life without Nancy.

Fisher said, "After you fell asleep, what happened?"

"The next thing I remember, it's morning, and I was woken up by a police officer. I asked what was going on, and Sharon told me about Kyla. I didn't believe her at first. Sharon was hysterical and not making any sense. I rushed over to the house to see for myself, and that's when I saw you guys."

So far, Gardener's story matched what they had learned from the surveillance footage and Sharon's statement. But there was one thing missing. There was blood on the side of the Audi's passenger door, which prompted the CSU officer to examine the car. Holt believed the blood could only have come from Gardener's shirt, and the blood on the shirt could only have come from Kyla.

Holt said, "We found a knife covered in blood in the glove compartment of your vehicle. Do you want to explain how it got there?"

Gardener's face turned pale. "I think I would like to speak to my lawyer now."

"That's a good idea," Holt said. He turned to Fisher and nodded.

She stood up and said, "Paul Gardener, you are under arrest for the murder of Kyla Gardener."

ELEVEN

Callaway decided to go to a diner and have breakfast. He had enjoyed a cup of coffee at the beach house, but there was no solid food there.

His stomach rumbled as he walked the block to the restaurant.

Joely Paterson was behind the counter, serving hungry customers. She had blonde hair she liked to keep pulled back in a ponytail. She had on a tight-fitting t-shirt with an apron on top.

The half-full restaurant had plenty of places to sit this time in the morning. Normally, Callaway would sit in one of the back corner booths, keeping away from the crowd, but today he grabbed a stool and sat at the counter.

Joely came over. "I've only seen you once since you came back from Fairview. Were you working on another case?" she asked.

Unlike other people, Joely was enamored with Callaway's chosen profession. She, too, wanted more out of life. She dreamed of being a singer, but instead of following her dreams, she got married and then pregnant. Her then-husband worked as an equipment manager for a local rock band. He was away for long periods at a time when the band was on the road. After their last tour, he never came back. He called her from some town and told her he did not see himself married or as a father. He promised he would send her money, but he never did. Joely now had a four-year-old boy to take care of. Fortunately, she had a mother who was willing to help out.

Callaway found her attractive, and he almost convinced her to go out with him. But the moment she became aware of his history, her interest vanished. He reminded her too much of her ex-husband. Callaway had left his wife and daughter to pursue a life of adventure, and he was always behind in his child support payments. He was what she despised in men. They were always looking for a good time but never wanted the responsibility that went with it.

She warmed up to him when she found out about the cases he was involved in, the most important being the murder of Julia Seaborn.

Julia's body was found underneath Milton's Westgate Bridge. When her case turned cold, her family hired Callaway to find her killer. Callaway's search led him to Fairview, and with the help of a reporter, he solved not only Julia's murder but also another girl's. Callaway had hoped the case would be his calling card to fame and fortune, and he would work on more intriguing cases from then on. Unfortunately, not everyone thought private investigators were reliable in solving serious crimes. They trusted the police detectives to do the job. When the money from the Seaborn case ran out, Callaway went back to photographing cheaters and adulterers.

Callaway sighed. "I'm not working on anything worth talking about. What have you been up to?"

"I got a call from a music producer," Joely replied with a wide smile.

"You did?" he asked, surprised.

"He's only worked with local talent, but it could lead to something big, right?"

"Definitely, but how did you find him?"

"He found me. I started posting songs online, which I shared on my social media page. People started listening to them, and they started sharing them with their friends and families. It's not a big following—only a couple hundred people—but I figured I have to start somewhere, you know."

Callaway smiled. "Yeah, sure, good for you. Congrats."

"You're just saying that so I will go out with you."

He shook his head. "No, I really mean it. I hope this is your big break." Callaway knew she desperately wanted a better life for herself and her son. It must not be easy raising a kid on her own. He felt like human waste for the way he had treated his ex-wife. If he could go back and change one thing, it would be the way he walked away from his marriage.

Joely was now beaming. "You know, you just made my day. And for that, you get a free coffee."

"Can I get something to eat too? I'm short on cash."

"Fine, but this is the last time. Bill is already on my case for giving freebies to customers," Joely replied. Bill was a somewhat stingy manager with a by-the-book attitude.

Callaway smiled again. "You have a heart of gold and the voice of an angel."

Joely smiled back. "Stop it. Flattery will not get you an extra meal."

Callaway looked around and found the morning newspaper on a stool. He was flipping through the pages when his breakfast came. It was eggs with toast. There was also a cup of piping hot coffee.

"Enjoy," Joely said.

"Thanks, I will."

He dug in like he had not eaten in days. The plate was empty in a matter of minutes. He was sipping coffee when he saw what was on the diner's TV.

"Do you mind turning up the volume?" he asked Joely.

The TV was showing a police press conference. He recognized Detective Greg Holt, and behind him was Detective Dana Fisher. Microphones were shoved in front of Holt.

Must be another murder, Callaway thought.

Callaway lifted the coffee cup to his lips, but then he quickly set the cup down. He squinted. He then got up and went around the counter, his eyes still glued to the TV. The set was an older model, placed on a top-shelf. Callaway closed in until he was inches away from the screen.

"Hey, you're blocking the view!" a middle-aged man at the counter shouted.

But Callaway was transfixed. He was staring at the house in the background.

"You okay, Lee?" Joely asked.

Without answering her, he turned around and rushed out of the diner.

TWELVE

He was dressed in a two-thousand-dollar Italian suit. His shoes were the finest leather money could buy. He was clean-shaven, and his hair was slicked back. On his wrist was a gold watch with a dial encrusted in diamonds.

Evan Roth was a high-priced lawyer. His clientele were individuals with a net worth in the millions. He earned his B.A. *magna cum laude* from Cambridge University and his law degree from Yale University. His father, Ezra, was a well-known lawyer who kept the infamous mobster, Lou "Shotgun" Marconi, out of prison. Marconi got the nickname after he mowed down a group of rival gang members outside a barbershop.

Ezra had suddenly died in the middle of his closing argument in a high-profile case. Some said he got what he deserved for the way he kept murderers, rapists, and even citizens charged with treason from getting the death penalty.

Roth was in court the day his father fell to the floor in front of the jury. He was as shocked as everyone else. His father was a model of good health. He ate well. He exercised regularly. He even stayed away from tobacco and alcohol. What killed him, Roth found out later, was a heart defect.

His father worked seventy to eighty hours a week. He lived and breathed the law. Every day he was not in court was a bad day for him. This led him to miss his regular health check-ups. Had he gone to the doctor even once, his heart condition would have been noticed, and perhaps he would still be alive.

Roth did not look back in regret. His father was a smart man, and he died doing what he loved. Roth, however, learned from his father's mistakes. He chose not to represent individuals with violent histories, such as drug lords, serial killers, or terrorists. The exposure he could get from such cases would be great, but not the pay. Instead, he went after clients with legit money and who found themselves in difficult situations.

Paul Gardener was such a person. He sat across the table from Roth with his head bowed. Paul had the look Roth had seen too many times over his career: shocked, confused, and scared. Shocked because he never imagined he would be in this position. Confused because he did not know why it happened to him. Scared because he did not know what was going to happen next.

In Roth's experience, it was the innocent that felt the severe effects of the various stages of emotions. Their shock, confusion, and fear was genuine. To them, this was a nightmare they could not wait to wake up from.

Roth believed all his clients were innocent. If he did not, that would make his job more difficult. He never asked his clients if they had done what they were accused of. Even if they tried to confess to him, he simply told them he was the wrong man to confess to. If they wanted to admit their guilt, they should tell the police or their priest. Roth's job was to defend his clients and prove them innocent.

The jury needed to see the conviction in Roth's eyes. If he argued his client's innocence, the jury needed to believe him, and to believe him; they needed to trust him. The only way for that to happen was for him to lay out the facts in such a way the jury had no choice but to give a verdict of not guilty.

Roth unlocked his designer briefcase and pulled out a legal pad. From his suit pocket, he removed a gold-plated pen. "Tell me what happened last night," he said.

THIRTEEN

The press conference had ended when Callaway showed up. To his surprise, the reporters had not dispersed. He realized why when he saw them huddled around Detective Holt.

Callaway had had a few run-ins with Holt, and if you asked him, they were not pleasant. To say Holt did not like private investigators would be an understatement.

Holt had said to Callaway there was no use for people like him. Crime was the police's business. Callaway always replied that with the crime rate so high and the solve rate so low, there was definitely a need for people like him. The police had limited resources, and there was only so much they could do to solve a case. If a private investigator was working in tandem with them, there was no telling how fast a case could be solved. Callaway had even proposed during one of their brief encounters that the Milton PD hire him as a consultant. Holt had shot down the idea even before Callaway had finished his sentence. There was no way he would take such an absurd idea to his superiors. Callaway could not entirely blame him, though. Thanks to his time as a deputy sheriff, Callaway knew the rules and regulations a detective had to follow in order to solve a case. The arrest must be in accordance with procedures. The evidence must be attained within certain guidelines. A witness must not be coerced into providing a statement in favor of the prosecution. Without these policies, a case could be thrown out of court.

Callaway was not bound by any rules except his own. He knew right from wrong. His time in the sheriff's office also gave him the ability to discern what was admissible in court and what was not, but he also was not afraid to bend the rules from time to time in order to solve a case.

When clients hired Callaway, they were fully aware they were hiring not a police officer but a person who was willing to go above and beyond to solve their problems. No police officer would sit in a cold vehicle for hours to catch an adulterer. Their time was better spent on a stakeout to catch a big-time drug dealer or a high-profile criminal.

Maybe that's why Callaway was always struggling for money. People did not value the service he provided to them. He should have known better when he chose to go independent.

He was moving around the crowd when he spotted a familiar figure standing in the corner. Detective Fisher had her arms crossed over her chest and a frown on her face.

"Why so sad?" Callaway asked, walking up to her.

Her frown melted when she saw him. "Lee, what're you doing here?"

"I figured I'd drop by and see what all the commotion is about," he replied.

Callaway and Fisher had once dated—that was another reason Holt did not like him very much. He was new to the city, and she was single and available. She realized at that time that Callaway was not serious about a long-term relationship. She felt he was still dealing with unresolved issues stemming from his marriage.

"You caught the press conference on TV?" she asked.

"Live and in full color."

Fisher shook her head. "I don't think it's a good idea, but Holt disagrees."

"He's relishing every minute in front of the cameras," Callaway said, looking in Holt's direction.

"It's not his fault. The department has been under a lot of pressure from the public, the media, and the mayor. They keep cutting our budget, but they still expect us to meet our mandate."

"Oh, the travesty," Callaway quipped.

Fisher laughed, knowing Callaway was joking. Callaway had been through his share of cutbacks when he was in the sheriff's department. In fact, police department cutbacks were the topic of the first conversation between them.

Fisher was at a party hosted by a friend of hers when Callaway approached her. He knew someone at the party as well, and over a round of drinks, they hit on a topic they were both passionate about. She was furious the government was willing to give tax breaks to the wealthy but not invest more money in those who protected the general population. He did not disagree with her, but he also expressed his belief that people got the politicians they deserved. After all, it was they who elected them.

Fisher said, "Holt feels this case is a slam-dunk, so he wants the public to see the good job we are doing at the Milton PD."

"So, is it a slam-dunk?" Callaway asked with a raised eyebrow.

Her eyes narrowed. "Why're you so interested, Lee?"

"Let's say I may have a vested interest in what happens."

She blinked. "Do you mind explaining what that means?"

"I wish I could, but I can't," he replied. "So, what evidence do you have against Paul Gardener?"

"I wish I could tell you, but I can't."

He grinned. "Touché. Can you at least tell me where he is?"

"Milton PD."

"He got a lawyer yet?"

"The moment we charged him. It's Evan Roth."

"He's good and expensive."

"It's the guilty who hire the best lawyers money can buy."

"I'm not gonna argue with that," he said, moving away from her.

"Where're you going?" she asked.

"I need to talk to Roth."

FOURTEEN

Roth stood before the reporters who were assembled outside the Milton Police Department. He could have made a statement at some other location, but he knew the value of optics. He wanted the public—correction, the potential jury—to see where they were keeping his client.

The building resembled a giant concrete block. The structure was gray, cold, and uninviting. No person would want to spend even a minute inside there, but his client, an upstanding citizen of Milton, was locked up inside.

The narrative was vital in cases of this nature. The police wanted to show there was overwhelming evidence against the accused. Roth's job was to refute this so-called evidence.

The press conference held by the detectives outside the victim's residence was nothing more than an attempt to make a statement. The victim lived and died in a place she called home. She had also died at the hands of someone who was meant to protect her—her father.

Roth waited as the reporters rushed to prepare themselves. Batteries were checked on voice recorders. Camera lenses were double-checked for the perfect shot. Video equipment was adjusted and readjusted to capture the right angle.

Roth loved every minute. This was why he chose to follow his father's footsteps and become a criminal defense lawyer. He relished the surge of adrenaline he felt at the start of a new case, and on top of that, there was the money. His fees were exorbitant, but most clients would pay just about anything to get out of the predicament they were in. Roth was what stood between their freedom and life inside a concrete cell.

Roth started with a standard opening. "I have just spoken to my client. He is doing well under the circumstances. He is shocked and upset by the death of his daughter. He is a devoted father and a loving husband. Now I will take a few questions."

Hands shot up in the air. Roth had already scanned the group for reporters who asked tough questions and those who did not. Who wrote favorable stories on the cases about his defendants and who did not. Who was biased and who was not.

He pointed to one reporter, who quickly asked, "What do you have to say regarding the evidence against your client?"

"The prosecution has not yet provided me with a list of the charges against my client. It is something I will be asking the DA's office right after I leave here."

Another hand shot up. "Is it true your client was caught red-handed?"

Roth made a dramatic face, but his expression was more for the cameras than a reaction to the question. Roth had prepared himself for every question imaginable. "I'm not sure where this rumor was started, and if I were you, I would check my sources. My client is an upstanding citizen who has donated thousands of dollars to the local community. He has a very successful business, and a majority of his employees are from this city."

"Why would the Milton Police Department make an announcement so suddenly if they did not believe your client was guilty of the crime?" another reporter asked.

Roth almost chuckled, as if the question was beyond absurd. "This is something you will have to ask the fine officers at the Milton PD. I have no idea. My client has never been charged with any crime in his entire life—not even a speeding ticket. This entire ordeal has been nothing short of a nightmare for him. He has lost his only child, whom he deeply cares about. He would rather be with his wife, mourning this tragic loss, than be alone inside a cold prison cell."

Another hand shot up. "When will you be requesting bail?"

"We are hoping to go before a judge later today so my client can be home with his family."

Roth answered a couple of questions that were in the same vein as the previous ones. He finished by saying, "We intend to fight vigorously any and all charges against my client."

He walked away from the group of reporters with a smile on his face. His goal was to get the message across that his client was not the person the police had made him out to be, and he felt he accomplished this and much more.

FIFTEEN

Callaway had watched the question-and-answer session with great interest. Lawyers were a particular breed. They revealed only what was necessary and what would win them the case.

Callaway's clients were mostly wives who had hired him to dig up dirt on their rich husbands. That information was then used to extricate a divorce settlement that was in their favor. This gave Callaway a front-row seat when it came to lawyers. He had more than his share of run-ins with them, and the experience was something he would rather avoid.

Provided with proof of their clients' infidelities, the husbands' lawyers often threatened to sue Callaway and his clients for absurd amounts of money. They tried to get the judge to dismiss the evidence in court, arguing it violated their clients' right to privacy. They even went so far as to try to have Callaway charged for voyeurism.

Callaway tried to take it all in stride. The lawyers were paid handsomely to defend their clients, and even with hard evidence—photographs of their clients caught in compromising positions—they did everything in their power to have that evidence ruled inadmissible in court.

When they attacked Callaway's character, however, it was when he took it personally. They would speak of his infidelities. They would mention his gambling habits. They would show his run-ins with the law—Callaway had been booked for disorderly conduct on a few occasions, and if you asked him, he blamed the booze for his behavior—anything to discredit him and his work.

Fortunately, the presiding judges would counter it was their clients who were on trial, not Callaway. Also, Callaway was careful in the manner he went about his business. The photos were taken from outside the rendezvous point. He never tried to hide inside a closet to get the perfect shot. It was not his fault if some people did not pull the drapes before they began frolicking in bed.

He never planted hidden cameras or tapped telephones. He was smart enough to know anything procured illegally would not hold up as evidence. The last thing he wanted was to do anything that would leave *his* clients in a worse position than when they hired him.

He watched as Roth made his way to a shiny Bentley. He hurried to catch up with him.

"Mr. Roth," Callaway said. "I need to speak to you."

Roth was typing away on his cell phone when he turned. He eyed Callaway up and down and said, "You can make an appointment with my secretary." He did not even bother offering his business card. Callaway's rumpled attire did not give off the impression he could afford his services.

"It's about Paul Gardener."

Roth's eyes narrowed. "What about him?"

"I need to speak to him."

"Are you a lawyer?"

"No. I'm a private investigator."

Roth frowned. "I already have a PI on my payroll, so I don't need another."

"I'm not looking for a job."

"Then what are you looking for? Money?"

"More money would be nice, but your client already gave me some."

Roth blinked. "What?"

"Your client is my client."

"Okay, now I am even more confused."

"Your client hired me for a job, and that's why I need to speak to him."

"What was the job?"

"I can't say."

"Then no, you can't speak to my client."

Roth moved toward his car.

"It's about last night," Callaway said.

Roth stopped. "What about it?"

Callaway was silent. He was not sure how much he could reveal just yet.

Roth asked, "Was my client with you last night? Are you his alibi?"

"No."

"Then you can't help him escape lethal injection because that's what the prosecution will ask for, murder in the first degree, which will automatically qualify him for the death penalty."

"Call your client," Callaway said. "Ask him if he is willing to speak to me."

Roth stared at him, still unsure.

"I have something that is of great interest to your client, but first, I need to show it to him. If he gives me his approval, then I'll show it to you."

Roth exhaled. "Fine. What's your name?"

SIXTEEN

Roth made the call. He then took Callaway inside Milton PD, but only because they were already standing next to the station. Roth's time was too valuable, and he did not like anyone wasting it.

The accused was allowed access to legal counsel at any time, including anyone on his lawyer's legal team. Roth introduced Callaway to the desk sergeant as a member of his firm.

Before leaving, Roth warned him, "Don't make me regret this."

Callaway had no intention of getting in the crosshairs of Evan Roth. He had his own share of problems to deal with and did not need another.

Unlike regular visitors, Callaway did not have to go through a rigorous screening. The sergeant did, however, review the items Callaway had on him. He held up a camera and asked, "What's this for?"

"Well, I wish to take photos of the accused, in case you rough him up," Callaway quipped.

The sergeant's eyes hardened. Police brutality had always been an issue, and thanks to cell phone cameras, it was a hot topic. In this day and age, no police officer could so much as slap a suspect without some civilian bystander recording the act on a smartphone. But the officer had no reason to disallow Callaway's camera, so he grunted and gave the camera back.

Callaway was given a visitor's pass and was made to sign a ledger. He was then escorted into a windowless room.

When the door slammed shut behind him, Callaway immediately regretted coming here. The walls were painted dark gray, and over the years, grime had accumulated on them. The floor was rough and concrete. The table was metal, but it was covered in scratches.

The room suddenly felt hot and stuffy. Perspiration broke out under Callaway's collar, and he began to feel like he was suffocating.

He closed his eyes and took a deep breath. It did not help that the space smelled of sweat and urine. He suddenly had the urge to run out of the room and never come back.

He was relieved to hear the door open and see Paul Gardener come in. He was wearing an orange jumpsuit. His hands were shackled, and he had a day-old growth of beard on his cheeks. His eyes were raw. *He must have been crying before they led him here*, Callaway thought.

Gardener sat down across from him, and the officer removed the cuffs around his wrists. The officer left the room before shutting the door behind him.

Callaway stared at Gardener and suddenly felt overwhelming guilt. He could get up and leave at any time he wanted, while Paul had no choice. Whatever Callaway had felt coming to the Milton PD, Paul was feeling it ten times worse.

"How are you, Paul?" Callaway finally asked.
Paul rubbed his hands. "I'm good, I guess."
"You know why I'm here."

He nodded. "I forgot about it until I saw you just now. I've had an eventful day."

"I know."

They were silent a moment.

Callaway said, "We don't have to do this now. We can always do it later. But I figured I should show it to you. You did hire me for a job."

Paul sighed. "I'm not sure what use it has now. I've got bigger problems to deal with. Do you know they are charging me with murdering my own daughter?"

"I heard," Callaway replied.

Paul lowered his head. "I would never hurt Kyla. She was my baby. I don't even…"

Callaway put his hand up to stop him. "I'm not your lawyer, Paul. Client-attorney privilege doesn't come into play with me. If I am subpoenaed, I will have to disclose our discussion in court."

Paul nodded. "Okay, show me," he said.

Callaway pulled out the camera, turned it so Paul could see the LCD screen, and began to scroll through the photos.

The pictures showed Sharon Gardener leaving the house and driving away in the middle of the night. They then showed her arriving at an apartment building. Two hours later, they showed her leaving the building with another man.

Paul stared at the last image.

"Do you know him?" Callaway asked.

"No."

Callaway leaned forward. "I think it would be best if Evan Roth saw them."

"Why? What good would it do? I had a feeling my wife was unfaithful, and I wanted to see proof of it. I thought it might help me in the divorce." He shook his head. "That's the least of my worries now."

"As a former deputy sheriff, I am familiar with how investigations go. The detectives will be getting statements from everyone who was at your house last night, which means you and your wife. And it might end up including me because I was also there. I don't want to explain myself to them without you seeing what I found first."

Paul said nothing, but he still stared at the image. Callaway could not imagine what he must be going through. His daughter was dead, his wife was cheating on him, and he was stuck in a six-by-eight cell. He looked like the loneliest person on the planet.

"Just show it to your lawyer," Callaway said. "It might mean nothing, or it might mean everything."

SEVENTEEN

The District Attorney's Office was located on the eighth floor of a government building, and like many government buildings, it was massive, imposing, and ugly. The office of the DA, however, was the polar opposite. It was spacious, colorfully decorated, and the windows did not have any drapes or shades, allowing natural light to flow in.

District Attorney Judy Barrows was in her sixties. She had a wiry frame and deeply etched skin. Her teeth were stained yellow from many years of heavy smoking. Her eyes were small and narrow but were always focused and steady. During a cross-examination, if she had you in her gaze, you could not look away.

Barrows had graduated with a Bachelor of Arts degree from Cornell University. She received her Juris Doctor from the University of Michigan Law School. When she moved to Milton, she took a job in the DA's office, quickly moving up to become the Chief Deputy District Attorney until finally becoming the District Attorney a few years later. It was a position that was never held by a woman before her. She was currently serving her fifth term in office.

During her years as a prosecutor, she worked on hundreds of cases, ranging from assault to sexual assault to child abuse to rape, and she was now focused on murder cases. She was a member of several boards, which included the Milton Rape Victims Advocates, the Milton Women's Shelter, the Milton Bar Association, and she was the president of the State District Attorney's Association.

She was married for close to forty years. She had three adult children and five grandchildren.

Holt and Fisher were seated across from her as she read the evidence against Paul Gardener. They did not utter a single word until she was finished. Barrows was cheerful when it came to her family, but she was brutal when it involved her work.

She removed her reading glasses and leaned back in her ergonomic leather chair. She glared at Holt. "You should have spoken to me first before going in front of the cameras and giving a statement. I would have advised you against it."

Holt adjusted himself in his chair. He was not used to being scolded like a child, but those who dealt with Barrows had come to expect this.

"The evidence was overwhelming…"

"Was it?" she asked, cutting him off.

"We found the suspect inside the house where the murder took place. We found blood on the suspect's clothing. And we found a bloody knife in the suspect's vehicle."

"Don't you find it a little suspicious that the suspect left the victim's body in her bedroom while he went to sleep in the guesthouse?"

Holt opened his mouth but then shut it.

"Don't you find it even more suspicious that the suspect decided to leave the murder weapon in *his* vehicle rather than dispose of it someplace else?"

Holt was quiet.

"Now, as far as the blood on the clothing is concerned, the suspect may not have realized it was there."

After a brief moment of silence, Fisher spoke up. "Are you saying we don't have a case?"

"I'm not saying that, nor am I saying you shouldn't have charged Mr. Gardener. The facts are what they are, and you did your job. But I have to look at this case differently than you. I have to see if I can get a conviction. All the issues I just raised are ones the defense will raise as well." She leaned on the desk. "We need to be prepared for this and for much more, especially now that Mr. Gardener has retained Evan Roth."

Holt now understood the prosecutor's concerns. Roth was one of the most ruthless defense lawyers in the city. Barrows had had her share of battles with him, and she did not win them all.

He could tell she did not want to lose this one either.

She said, "If I know Roth, he will be seeking bail as soon as he gets in front of the judge."

"We can argue Gardener is a flight risk," Holt said.

"How?"

"His family is worth millions. He's got resources and connections. His father-in-law is a senator. Last year, he and his wife traveled to three countries."

"How do you know that?" Barrows asked.

"During our search of the house, we found their passports, and from the entry and exit stamps, we discerned when and where they went."

"How does that assist us?"

"We tell the judge that he has links to other countries."

Barrows thought a moment. "Where did they go last year?"

Holt looked over at Fisher for assistance. Fisher squinted and said, "I think it was South Africa, the Cayman Islands, and Switzerland."

Barrows considered this. "If my memory serves me correctly, all three of those countries have extradition treaties with the United States."

"But two of those countries are known for their lax banking policies."

Barrows shook her head. "It may not be enough to deny bail. Get me something I can take to the judge."

EIGHTEEN

Callaway returned to the beach house, feeling a little deflated. He had a duty to let his client know what he found. What his client did with that information was up to them. Callaway always completed the job he was hired for. If he could not, or if he failed due to his own actions, he would refund the client's money.

That was the right thing to do.

He never understood why he was always struggling for money when, over the years, he was fortunate enough to snag rich clients. But debts always followed him, and the debts were not all owed to financial institutions. Some of his loans had come from shady people, and they did not believe in installment payments, waiving interest, or loan forgiveness. What they wanted was the money, in cash and on time. Any deviation from those rules meant physical harm would come his way.

Callaway always tried to pay off his debts. In some cases, he had no choice. But whenever he was clear of one debt, he somehow managed to take on another. Once, after completing a job for the wife of a politician, which resulted in a nice payday, Callaway was feeling good about himself. Instead of depositing the money in the bank as regular folks did, he decided to try his luck at the racetrack. He was only going to bet on one or two races. He did not, and he ended up wasting virtually all the money. Seeking to lick his wounds, he decided to get a drink at the racetrack bar. When he was in between shots of whiskey, he overheard a group of people at the next table talking about a guaranteed investment. They were bankers, and they knew a way to get a high rate of return in the stock market. Callaway, reeling from his latest self-inflicted financial loss, decided to invest with them. He wanted something that was secure, and that would replenish his pockets. But there was a problem. Thanks to blowing his latest payday, he had no money to invest. So, he did what he always did whenever he needed a quick loan: went to individuals who had criminal records to borrow money.

After he made his investment with the bankers, he felt he could pay these new debts back in no time. What he did not know at the time was that the FBI was already investigating the bankers for an alleged Ponzi scheme. A few days after Callaway handed the bankers the money, they were arrested. The money disappeared, probably to some numbered account in the islands, and with it, his hope of ever getting the money back and the return he was promised.

He then spent the next several months taking on any job that came his way, no matter how menial. If someone wanted him to find their lost pet, he did it. Anything to pay back the loan he had taken.

Paul Gardener was a good client. He said he had found him through an online search. Callaway believed him. Paul gave him the first installment of his pay without asking too many questions. All he wanted was evidence that his wife was cheating on him.

Callaway was hoping he would spend a week or two trailing Paul's wife. The billable hours would have racked up to some serious cash.

Callaway had no opinion on Paul's current predicament. Whether he was guilty or not was to be determined in court, not by him.

Callaway just did not want to be caught in the middle. That was all he wanted.

If any fingers pointed in his direction, he could always plead the Fifth. He did not hear anything. He did not know anything. He was just an innocent bystander who somehow was caught up in a mess.

He sighed.

With the Gardener job over, he would have to find more work.

He checked his phone and realized there was a message for him. He frowned when he saw who it was from. On any other day, he would have ignored the message or deleted it, but today was not that day.

He dialed the number.

NINETEEN

A court-appointed officer was standing by the Gardener residence's front door when Holt and Fisher drove up. The officer's duty was to make sure the detectives did not tamper with something that might turn out to be evidence. There had been cases of detectives returning to the scene of a crime and planting evidence favorable to the prosecution. The chance of this occurring on a regular basis was rare, almost never, but even one time could taint the entire legal system. A suspect was entitled to due process that should be fair and impartial.

Holt and Fisher signed a piece of paper, and the officer held the front door open for them. They pulled on latex gloves and began the arduous task of combing through the house, looking for clues.

They could not split up because there was only one officer at the scene. They had to work in tandem as they first went through the guesthouse and then the kitchen where the murder weapon was taken from. They then moved to the bedroom where Kyla Gardener's body was discovered.

The two detectives were not sure what they were looking for, but they would know it once they saw it.

Half an hour later, they had come up empty. Anything that was of use had already been tagged, photographed, and taken as evidence. Even Paul Gardener's Audi had been towed to a police facility in order to be stripped for further clues.

Holt pulled off his gloves. "This was a waste of time," he grumbled.

Fisher said, "We still haven't checked the office."

"And what do you expect to find in there?"

"I don't know, but we should take a look."

"You do that while I go sit down."

He saw the officer staring in his direction. There was no way Holt could be in the living room while Fisher was in the office. "Fine," Holt huffed. "But make it quick."

Fisher went through the room. Holt looked on, his arms crossed over his chest, feeling a slow burn of impatience. The officer stood next to him, keeping his eyes on Fisher as she pulled open the drawers, ruffled through the documents inside, then moved on. She picked up a couple of envelopes, and after taking a quick look, she put them away. She opened a couple of Bankers Boxes, but all she saw were invoices and statements related to Gardener's business.

"You done? Can we go now?" Holt asked. He was normally very methodical on the job, but when he became disinterested, he was prone to childish exasperation.

Fisher was about to leave when something caught her eye. She moved to the bookshelf in the corner. A yellow piece of paper was stuck between two hardcover books. She pulled the paper out and unfolded it.

A smile crossed her face when she saw what it was. She turned and held the paper out for Holt to see. He examined the printed words and said, "It might just do. Good job, Fisher."

She informed the officer of their intentions. The officer pulled out a Ziploc bag, placed the document inside, and made a note of the discovery for the record.

TWENTY

Roth stared at Judy Barrows. He found her intimidating, but he kept his feelings hidden. Barrows' courtroom exploits were well-known among the legal community, and even if you had not seen her in action, you had heard of her.

Roth had won a few cases against her, but it still did not diminish the effect she had on him. She was relentless, determined, and tough as nails. If you did not bring your A-game, she would eat you alive.

There were too many lawyers whose careers were tarnished or destroyed by Barrows. They made the fatal mistake of underestimating her. They viewed this small woman as a pushover. What they got was an onslaught of legal expertise.

Roth was determined never to make that mistake. In fact, if he could avoid going to battle with her, he would. So, when she called him to discuss the Gardener case, he rushed over.

"Thank you for coming at such short notice," she said.

They were seated across from one another on small sofas. They looked like two colleagues having a casual conversation. She had offered him coffee, and he had declined.

"It's no trouble," he replied. "I'm more than happy to oblige."

She smiled, but it was not affectionate. "I thought it was better that we meet first before we get fully invested in the case."

"I agree."

"I am going to ask the judge to deny bail," she said, quickly getting to the point.

Roth was not the least bit surprised. This was a tactic used by most prosecutors in order to apply pressure on the accused. The longer they were locked up, the more they were willing to cut a deal, even if that deal sent them back to prison, albeit for a shorter period of time.

"On what basis?" he asked.

"Your client is a successful businessman."

"All the more reason for him not to be a flight risk," Roth countered. "He wouldn't leave behind everything he's worked so hard for."

"But he does have connections and access to resources. Last year, he went on three trips overseas. To South Africa, the Cayman Islands, and Switzerland."

Roth was not aware of any trips, but he would confirm this with Paul later. He knew Barrows was preparing a case to convince the judge to deny bail and that she wanted to see his rebuttals. "All three have extradition treaties with the US," he said.

"Yes, but I will argue that if he can visit those countries, what is stopping him from going elsewhere?"

Roth believed Barrows was grasping at straws, hoping one of them would achieve her objective. He said, "I know people who have traveled to many more countries than that in a given year."

"Many of those people are not charged with murdering their daughter."

He smiled. This was the opening he was waiting for. "My client did not murder his daughter. He had no motive to harm her."

"The motive will become known in due time," she said. "Your client was at the scene of the crime. The victim's blood was on him. The murder weapon was in his vehicle. When provided with these facts, a jury will return from their deliberations with a verdict of guilty."

"But when presented the other way, they may not," he said.

She waited for his explanation.

"It doesn't make sense that a man would kill his daughter, hide the weapon in *his* car, and then decide to stay on the premises and fall asleep. If he had committed the murder, should he not be fleeing the crime scene instead of going back?"

"Maybe he decided to flee and had made it all the way to the car but then realized he couldn't drive in his condition."

Roth was confused. "Condition?"

"Your client had been drinking that night. A bottle of scotch was found in the guesthouse."

"He only consumed half a glass."

"So you say."

She was testing him. She wanted to see how hard he was willing to fight back.

Barrows continued. "In his inebriated state, he decided to sleep it off, and thus was woken up by his wife the next day."

Roth could punch a dozen holes in her theory, but he was not willing to get into it now. He would leave that for when they were before a judge and jury.

"Speaking of the wife," he said, "if my client stayed put to sleep from the alcohol, as you say, wouldn't he have been worried his wife would eventually find out what he had just done?"

"She did find out when she went into her daughter's room."

"Yes, but why didn't she hear anything during the night?" he said. "The couple's bedroom is next door to their daughter's."

"She couldn't because she was under the influence of sleeping medication."

His smile widened even more. "She wasn't home that night."

Barrows was taken aback. "What?"

Roth removed a set of photos from his briefcase and placed them before her. "These were taken on the night Kyla Gardener was murdered. You can see from the date stamp that Mrs. Gardener had left the house for almost three hours. My client could have used that as an opportunity to make his escape."

The surprise was still visible on her face. "Who took these?"

There was no point in hiding the truth, Roth knew. Sooner or later, he would have to reveal this fact, whether it was now or through a judge's order. "My client was suspicious his wife was cheating on him, and to verify this, he hired a private investigator. I will be submitting these photos as evidence."

Barrows face was grim. Roth was beaming on the inside. He had scored one for the defense. If the prosecutor was going to use Sharon Gardener as a witness against her husband—there was a strong possibility of this because the couple was in the process of divorcing—they would think twice now.

She cleared her throat and said, "We're not here to argue about your client's guilt. We'll have plenty of time for that. We are here to discuss whether he should be set free before the trial."

"My client is not a threat to himself or anyone else. If you go to the judge with what you've just told me, I guarantee the judge will grant my client bail."

Barrows smiled.

Roth suddenly felt unnerved.

"Detectives Holt and Fisher were at the scene of the crime, and they discovered something interesting."

He sat up in his seat. He now regretted not visiting the crime scene before he came here. "I hope everything was as it should be."

"It was. An officer appointed by the court made sure of that." She opened a desk drawer and pulled out a plastic bag. Inside was a yellow piece of paper. "It's a purchase agreement between your client and a company located in Milton. It's dated less than a month ago."

Without looking at the document, he asked, "What's it for?"

"Your client bought a small boat."

It was his turn to be taken by surprise, but he controlled his emotions as best as he could. "Maybe he likes to fish."

"We found no fishing equipment in the house. In fact, your client doesn't even have a fishing license to his name. We will argue that it was all premeditated and that after killing his daughter, your client had planned to sail away." She dropped the bag on the desk. "I'll be filing this as evidence."

She had just scored one for the prosecution.

The silence hung in the air as they both stared at each other, wondering who would blink first.

Barrows said, "I'm willing to offer a plea deal. I already have too many cases on my desk that need my immediate attention. We will drop murder in the first degree and instead go for a lesser charge if your client pleads guilty. He's only forty-six. He'll be out in twenty years and be able to resume his life."

"Let me think about it," Roth said.

TWENTY-ONE

Callaway knocked on the steel door and waited. He was in a spot located behind a strip club. A second later, a small window slid open, and two eyes appeared. He felt like he was in some bad cop movie.

"What do you want?" the man demanded.

"Baxter, open the door. It's Lee Callaway," he replied, annoyed.

"Who?"

"Do you want me to leave? I'll go. Then you'll have to answer to Mason."

A bolt was turned, a chain was removed, and the door was unlocked. Baxter was six-four, two hundred and fifty pounds of pure muscle, and he sported a buzz cut. He always wore a tight t-shirt, which made his big arms look even bigger.

Callaway moved past him and went up the stairs. He could hear sounds from the club coming through the wall. He was confronted with another door. He waited as Baxter trudged up behind him. He was always surprised at how the man was able to fit through the narrow stairs. It was Baxter's duty to let people in—with his boss's permission, of course. One time, Callaway barged in, and Baxter almost lost his mind. The man was a little loose in the head, Callaway figured. But he took his job seriously. He had to give him that.

The office was small and narrow. A wide desk took up most of the space. A man was seated in a leather chair behind the desk. Mason was short and rail-thin with every inch of his arms covered in tattoos. He sported a small goatee and he wore wire-rimmed prescription glasses.

"Lee, my friend," Mason said with a smile. "Come in and have a seat."

"I didn't know I was your friend," Callaway said.

Mason made a melodramatic gesture, acting as if Callaway had insulted him. "You were always my friend."

Callaway shot a look at Baxter. "If I was your friend, then why was your guard dog ready to break my leg the last time I was in here?"

"That was just business, you know that," Mason replied.

Callaway had found himself in a tight spot, and with nowhere else to go, he showed up at Mason's doorstep. Mason was more than willing to extend him the loan, but when Callaway fell behind, Mason sent Baxter to recoup the money. Fortunately, Callaway was able to talk his way out of serious injury.

"I've got a job for you," Mason said.

"I'm not taking any more jobs from you."

"You took the last one."

"Only because I owed you money."

"Listen, I'm interested in hiring you, Mr. Private Investigator." Mason gave him a smile, which was anything but pleasant. "I bet you need the cash. Why else would you be here?"

Callaway hated that Mason was right. Why could he not just get a stable nine-to-five job and be done with dealing with lowlifes like Mason?

"I only came to see what you wanted," Callaway said.

"Well, I want you to find someone for me."

"I bet this person owes you money."

"Yes."

"Then, no thanks. I'm not going to find this person, so Baxter can hurt him."

"We don't want to hurt him, Lee. He made an agreement with us, which he reneged on. We just want our money."

Callaway stared at him.

Mason's expression hardened. "We *will* find him, with or without your help."

Callaway did not like the sound of that.

"How much does he owe you?"

"Ten grand, but after interest and late penalties, it is twelve grand. And if you collect in full, you keep ten percent."

That's over a thousand dollars, Callaway thought. *That would come in handy right about now.*

"What if he doesn't have the money?" Callaway said. "I'm guessing he doesn't, which is why he has become scarce."

"He owns a classic Plymouth Road Runner. He put it up as collateral. It's gotta be worth at least twenty grand. You find him. You'll find the car."

Callaway thought Mason's offer over. "Okay, I'll do it. But if I find him, you don't hurt him. You sell the car and get your money."

"That's what I keep saying. I just want my money. That's all," Mason said, spreading his arms out.

"What's his name?" Callaway finally asked.

TWENTY-TWO

Paul Gardener shook his head. "I'm not pleading guilty. I did *not* kill my daughter."

Roth was back at the Milton PD. After his meeting with Barrows, it was his duty to inform his client of all his options. Roth did not have to agree with them, and in some instances, he would wholly advise against them, but he still had to convey them.

"These aren't options you are bringing me," Gardener said. "They all lead me to spending time in prison."

"Yes, but at a reduced sentence."

Gardener shook his head and pointed a finger at Roth. "I'm not going to prison for something I did not do. I had no reason to hurt my daughter."

"Are you sure?" Roth asked.

Gardener blinked. "What do you mean?"

"The prosecution believes that you were drunk and you had a fight with your daughter. In a fit of anger, you strangled her and then stabbed her."

"That doesn't make any sense. If I strangled her, then why would I stab her?"

"You tell me."

"I can't. I don't remember anything."

"How can you remember nothing when all signs point to you as the killer?"

Gardener opened his mouth but then shut it. He lowered his head and stared at his hands. Roth was not trying to get a confession out of him. Far from it. What he wanted to see was how he handled himself under questioning. If Roth put him on the stand, and he would only do that if there was no other choice, Barrows would come at him from all sides. He better have his story straight, or else Barrows would expose him in front of the jury.

Gardener stood up and walked over to the wall. "What about my bail?" he asked.

"Prosecution will try to get the judge to deny it."

Gardener turned to him, his eyes full of terror. Roth did not blame him for wanting to avoid another day being locked up. "Why?" he asked in a low voice.

"Last year, you took three trips abroad. They will argue that it makes you a flight risk."

"But, I'm not."

"What were you doing in South Africa?" Roth asked.

Gardener searched his memory. "My wife and I went on a safari for our twentieth wedding anniversary."

"The Cayman Islands?"

"Her family is wealthy. They have money stowed away in numbered accounts all over the world. I went there with my brother-in-law to check up on one of those accounts." Gardener did not sound like he wanted to hide this information. He had bigger things to worry about than tax evasion. His freedom was far more important. "We were only there for three days."

"Do you have an account there?" Roth asked.

He shook his head. "I don't make enough to warrant one."

Roth nodded. "And what about Switzerland?"

"I was there on a business trip to raise capital for my firm."

"And did you raise the money?"

Gardener shook his head again. "Not everyone is willing to invest in technology, specifically tech geared toward the app market."

This is good, Roth thought. They could argue he did not have the means to become an international fugitive.

"One last thing," Roth said. "They know you bought a boat recently."

"I did, but why is that a problem?"

"You never owned one before. In fact, you don't even have a fishing license. So why did you buy one now?"

Gardener stared at him. His shoulders slumped. "I've been under a lot of stress. My business is not doing as well as I had hoped. I knew my marriage was coming to an end. I just wanted to get away from everything. The thought of being out in the ocean with not a care in the world, with no place to be and no place to go, was alluring, and that's why I purchased the boat. I know it was more of a dream than reality, but it gave me some hope for the future."

"This doesn't help us. In fact, it gives the prosecution more ammo. They will argue that you had planned it all and after you murdered your daughter, you were going to sail away on your boat."

"I'm not a murderer," Gardener said. "I don't belong here. You have to get me out."

TWENTY-THREE

The bungalow was at the end of a quiet street. It had a two-car garage with a white picket fence. The lawn had recently been mowed, and grass still littered the edges of the driveway. Children's toys were scattered on the front porch. Callaway tiptoed over them as he made his way to the front door.

He rang the doorbell and waited. A minute later, the door slid open a notch. He could see a woman behind it.

"Can I help you?" she asked.

"Is Mike Grabonsky home?"

"No, Mike's not here."

She was about to shut the door when he stuck his hand in to stop her. "Wait," he said.

"Leave me alone," she said. "Or else I'll call the police."

"Give me a minute to explain, *please*," he said. He stuck his other hand inside his pocket and pulled out a card. It was the one with his pseudonym. *Now's not the time to be deceitful*, he thought. He stuck his hand back inside, pulled out the card with his real name, and held it out for her to take. She snatched the card. A moment later, she opened the door.

"You're a private investigator?" she asked.

"I am."

"Sorry, I thought you were with the people who came by earlier."

"What people?"

"There were two of them. One was short, but he had a lot of tattoos, and the other was big, and he looked mean."

So, Mason and Baxter were already here, Callaway thought. *Figures.*

"What did they want?" he asked.

"They wanted to know where Mike was. I told them I didn't know. Then they did this." She held the door, so he could see.

The interior of the house looked like a tornado had hit. The furniture was smashed or tossed aside. The walls had holes the size of fists, likely from Baxter's hand. The TV was broken and lying on the floor.

Callaway's face was hard. It was one thing to rough up a guy for not paying up; it was another to go to his house and threaten his family. "Did you file a police report?" he asked.

"They told me if I called the police, they would come back and burn the house down."

He doubted very much they would go that far, but Baxter did have a few screws loose in his head. There was no telling how literal he would take any of Mason's instructions. One time, a guy was not forthcoming with information, and Mason told Baxter to make him spill his guts. Baxter took out a knife and split the guy's stomach open.

"We've got two kids," she said. "They are staying with my sister right now. Fortunately, they were at school when those guys came to the house. I'm worried for their safety."

"Nothing will happen to them. Those people just want the money Mike borrowed from them."

"But why would he go to them? We have our savings, and we also have a home line of credit."

In Callaway's experience, most husbands never told their wives the entire truth. Mike must have already gone through the savings, and he must have tapped the line of credit dry.

No one with a good credit score would go to a loan shark. They were the last resort when all other options were closed. Mason and people like him in his profession preyed on the desperate. They were a modern version of the feudal lords who lent money to farmers at exorbitant interest rates, knowing full well the farmers could never pay them back. When they could not, the lords seized the farms and made the farmers work for them.

Mason must have known Mike could never pay him back, which was why he had made him sign the Road Runner as collateral. He knew he could double his investment if he got his hands on the classic car.

"Do you know where Mike is?" Callaway asked.

"If I knew, I would have told those guys when they were destroying my house," she replied. "I've called his cell phone. I've called his work. I've even called all his friends. No one has any idea where he is."

Callaway rubbed his chin. *This isn't promising*, he thought. "Does Mike have family in Milton?" he asked.

"No, but his dad lives about fifty miles away in Maryland."

"Did you call him?"

"I did, and he's not heard from him either. He and Mike don't get along too well, so I doubt they'd keep in touch."

TWENTY-FOUR

Roth entered the Gardeners' residence with his assistant in tow. Accompanying them was the court-appointed officer.

Roth pulled on a pair of latex gloves, a box of which he always kept in his car. As a criminal defense lawyer, there was no telling what he would have to do in order to win a case. He once had to dig through the garbage outside a crack house to find evidence that ended up exonerating his client. He could have asked his assistant to do it, but Roth was not sure what he was looking for until he saw it with his own eyes. This was why *he* had come to the Gardeners' home. He wanted a first-hand view of the crime scene. During the course of a trial, he might have to take the jury step-by-step through the entire house. In order to make them feel an emotion or get a reaction, he had to feel and react first.

He pulled out a voice recorder, and after reciting the time, date, and place of recording, he began his tour.

He started with Kyla Gardener's bedroom. The bed sheets, pillowcases, and mattress had been removed. At the trial, the bloodstains on them would be analyzed in great detail. Roth was not too concerned about this. He was certain the blood was hers and hers only. Paul Gardener was not cut anywhere on his body, so there was little chance his blood was on any of the items in the room.

Roth thought of something. His eyes scanned the floor, moving from the bed to the hall. There were no drops of blood anywhere. If Paul was drunk and in a rage, as the prosecutors were going to paint him to be, there would have been blood everywhere. The fact that blood was only confined to the mattress spoke volumes to him.

He motioned for his assistant to take photos of the bedroom and the hallway.

He moved to the stairs. Again, there was no blood. He got down on his haunches to confirm.

According to Barrows, after stabbing his daughter, Paul had proceeded to go downstairs to his car in order to hide the murder weapon. Yet there was no trail of blood leading from the bedroom to anywhere on the main floor.

Could someone under the influence of alcohol have the clear mind to know where to hide the weapon? And could they have done it without spilling a single drop? If they were fully aware of their actions, why did they not just dump the knife in the gutter somewhere instead of leaving it where it would end up incriminating them?

There was also the matter of the bloodstain on Paul's golf shirt. Even without the blood analysis, he was sure it belonged to Kyla. Paul had no visible cuts on his skin. But how did Kyla's blood get on him, and why only on a certain part of the shirt? The rest of his clothes were clean, including his pants.

Roth moved to the kitchen and then the guesthouse. He stared at the spot where Paul was found asleep by his wife. If he had the presence of mind to know what he was doing, then why not just run away? Why stay at the scene of the crime?

Roth's job was not to have answers to all the questions. His job was to raise additional questions *against* the narrative the prosecution was forming.

He had his assistant snap photos of the guesthouse. Again, he saw no blood anywhere. How could someone so drunk be so careful?

The only spot that had any blood was on the recliner where Paul was sleeping. The recliner was sitting in the evidence locker at the Milton PD, and the blood could only have come from Paul's shirt.

Roth spent another hour surveying the scene before he left.

TWENTY-FIVE

There was something about what Mike Grabonsky's wife said that stuck in Callaway's head. He was now on his way to Maryland. The home of Mike's father was the very last place Mike would be, and that was what made it *the* best hiding place.

The house was on a winding road. Callaway almost missed the exit when he drove up. Luckily, he had the GPS on his phone to guide him.

The residence was a two-story house with a long, open porch. A Ford 4x4 was parked in front. Callaway pulled up next to it, parked, and got out of the car.

The front door swung open. A man came out, holding a shotgun at the ready. He wore a trucker's hat, white t-shirt, camouflage vest, blue jeans, and black boots. His face was hard, and his gray eyes were focused on Callaway.

"You're trespassing," the man growled.

Callaway put his hands up. "There's no sign that says I am."

"I don't need a sign. You're still on my property."

"My name is Lee Callaway, and I'm looking for Mike."

"I don't know any Mike. Now get lost before I start putting holes in your vehicle."

Callaway did not like having a gun aimed at him, and he detested being threatened.

"I'm not here to cause trouble," Callaway said. "Some bad people are looking for your son, and I want to make sure I speak to him before they do."

"This got nothing to do with me. I haven't talked to Mike in years."

"Then I'm sorry to have wasted your time."

Callaway was about to get back in his car when he said, "You might be interested to know that the guys who are looking for Mike were over at his house. They tore up the place pretty bad. Scared your daughter-in-law. She's worried about your grandkids. Just thought I'd pass that along to you."

The man said nothing. His steely eyes were fixed on Callaway.

Callaway got in his car and left. When he was back on the main road, he drove up a bit and then pulled into a neighbor's property so he could keep watch.

The Ford 4x4 drove by a couple of minutes later.

Callaway followed.

TWENTY-SIX

Fisher got off the phone and said, "It was Barrows. She spoke to Paul Gardener's lawyer, and Gardener refused a plea deal."

Holt smiled. "That's the best news I've heard all day. Now we can hang him for murdering his daughter."

They were at a hotdog stand located outside the Milton PD. They had already braved the long line and were enjoying their lunch.

"Barrows doesn't think it's a slam-dunk case," Fisher said. "We still don't have a motive."

"We don't need a motive," Holt said. "We know he was at the house when she was murdered. We have the murder weapon, and we have the victim's blood on him. If that's not a slam-dunk, then I don't know what is."

Fisher did not look convinced. "There was something else Barrows mentioned."

"What?"

"We need to go and speak to Mrs. Gardener."

"Why?" Holt asked.

"I'll fill you in on the way over there."

The drive was close to an hour. They pulled up to a house that resembled a mansion. The house was all white: white exterior façade, white columns, and white window frames. The home came complete with a white fountain with two angels spraying water from their harps.

Fisher drove around the fountain and parked by the front door. They got out and rang the doorbell.

A Filipino lady answered the door. They introduced themselves and asked for Sharon Gardener. A few minutes later, they were escorted into a spacious room. The first thing they noticed was that it too was white, from the white paint on the walls to the white furniture and white rug. *This room is so bright; it could put your eyes out*, Holt thought.

Sharon Gardener entered the room. She was wearing a dark green robe and no shoes. She wore no makeup, and her hair was disheveled. Her eyes were puffy and red. She looked like she had not slept since the night her daughter was killed.

"Please have a seat," she said.

Holt and Fisher sat on the sofa. Sharon took one of the chairs. "Can I get you anything to drink?" she asked.

Holt and Fisher shook their heads.

"If you change your mind, I can have Margaret get you something," Sharon said.

Holt and Fisher assumed Margaret was the Filipino lady who opened the door for them.

"This is a nice place," Fisher said, looking around.

"It's my brother's house. He's a doctor, and he's done well for himself." Sharon then got straight to the point. "Do you have any news regarding my husband? Isn't that why you came here?"

Fisher looked over at Holt. He let her take the lead. "We came to ask you a few questions."

"*Me?*" she said, genuinely surprised. "I told you everything I know back at our house."

"You didn't tell us everything, Mrs. Gardener," Fisher said.

"Call me, Sharon. And I'm not sure what you are talking about."

"On the night of your daughter's…um… death…" Fisher was careful not to say *murder*, or else Sharon might break down in sobs. "You said you had taken sleeping medication and slept through the entire night."

"I did."

"We have information that contradicts that."

Sharon sat up straight. "What information?"

"There are photos of you leaving the house that night."

Sharon's face turned pale. "How?" she asked.

"Your husband had hired a private investigator to follow you. He caught you on camera."

Sharon looked like she was about to faint. Her hand shook as she placed it over her mouth. She looked away for a few seconds. "What was on the photos?" she asked, her voice barely audible.

"We don't know, but the prosecutor has seen them. And according to her, it clearly shows you with another man."

Sharon put her hands over her face. "Oh, my God."

Fisher paused to let the information sink in. "Did you turn off the security cameras that night?" she asked.

Sharon dropped her hands to her side and nodded.

"Why?" Fisher asked.

"Why do you think?" she replied. "I was going out to meet another man that was not my husband."

"You were having an affair?"

"Yes."

"Why didn't you tell us this when we first spoke to you?"

"I was embarrassed and horrified. I'm not proud of what I have done, and I didn't want the world to find out. I also didn't…"

She let her words trail off.

"You also didn't what?"

"I also didn't want Kenny's wife to find out."

"Is Kenny the man you were with that night?"

"Yes."

"What's his full name?"

"Kenny Goldman."

"What does Mr. Goldman do?"

"Kenny is a yoga instructor. I met him at his yoga studio. I never intended things to get personal between us, but Paul and I were having problems, and I needed someone to make me feel beautiful again."

Holt and Fisher were silent.

"I'm sorry I lied to you. I never intended it that way. I just never thought it was a big deal," Sharon said.

"It is a *big* deal," Holt said. "We always thought your husband had turned off the cameras to hide the crime he was about to perpetrate. We now know that's not the case. This means because of your actions, we don't have any record of what happened that night."

Sharon Gardener put her hands over her face and began to sob uncontrollably.

TWENTY-SEVEN

Paul Gardener made his first court appearance. He was dressed in a simple suit, a plain white shirt, and a tie without any pattern. He was clean-shaven, and he wore nothing that was expensive or attracted attention. The media had gathered inside and outside the courtroom, and whatever they captured, whether in photographs or the written word, would influence potential jurors' minds as to whether he was guilty or not. Roth did not want Paul to come across as someone who was wealthy and privileged. Jurors could use that information to punish him.

Paul was read the charges against him. He pleaded not guilty to all counts.

This came as no surprise to those present. What did surprise them was the absence of Sharon Gardener. The media was salivating at the chance of getting a photo of her. There was a strong belief that she would appear. It was her daughter who was murdered, and it was her husband who was accused of the crime.

The reporters and photographers were also surprised that no one from Sharon's family was there either. Her father was a senator, and her brother was a prominent doctor. Their presence would have made for great copy.

Paul's mother was in court, and she made sure to give her son a reassuring smile whenever he looked at her.

The prosecution and the defense spent over two hours presenting their case as to why Paul should or should not be granted bail. The judge listened to each with great interest. He then deliberated for almost an hour. When he returned, he announced his decision to grant bail, but it came with conditions.

The amount was set at half a million dollars. Paul's mother pledged her house as security. Paul was required to hand over his passport, which he promptly did, and he had to stay with his mother for the duration of the trial if no plea agreement was reached before that.

When the court was adjourned, Roth and Paul left the courthouse and were promptly surrounded by a throng of media as Roth led Paul by his elbow to a waiting SUV. They ignored the microphones thrust in their faces, and the questions shouted at them.

The moment they were in the SUV, Paul collapsed on the seat. The entire ordeal had left him exhausted. He did not expect this much media would show up at his arraignment, and he did not expect the judge to take almost an hour to make his decision regarding his bail. Paul could not imagine spending another minute inside a six-by-eight cell.

Roth put a hand on Paul's shoulder. "This is just the beginning, I'm afraid. From now until the trial, you will be scrutinized and vilified by everyone with an opinion. Some have already reached a verdict in their minds as to your guilt. We don't care about them. We just care about the twelve people who will ultimately decide your fate. So until we get to that point, my advice to you is not to focus too much on what's going on around you. It will only wear you down. And we need you ready and focused for the time when we go to trial. Do you understand?"

Paul gave a noncommittal nod, and then he turned to the window.

They were driving in silence when Paul said, "I would like to visit my house first."

"I don't think it's a good idea," Roth said.

"Why not?"

"A terrible crime was committed there, and you're the primary suspect. If you go back, the prosecution could use that against you. They could argue that you only went back to clean up the scene. They might even request that your bail be revoked."

Paul nodded in understanding. "What about Sharon? How is she doing?"

"I'm not sure, but I doubt she's doing well considering..."

Paul did not need Roth to say the rest. "Can I see her or speak to her?" he asked.

"I don't think she wants to speak to you."

Paul turned to him.

"She knows about the photos your PI took."

Paul frowned. "How did she find out?"

"Through the prosecutor, most likely. In fact, it's now all over the news."

Paul shook his head. "I never wanted it out in public. It was a personal matter between Sharon and me."

"It was the only way we could cast doubt on the prosecution's case against you. Your wife turned off the security cameras, not you. She lied to the police that she was there all night when in fact she was not. They were going to use her as a witness against you. They always use one spouse against the other when there is a homicide in the family. With you and Sharon on the brink of divorce, I have a strong feeling she would have gone in whatever direction the prosecution wanted her to. She would have done so out of spite to hurt you. Now she can't say she saw or heard anything that night when she was not even there."

They were silent again.

"Can I at least see my daughter's body?" Paul asked.

"Again, that's not a good idea."

"Then, what *is* a good idea?" Paul snapped.

Roth was quiet. He knew Paul was angry and confused. He was trying to reach out and touch anything from his life before this nightmare started.

Paul whispered, "I didn't kill Kyla. I couldn't have."

Roth had seen this before. His clients who were accused of murder would repeat to themselves over and over that there was no way they were capable of committing such a horrific act. Roth was pleased with this. The more Paul convinced himself he was innocent, the better chance Roth had of convincing the jury that this was true.

Roth said, "In a few days, when the heat dies down and something else catches the media's attention, maybe I can try to arrange for you to see Kyla's body. Right now, though, the perception is that you killed her."

"I didn't," Paul replied.
He faced the window again.

TWENTY-EIGHT

Holt huffed and puffed as he paced inside the DA's office. Barrows had worked with enough police detectives to let him vent. Detectives were a very special breed. When they had someone in their sights, they became obsessed with them.

All evidence pointed at Paul Gardener being the suspect, and Holt wanted him locked up. It bothered him when a criminal was allowed to walk free.

"It wasn't up to me," Barrows said. "The judge wasn't convinced Gardener was a flight risk."

Holt shook his head and continued pacing.

"He put up enough assurances to satisfy the judge's requirements," she added.

Holt stopped and said, "It was his wife that screwed us. We should bring her in and charge her for obstruction of justice."

"And how would that look?" Barrows asked. "She is a grieving mother whose daughter was potentially murdered by her husband."

"What if she murdered her?" Fisher replied. She was sitting in the back and had her arms crossed over her chest.

"What?" Holt growled.

"Our job isn't to focus on one suspect but *all* suspects."

Holt did not look convinced.

Fisher said, "Sharon Gardener turned off the cameras."

"Yes," Holt said. "So that her husband wouldn't have any proof of her affair."

"What if her daughter caught her leaving the house, and she threatened to tell her father? So far, we have no information indicating the victim and Gardener had a strained relationship. In fact, Gardener's reaction wasn't an act when he saw his daughter's bloodied body in bed."

"How can you be so sure of that?" Holt asked.

"I can't, but it is something to keep in mind. What if Sharon got into an argument with her daughter, and it got so heated, she stabbed her?"

Holt tried to wave Fisher's suggestion away.

"Just think about it," Fisher insisted. "Gardener was asleep in the guesthouse. He couldn't have heard any commotion all the way there. But Sharon could have heard something from her bedroom, which was next to the victim's."

"No, she couldn't have," Holt corrected her. "She wasn't even at home at that time, remember?"

Barrows put her hand up to stop them. "This is no time for you two to be arguing. Your job is to find me a suspect with enough evidence for me to get the jury to convict that person." Barrows paused to collect her thoughts. "I could have made more money in a private firm, but I chose to work for the DA's office instead. Believe me. There were many opportunities for me to switch sides. Every time I won a big case, the offers came flooding in. Do you want to know why I didn't leave this position? Because I wanted to feel like I've righted a wrong in this world. It's a simple way of thinking, but it is the only way I know how to keep doing this job. What I'm saying is that so far, we have evidence against Paul Gardener, but if you bring me something against Sharon Gardener, I will keep an open mind and give it serious consideration."

TWENTY-NINE

Callaway followed the Ford 4x4 for twenty minutes on the remote road. The Ford then turned right onto a narrow dirt path. Callaway did the same.

He was surrounded by tall trees and bushes on either side of him. He had no idea where he was, but he hoped his trip was worth it. If his hunch did not turn out right, he would have to start all over again. He was not sure what he would do then.

The Ford slowed down and then moved up an incline. As the Ford drove along, Callaway spotted a house that had been shielded by the tall trees.

Callaway did not go any further. He pulled the car off the dirt path and parked behind a giant tree. Callaway got out and approached the house on foot. The home looked more like a cottage than a house. The structure was small, made entirely of wood, and had a triangular roof.

Callaway thought about going up to the door, but there was no telling what awaited him inside. He already had a shotgun pointed at him, and he did not want to take any chances.

Even though he had a permit for concealed weapons, he hated carrying his gun. He always worried about what would happen if he had to use it. If he did, it could only mean he put himself in a situation that ended up in a shoot-out. The outcome from that would definitely not be what he wanted. Callaway had no desire to spend any time in prison, which was why the gun was currently locked up at the beach house. But today, as he contemplated his risky situation, he suddenly felt vulnerable.

Maybe I should have brought the gun, he thought.

The Ford pulled away from the house. When it was out of sight, Callaway made his way up to the front door.

He knocked on the door. It swung open. A man wearing a t-shirt, pajamas, and no shoes stared at him in shock.

"You're not my father," he muttered.

Before the man could shut the door, Callaway pushed his way in. The man stumbled and fell to the floor.

"Mike Grabonsky?" Callaway asked.

Mike's eyes filled with horror. "Please don't hurt me. I don't have the money. I swear."

"Get up," Callaway said.

Mike stared at him.

"Listen, Mason sent me to look for you. Do you want me to tell him I found you?"

Mike shook his head.

"Then, get up and we'll talk."

Once they were seated across from each other on small sofas, Callaway asked, "How did you get involved with someone like Mason?" Mike did not look like the type of guy who gambled. But then again, most gamblers were ordinary people who had a family and a decent job.

"It's not what you think," Mike replied.

"Okay, then tell me."

"I didn't go to the racetrack or lose money at a poker table. I invested in something that was supposed to be risk-free."

"It always is until it's not."

"No, seriously. On the advice of my real estate agent, I bought a property. The place was in real bad shape. The neighborhood was up-and-coming, and I figured this was the best time to jump in. I borrowed money from the bank, I tapped my lines of credit, and I even took money from our savings. I was certain I could pay it all back once I flipped the property for a profit."

"What happened?"

"I got conned by a shady contractor. I should have seen the red flags when he promised to have the project completed in half the time I thought was needed. I was glad to save some money. I really didn't have enough cash to complete the project anyway. I didn't even have a contingency fund in case the project went over budget. The construction began on schedule, but the contractor kept asking for money because he had to buy supplies, pay his employees, and get permits, and so I kept paying him. The place quickly turned into a money pit. Then, one day, the contractor suddenly disappeared. The house was only halfway done, and I was out of money."

Callaway sighed. "So, you went to Mason?"

Mike shrugged. "I had no choice. I needed ten thousand to keep the creditors away. If I didn't come up with it fast, the bank would've taken the house, and I would've lost everything."

"And how were you going to pay Mason back?" Callaway asked.

"I was hoping to buy enough time to find a buyer who was willing to take over the property in mid-construction. I have all the required permits. I have enough materials to move the project further. I just didn't have the manpower to get it done. I am sure some builder would be willing to finish the job."

"So, what went wrong?"

"I had a builder seriously interested, but he backed out right at the last minute. I quickly lined up another, but by then, Mason was after me."

"So, you ran?"

"I had no choice."

"You know they were at your house."

Mike's shoulders slumped. "I just found out from my father. He and I never saw eye to eye, but when I told him what I'd gotten myself into, he let me stay here."

"How long were you expecting to hide?"

"Long enough for them to go away."

Callaway gave Mike a stern look. "People like Mason never go away. With them, you can't even declare personal bankruptcy and hope the debt is wiped out. It stays with you until you die."

Mike's eyes widened.

"What about your car?" Callaway asked. "The Plymouth Road Runner. Why don't you sell it and pay Mason back?"

"I would, but it's gone."

"What?"

"Do you think I'd leave my family and run if I still had the car?"

"Where is it?"

"It's repossessed."

"Why?"

"I had to finance it to fix it up. But then I fell behind on the payments."

"By how much?"

"Three thousand."

Callaway pinched the bridge of his nose in frustration. "So, let me get this straight. You owe money to the bank and other creditors, you owe money to Mason, and you owe money to the finance company. How much money in total are you in the hole?"

"If I had to make an estimate, I'd say eighty."

Callaway almost fell off the sofa. "Eighty thousand?"

Mike lowered his head and nodded.

Callaway stood up. "I guess you deserve what's coming to you." Callaway was terrible with money, but even he knew never to get in too deep, especially with scumbags like Mason.

Mike jumped up. "You gotta talk to Mason for me. Make him understand my situation."

"Why would I do that?"

"You seem like a reasonable person."

"I am, and that's why you're still here and not in front of Mason."

Tears formed in Mike's eyes. "Please. I've got a family. You have to help me. I just need enough time to find a builder, sell the house, and pay off my debts. I swear I won't jump into another scheme ever again."

"What you're telling me requires time. I can talk to Mason, but I doubt I can convince him to wait that long."

Tears flowed down Mike's cheeks. Fear glinted in his eyes. Callaway knew Baxter would hurt Mike the moment he got a hold of him. Mike was not a bad person. He was just someone who fell into a bad situation."

"Okay, I'll try to get you out of this mess, but you have to do whatever I say, got it?" Callaway said.

Mike nodded. "Just tell me what you want me to do."

THIRTY

Outside the District Attorney's office, Holt stormed toward his car with Fisher right behind him. He knew Fisher was right when she said they should keep an open mind as far as other suspects were concerned. He just could not believe Sharon Gardener would have killed her only child. The woman was distraught to the point where Holt wondered if she needed counseling. Maybe it was guilt that was eating away at her. As for Gardener, he might be feeling no guilt because he had given his daughter what he felt she deserved.

As for suspects, Holt had come into this investigation with an open mind. It was when he saw the bloodstain on Gardener's shirt that he became suspicious. Then other things began to fall into place. There was the murder weapon found in his car. How did it get there? And what about his story of not remembering what happened that night? How was that possible? He did not consume enough liquor to blackout.

Maybe Paul Gardener has a low tolerance level for liquor, Holt thought, but he quickly dismissed the possibility. During their sweep of the house, he had spotted empty bottles of alcohol in the guesthouse's garbage can. Gardener may have been a casual drinker once, but lately, he was consuming far more than average. Regardless, his lack of memory seemed too convenient for Holt.

He was unlocking his car when a black Lincoln Town Car pulled up next to him and stopped. The driver's side door swung open, and a man in a dark suit stepped out. He was tall, had a thick mane of white hair that was combed to one side, and he had smooth, tanned skin.

He extended his hand and introduced himself as if Holt did not know who he was. He did. Everyone in the state knew him.

Senator Barron Lester had been elected three times to the upper chamber of Congress. He was currently up for re-election, and very few people thought he would lose. His popularity was high, as his platform focused on the poor and the middle class.

Holt shook his hand and introduced his partner.

"I'm sorry to surprise you like this," Senator Lester said. "I didn't want to show up at the police department and make a big scene."

"It's alright, sir. What can we do for you?" Holt asked.

"It's about Kyla."

"I'm so sorry for your loss," Fisher said.

"Thank you," Senator Lester replied. "As you can imagine, this tragedy has shaken my family and caused me great distress. I've had to take time off my campaign to mourn the loss of my only grandchild. I didn't get to see Kyla as often as I should have. My position in the Senate has kept me busy and away from my family. I now regret that deeply. It is why I want to be as much help as possible."

"Help, sir?" Holt asked, confused.

"I know my son-in-law is under investigation. If there is anything I can do to assist, I want you to know I am available."

"Thank you, sir, but we have everything under control."

"I'm sure you do. Your services to the city and state are greatly appreciated."

Fisher said, "I have a question if you don't mind."

Senator Lester smiled. "Of course not. Please ask."

"Did you ever get any wrong vibes from your son-in-law?"

He frowned. "How so?"

"Did he have any anger issues? Or maybe a temper?"

Senator Lester shook his head. "I can't say he did. In fact, I think he's one of the politest people I've ever known. I've never seen him raise his voice at anyone. Not even at Kyla when she was young."

Fisher was surprised. "Never?"

"I'm sure once in a while, he must have gotten frustrated and snapped at someone. I know I've said many things under pressure. But I wouldn't say Paul had a bad temper."

"What is your son-in-law like?" Fisher asked.

"He's always come across as an honest, hardworking, and dedicated family man. He's an upstanding citizen."

"Are you aware that he and your daughter were having marital problems?"

"Sure, Sharon mentioned it to me. I always want my children to be happy. If the marriage was causing her pain, then she has my support in whatever decision she makes."

"I apologize for being so blunt, sir," Fisher said. "But do you think your son-in-law could have murdered your granddaughter?"

Holt grimaced. The last thing they wanted was to offend a sitting senator whose dedication to the office was beyond reproach. Fortunately, Senator Lester smiled again. "It's a fair question, and I am more than happy to answer it. No, I don't think Paul killed my granddaughter. I refuse to believe it. But I am old enough to understand you never know what people are capable of under duress."

Fisher's brow furrowed. "What do you mean, sir?"

"I know I shouldn't say this, I don't want to influence your investigation, but Paul's business has been suffering lately. I know he was under a great deal of financial stress."

There was a moment of silence.

Senator Lester looked at his watch. "I should be going. I have an important meeting to attend." He stuck his hand inside his jacket pocket and removed a card. "I would greatly appreciate it if you guys kept me abreast of the investigation. My personal cell number is on the back. You can call me day or night."

THIRTY-ONE

Holt and Fisher watched as the Lincoln disappeared from view.

Fisher turned to him. "Why do you think Senator Lester came to see us?" she asked.

"Maybe he wants us to know how important this case is to him," he replied.

"Sure, I get that. But why does he want us to keep him abreast of the investigation?"

"He wants to know if we dig up any dirt on his family. You have to remember; he's up for re-election."

Fisher nodded. "It can't be good for him having the public see his son-in-law charged for murdering his granddaughter. The optics look really bad."

"Or it might end up helping him get re-elected," Holt said.

"How so?"

"Senator Lester has a flawless record, but even that doesn't guarantee victory. There is a strong group of candidates this time around. If one of them catches the voters' interest, Senator Lester is looking at a long, hard fight."

Fisher frowned. "Okay, but you still didn't answer my question."

"No one from Sharon's family was in court for Paul Gardener's bail. Even Sharon was a no-show," Holt replied. "I think the family is distancing itself from the entire situation. Paul Gardener came into the family by marriage. He is not related to them by blood. Isn't it suspicious that no family member has made a public statement in support of Gardener?"

"Maybe they are waiting to see what we find first."

"Maybe."

Holt opened his car door, but he paused before getting behind the wheel. "I'm curious. Why did you ask Senator Lester if his son-in-law had anger issues?"

"Someone strangled and then stabbed Kyla Gardener. The act had to be committed in a fit of rage."

"Are you saying it's a crime of passion?" Holt asked.

"Maybe."

Holt made a face. He did not like the sound of that, and she knew why.

"This means it might not be premeditated and therefore not murder in the first degree," she said.

"That's not for us to decide," Holt said. "We lay the charges, we gather the evidence, and we leave it up to the jury to decide whether it's the right punishment or not. And you always go for the extreme charge and hope the perpetrator pleads to a lesser one."

"I thought you didn't want Gardener to plead?"

"I don't. I still believe he murdered his daughter, and if his wife hadn't lied to us, he might still be in jail right now."

Holt got in the car.

"Where we going?" Fisher asked.

"Let's go talk to the man Sharon met that night."

THIRTY-TWO

Callaway knocked on the steel door and waited. As he expected, Baxter slid the small window open, revealing his eyes.

"Baxter, it's Lee Callaway," he said. "Let me in."

"Do you have an appointment?"

"Are you seriously going to start with this?" Callaway asked, annoyed.

"Boss is a busy man."

"Just let me in, okay?"

"I'm sorry I can't."

"Okay, fine. Let's see what Mason thinks when he finds out I came to talk money, and you didn't let me in."

Baxter huffed and unlocked the door. *I feel like I'm in a bad B movie whenever I come here*, Callaway thought.

He stormed up the steps, but then he waited for Baxter to hold the door open. Mason was on the phone, and his face lit up when he saw Callaway.

"Monday morning at nine, okay?" Mason bellowed into the receiver. "If you are late even one minute, I'll send Baxter to look for you." He slammed the phone down and turned to Callaway with a smile. "How's my favorite PI?"

Callaway raised an eyebrow. "I'm your favorite now?"

"You were always my favorite. So? Where's my money? Where's Mike?"

"I don't have your money, and I still haven't found Mike."

Mason turned to Baxter. "Did he just say he doesn't have my money, or am I going deaf?"

Baxter smiled as if this was his cue to inflict some punishment. "He said he doesn't have your money."

Down boy, Callaway dryly thought.

Mason said, "If you don't have my money and you don't have Mike, then what are you doing here?"

"I came to ask for a loan," Callaway said calmly.

Mason was taken aback. "You want to borrow money from *me*?"

"Yes."

"You sure about that?"

"Absolutely."

Mason's smile widened to the point where Callaway could see his tiny teeth. "You know if you don't end up paying me…"

"Yeah, yeah, I know," Callaway said, sounding bored. "You'll send your guard dog after me."

"Oh, yes, I will. And you know how much Baxter likes you."

Baxter was almost salivating at the opportunity to take a bite out of Callaway. *If he ever tried that, I would not mind plugging him full of lead*, Callaway thought. *I could always claim self-defense.*

"How much?" Mason asked.

"Three thousand."

"Three grand, huh?"

"Yep."

"What do you need it for?"

"Do I ever ask how you got your money?" Callaway asked.

"Hey, relax. It was just a question."

Mason punched in a code on the safe that was concealed underneath his desk. He pulled out stacks of hundred-dollar bills and placed them on the table.

"And how are you going to pay the interest?" Mason asked. "My rates are very high when compared to what the banks offer."

"I'll waive my fee for finding Mike."

Mason's eyes narrowed. "Why do I get the feeling I'm being played."

"How? You get your ten-grand that Mike owes you, you get back your three-grand I just borrowed from you, and you save over a grand from my finder's fee. The way I see it, it's a win-win for you."

Mason thought a moment. "It's now eleven thousand."

"What is?" Callaway asked.

"What Mike owes me," Mason replied.

"It was ten grand just a moment ago."

"I have to apply penalty and interest for late collection."

"That's pretty steep, even for you."

"It's called smart business."

Callaway shook his head. "Good luck finding Mike. I'm sure you can send Baxter to sniff him out."

"Okay, okay," Mason said, putting his hand up. "I was just teasing you. We got a deal."

THIRTY-THREE

The yoga studio was located atop a clothing store. The walls were bare, the floor was polished hardwood, and the windows were without drapes, allowing ample natural light to flow in. The entire atmosphere exuded peace and tranquility. Mats were placed on the floor where students followed the yoga teacher's instructions.

Kenny Goldman wore a skin-tight black t-shirt and black pants. His hair was pulled back into a ponytail, and he sported a goatee, but he had no mustache.

Holt and Fisher stood outside the yoga studio's doors, watching. They did not want to interrupt the class, so they waited patiently. Goldman was not a suspect, so they had no reason to barge in.

Holt noticed the entire class was made up of women. Some were older, but most were not. They were all in relatively good shape, and they followed Goldman like he was a guru. When he gave them a reassuring smile, they brightened up. His approval meant a great deal to them.

When the class ended, Holt and Fisher entered the studio. The women gathered around Kenny quickly dispersed when they saw Holt and Fisher approach. They probably sensed negative vibes from the two detectives.

"Kenny Goldman?" Holt asked, even though he knew who he was.

"Yes."

Holt flashed his badge. "Do you mind if we ask you a few questions?"

"Do I have a choice?" Goldman replied.

"Sure, you do. You say no, and we leave. But then we ask you to come down to the station and provide a formal statement."

Goldman waited to speak until the studio was empty. "It's about Sharon, isn't it?"

"It is."

He shook his head. "What happened to her daughter is truly tragic."

"How did you find out?"

"It's all over the news. Plus... Sharon told me."

"You spoke to her after the incident?"

"Yeah, I wanted to know how she was doing. She's devastated. She blames herself for what happened."

"Blames herself? For what?" Fisher asked.

"She feels maybe if she was home that night her daughter might still be alive."

"Did you and Mrs. Gardener meet in one of your classes?" Fisher asked.

He nodded. "She was one of my students. She used to come once a week, but then she started coming more regularly. I try to get to know my students on a personal level."

"I'm sure you do," Holt shot back.

Goldman was offended. "Sharon's the only student I ever got involved with. I've been married for over ten years. I have a son who means everything to me."

"Then why did you do it?" Holt asked.

Goldman looked down. "Sometimes you do things you know are wrong, but you still do them because you are too tempted, and you don't think anyone will find out."

"Does your wife know of the affair?" Fisher asked.

"I told her before she heard it on the news. I was worried once the story broke a reporter would show up at our door asking questions. My wife wants a divorce, of course. I'll give it to her and whatever else she wants. No point in fighting for stuff when I messed up. I just hope she lets me see my son."

"Do your students know?"

"I believe in openness and owning up to your mistakes. I teach this to my students, so I have to adhere to this as well. I told them what happened. A lot of them left. I don't blame them. I used to have three classes a day, sometimes even more. Now I'm not sure I can fill an entire week."

"Your class was full today," Fisher said.

"I asked for forgiveness, and some of my loyal students have forgiven me. Many are still on the fence. I broke the cardinal rule of not getting involved with a student. The teacher-student relationship is a delicate one. I know it's going to take a long time before I've earned everyone's trust again."

Holt realized the interview was going off-topic. "So, what happened that night?" he asked.

"I was at home when Sharon called me. She said she needed to see me urgently."

"Why?"

"She was feeling depressed, and she needed company."

"And so you left to meet her?"

"I know I shouldn't have—I kick myself over it every day—but I did. I told my wife there was a problem at the studio, and I left. I was hoping to be back quickly, but when I met Sharon, things got more intimate."

Holt was not interested in the sordid details. "Did Mrs. Gardener ever talk about her husband?"

"Not that much. She was unhappy in the marriage, and she never wanted to marry him to begin with."

"Then why did she?"

"I never asked—I figured she would tell me when she was ready—but I could sense that she felt trapped."

"Did she talk about her daughter?" Holt asked.

"Oh, yes. She adored her. I think her daughter was the reason the marriage lasted this long."

"Did she ever mention her husband and her daughter getting into any fights?"

Goldman shrugged. "She never went into too much detail, but what I gathered from talking to Sharon was that Paul Gardener was a good and loving father."

THIRTY-FOUR

When Callaway returned to the beach house, he was utterly spent. After borrowing the money from Mason, he drove Mike straight to the repo center. If Mason had any idea Mike was actually waiting outside his office the entire time, he would have gone ballistic.

At the repo center, Mike paid the amount he owed on the Plymouth Road Runner.

To Callaway's surprise, the Road Runner was actually in far better condition than he had expected. It needed a little cleaning, but they did not have time. Every hour Mason did not receive his money, he would add extra dollars to Mike's loan. He could raise interest rates based on his whims. He could also forgive a loan if he chose to, but Callaway seriously doubted he ever did that. Mason did not strike him as someone who cared for other people's plights.

With the Road Runner firmly in Mike's possession, he and Callaway took it to a buyer Mike had already lined up. The buyer examined the car with much interest. He found imperfections where there were none. Callaway wanted twenty thousand, and the flaws the buyer claimed he saw were a tactic to lower the price. The buyer countered with sixteen thousand dollars. Callaway held firm, to the point he was ready to walk away. The buyer finally raised the price to eighteen thousand, and Callaway, knowing time was of the essence, agreed.

He returned to Mason and handed over the ten thousand Mike owed him, plus the three thousand he had borrowed. Mason asked about what had happened to the Road Runner, which was really what he was after all along. Callaway told him a variation of the truth. Mike had sold the car, and he had ponied up the money he owed as soon as Callaway found him. "But why did you need three grand?" Mason asked. Callaway gave him no answer to that. He wanted Mason to rack his brains on this for a long time.

Mason was certain Callaway had pulled a fast one on him, but there was nothing he could do about it. Callaway had completed the job he had been hired to do.

Once all the obligations were paid out, Callaway was left with almost five thousand dollars. Mike figured he should get a piece of the leftover money, seeing as how it was his precious Road Runner that had saved his neck. Callaway reminded him that if he had told Mason and Baxter where he was hiding, which is what he was hired to do in the first place, they would have not only taken the Road Runner but also made sure Mike never walked again.

Mike could now safely return to his family and try to sell the investment property so he could become debt-free.

The beach house had a wet bar fully stocked with an assortment of spirits and beverages. Callaway poured himself a glass of brandy and walked out to the beach. He did not stop until he got close to the water.

He shut his eyes and let his senses take over. He could hear the gentle waves washing ashore. The air was cool and refreshing on his skin. The sand was warm from the sun. For a moment, he was in complete bliss.

He had money in his pocket, and there was no one chasing him for it.

His eyes snapped open.

There was someone who deserved the money more than he did.

He rushed back inside the house.

THIRTY-FIVE

Holt ended his phone call and leaned on the hood of his car. He had missed another dinner with Nancy, and she was not happy. Even after all these years, she still did not understand his obsession with work. Maybe she did but did not want to admit it. Whenever he was on a new case, he became so consumed he felt like a marathon runner who could not wait to cross the finish line. When he did finish a case, he vowed he would take it easy, maybe even quit the force entirely, but then he would long to start another investigation. Nancy knew before she married Holt that he was miserable when he was not working.

He sighed. Once the Gardener case was complete, he would take Nancy out to a fancy restaurant. He would even splurge on a show or even on a two-day retreat somewhere. She was the love of his life, and if she ever made him choose between her or his work, he would choose her. So far, she had not done that, which made him love her even more.

Fisher approached the car. She was holding a manila envelope. They had a warrant from the judge for Kyla Gardener's telephone records, and Fisher had gone inside the telephone company's headquarters to get them.

"They give you any trouble?" Holt asked.

"They weren't happy about it, but they had no choice."

No company wanted to disclose personal information on a client, even if that client was brutally murdered. Privacy advocates contended the law should apply to everyone, even after death. Holt disagreed, especially if reviewing records of murder victims allowed them to catch the killer.

"Anything interesting?" Holt asked.

"I took a look on my way out. On the day Kyla was murdered, she only made a couple of calls."

She handed him a piece of paper that had the call logs.

"Only a couple?"

"I guess young people don't make calls anymore. They would rather text or send photos."

Holt examined the log. "Do we know who these numbers belong to?"

"We can check."

Fisher pulled out her cell phone and punched in the first number. "Pedro Catano?"

Holt made a face. "How did you find that out?"

"It's called a *phone directory.*"

"I'm surprised you know it. I thought only old folks like me remembered it."

"I'm not that young, you know. My parents would get a phone directory in the mail once a year. I remember my dad going through it to see how many Fishers lived in our neighborhood."

"How many?"

"Quite a lot, actually. It's a very common name. What's the next number?"

Holt read the number out loud. Fisher punched it in. "No hits. Probably disconnected."

Holt read the third number.

"It's for Paul Gardener," she said.

"So, on the day she died, she called her father."

"Looks like it. What's the last number?"

Holt scanned it and frowned. "It says *Unknown.*"

"Oh yeah, I asked the telephone company about that. They said if someone chose to block their number, it wouldn't show up on the phone log."

"That doesn't help us much, does it?" he said, scratching his cheek.

"I asked the telephone company to also provide text messages from the day Kyla was murdered. I haven't had a chance to look at those."

She pulled out another sheet of paper and handed it to him.

Holt scanned the message, feeling utterly confused. "How can anyone understand this? It's all gibberish."

"Let me see," Fisher said, grabbing the list from him. "It's text shorthand. CT means 'can't talk.' TTYL means 'talk to you later.' LU means 'love you.' CUL8R means 'see you later.'"

"That's why I hate texting. Whatever happened to full comprehensive sentences?" Holt griped.

Fisher smirked. "I thought you hated texting because your pudgy fingers couldn't type on the keypad."

"The keys are so tiny, and to make matters worse, autocorrect kept changing what I wanted to say. I almost got in trouble a couple of times for that."

"You did?"

"I once had a sore throat, and it hurt when I talked, so I messaged the sergeant that I couldn't come to work because of germs. What I ended up sending was that I couldn't come to work because of Germans."

Fisher laughed.

"That's not the worst of it. One time, Nancy and I got into a big fight, and she refused to pick up the phone. I got mad, and I texted her that she was a hypocrite. What she saw was that I called her a hippo."

Fisher almost keeled over from laughter.

Holt frowned. "You think it's funny now, but it took a lot of begging and explaining to sort that flub out."

"I should teach you how to turn off autocorrect," Fisher said, wiping her eyes.

Holt's brow furrowed. "You can do that? I thought that stupid thing couldn't be turned off."

Fisher laughed again. "Yes, you can turn that stupid thing off. Some detective *you* are."

Holt sighed.

Fisher resumed reading Kyla's texts. Her face suddenly turned serious. "You won't believe this."

"What?"

"Kyla also had a text conversation with her father. And this one is in plain English."

"Let me see," Holt said.

A smile crossed his face as he read the exchange. "I think we may have found our motive."

THIRTY-SIX

The house was a two-story, single-family detached home located in an old neighborhood. The residence was a far cry from where Paul lived with his wife and daughter. The home was half the size of his current house. His mother's home had a solid foundation but could use an upgrade. The house had only one functioning bathroom, which he and his brother used to fight over when they were young. And during the winter months, he had to wear a sweater when he was inside due to the home lacking insulation. But even with all its faults, Paul had nothing but fond memories of growing up in this house. When the judge asked him to choose a relative to stay with, he chose his mother. She was a retired teacher who kept making the mortgage payments even after their father passed away in middle-age. He was hauling groceries from the car to the house when he collapsed from a heart attack. No one was home at the time. He died in the hallway leading to the kitchen. Had he suffered the attack in the driveway, perhaps a neighbor might have seen him and called for help. But that was all in the past. At the moment, Paul had more important things to contend with. Seated across from him on his parents' old sofa was his lawyer. Roth had called and said he needed to speak to him urgently, and he already was on his way. Paul agreed, of course, but now he wished the meeting was held in Roth's office.

Roth was seething, and he had not said two words since he arrived. Paul understood why. Roth did not want to blow a gasket in front of Paul's mother. After she had served tea, Paul asked her to give them some privacy. She left the house to run some errands.

When they were alone, Roth leaned forward and said, "Why didn't you tell me you had a fight with Kyla?"

Paul blinked. "What?"

"On the day she was murdered, you and she had gotten into some disagreement."

"How did you find out about that?"

"I got a call from the prosecutor. They have text messages between you and your daughter."

"I don't see what the big deal is."

"If a potential juror sees this, it could leave a negative impression of you. The media has already labeled you a killer. But I think there is a bigger problem here."

"Like what?"

"This helps the prosecution build a case against you for murder in the first degree. Until now, they had no reason as to why you killed your daughter…"

"I didn't…"

Roth cut him off. "I can see how they will present their case to the jury. They will say that you were angry or felt disrespected after your morning argument with Kyla. When you returned home from work, you were still seething. You went inside the guesthouse and drank enough alcohol to build your courage. When the time was right, you went upstairs to finish the fight with Kyla. You strangled her in the process and then you panicked. You ran downstairs to the kitchen, grabbed the knife from the knife block, and went back upstairs. Kyla was lying in bed, either still alive or dead, and then you stabbed her for good measure. You proceeded to hide the knife in the glove compartment of your Audi. You thought about driving away, but you feared getting pulled over by the police because of the amount of alcohol you had consumed. You decided to sleep it off, but your wife found out what happened."

Paul put his palms over his face. He suddenly could not breathe. The world around him began to close in.

Roth leaned closer. "Tell me that's not how it happened, Paul."

"I can't," Paul whispered.

"Why not?"

Paul looked up at Roth. There were tears in his eyes. "I don't remember anything from that night."

Roth stared at him for a long moment. He then relaxed and sat back on the sofa. In a calm voice, he said, "I'm sorry for putting you through this, but Barrows will be far more unrelenting than I am. She *will* make you remember what happened that night, whether it's the truth or not."

They were silent a moment.

Roth pulled out a sheet of paper from his briefcase and held it out for Paul. He took it. "Do you want to tell me what the fight was about?" he asked.

Paul scanned the transcript and nodded. "I remember it. Kyla was seeing someone, and she wanted to get married."

"Who?"

"She didn't say."

"And why did she want to get married?"

"She didn't say either."

"She loved this person?"

He shrugged. "I guess so."

"And you were against it, of course."

"I thought she was making a rash decision. She was still young. She had her entire life ahead of her."

"In one of the text messages, she mentioned she didn't care about the money. What was she referring to?"

Paul sighed. "My wife's family is well-off, far more than I'll ever be. Kyla's grandfather…"

"You mean Senator Lester?"

He nodded. "Before he got into politics, he ran a pharmaceutical hedge fund. He sold it for a lot of money. He gave each of his two children a significant inheritance. My brother-in-law is a doctor, so he invested the money in his private clinic. My wife bought the house we are now living in, and my father-in-law set up a trust fund for Kyla. She was supposed to receive a lump sum when she turned twenty-one."

"How much are we talking about?" Roth asked.

"Almost a million dollars."

"You feared it would be a marriage of convenience? That, someone, was going to marry her for the money?"

"Yes."

Roth mulled this over. "In her last text, your daughter said she would still take care of you. What did she mean by that?"

Paul's shoulders slumped even more. "Kyla knew my business was struggling, and she said the moment she received the inheritance, she would help me out."

Roth's face suddenly turned grim. "You know how the prosecution is going to spin this, don't you?"

Paul said nothing.

"They are going to say Kyla changed her mind at the last minute and you felt betrayed by that, and so you punished her for it."

Paul shook his head. "No, no, no. I never asked her for the money. She offered it to me."

"Doesn't matter. Money is one of the most common reasons for premeditated murder. The prosecution now has its motive."

Paul felt like someone had their hands around his neck and was squeezing it tight.

THIRTY-SEVEN

Holt and Fisher were at an apartment building in a rough part of the city. They had come to speak to Pedro Catano. They knocked on the door and waited. A few minutes later, the door opened, and a man stuck his head out. "Can I help you?" he asked. His voice had an accent.

They flashed their badges. Holt said, "We are looking for Pedro Catano."

"Pedro's not home," the man replied. "Is everything okay, officers?"

"And you are—?"

The man came out into the hall. He had weather-beaten skin, calloused hands, and he smelled of cigarettes. "My name is Luiz, and I'm Pedro's father," he said.

"Do you know when Pedro will be home?"

"I don't know. I have not seen him since two days ago."

That's the day Kyla Gardener was murdered, Holt thought.

"Is it normal for Pedro not to show up at home for a couple of days?"

"Not really, but sometimes he stays with his girlfriend."

Holt mulled this over.

Luiz said, "Is this about Kyla?"

"Did you know her?" Holt asked, surprised.

"Of course I did. She grew up right before my eyes."

Holt looked over at Fisher. She, too, was confused.

"Can you explain this to us?" Holt asked Luiz.

"I work for the family," Luiz proudly replied. "I do gardening for Mr. Lester for over thirty years."

"Mr. Lester?"

"Barron Lester."

"You mean Senator Lester?"

"Yes. And then I do gardening for his son and his daughter."

"Is that how Pedro met Kyla?"

Luiz smiled and nodded. "When Pedro was young, I used to take him to work. He used to play with Kyla while I did my work. When he got older, he started helping me more. I hope he takes over the business so I can slow down, you know."

"So, were Pedro and Kyla like friends?" Fisher asked.

"Oh, yes, they were." Luiz frowned. "What happened to her was so sad. She was a sweet girl, always saying hi to me. I will miss her so much."

Fisher asked, "You said you did work for Senator Lester's daughter, Sharon Gardener, as well. Is that correct?"

"Yes, I did."

"So, you must know Paul Gardener?"

"I do."

"What was he like?"

"He was very nice to me. The Lester family can be arrogant sometimes, but not Paul."

"Arrogant? How?"

Luiz looked away. He must have realized he said too much. If this ever reached the family, it might jeopardize his job.

Fisher said, "Don't worry. Whatever you tell us stays with us. We promise."

Luiz stared at her for a moment. "The Lesters don't respect the people that work for them. They are very rude to us and treat us like they own us."

"Even Senator Lester?" Fisher asked.

"Yes. He is very demanding and tough. One time, the lawnmower broke, and he took it out of my pay. That's why I bring my own equipment now."

"Why do you still work for them if they don't treat you properly?" Fisher asked.

"I need the money. I send it to my sister in Colombia. Her husband was killed during a government drug raid. He was riding his bicycle when everybody started shooting at each other. Her kids are bigger now, but I still help out."

"Was Mrs. Gardener also disrespectful to you?" Fisher asked.

Luiz nodded. "Oh, yes. One time, the sprinkler system stopped working. I was busy because my wife was sick, and I couldn't go fix the sprinkler. It was a hot summer, and the grass turn brown. Mrs. Gardener yelled at me in front of Mr. Gardener and their daughter. When everybody was gone, Mr. Gardener apologize to me. He gave me a bonus the next time he pay me. He was an honest man."

"Do you have Pedro's telephone number?" Holt asked. "We need to speak to him urgently."

"I called him a *million* times, but he does not pick up," Luiz replied.

"You said Pedro sometimes stays with his girlfriend," Holt said.

"Yes."

"What's her name?"

THIRTY-EIGHT

Callaway knocked on the door and waited. He was not sure why he was nervous, but he was. He fixed his hair and adjusted his shirt collar. He cupped his hand over his mouth and checked his breath.

Maybe I shouldn't have had onion rings for lunch, he thought. *Where's a pack of gum when you need it?*

He closed his eyes and took a deep breath. They said visualization helped calm the anxious mind. He tried to focus while taking deep breaths. He was walking on the beach. He was alone. There was no one as far as his eyes could see. The sun was up, the air was fresh, and the sound of birds chirping could be heard in the distance. He smiled as complete bliss overtook him. He was suddenly devoid of all worries.

His smile faded when dark clouds appeared in the sky. They were followed by harsh winds that bit his face. The water turned violent as if it was screaming at him. It crashed ashore at high speeds, making him feel pure terror.

He snapped his eyes open and saw his ex-wife. She was standing in the doorway, staring at him. "Glad you're awake, Lee," she said. "For a second there, I thought I'd have to shut the door and leave you out here."

Patricia "Patti" Callaway had dark hair that was cut short. Her eyes were brown, and they were also great lie detectors. No fib ever got past them. Her lips were always curled into a smile, even when the world around her was falling apart. Callaway had to admit he still found Patti attractive, even after all these years. And yet he had willingly released her when she was all his.

Callaway had fallen in love with her the moment he saw her. They had met at a bar in Spokem County. She was a waitress. He ordered a drink, and she brought it for him. He wished he could say she noticed him because he said something funny to her, or he had saved her from a group of goons who were bothering her, but that did not happen. What did happen was he had clammed up the moment she smiled at him. His hands became sweaty, and he felt like he was about to faint. He spent the rest of the evening sipping that one drink. When he asked for the bill, he saw to his surprise that Patti had written her name and number on the back. To this day, she never told him why she chose him over a dozen guys who were vying for her attention that particular night. Callaway liked to think she had chosen him because he was smarter and better looking than the other guys, but perhaps she was attracted to him by the way he acted like a little boy who had a crush on a girl in his kindergarten class. She probably was glad he did not try any lame pickup lines or crass comments on her.

They got married and had a daughter. Sabrina, or "Nina" as they liked to call her, was nine years old now. Callaway would not have minded if he was called a lousy husband but a great father. Unfortunately, he had failed at both.

He loved and adored his little girl. He doted on her when she was a baby, but then his restlessness took over. He could not see himself domesticated. He wanted to be free to follow his own path.

He was selfish when he walked out on his wife and daughter. There was no other way to say it. He still regretted this decision, but he knew deep down he would not have been able to make his family happy because he was not happy.

He moved to Milton and offered to buy a house for Patti and Nina in the city. He even offered to pay for Patti's nursing school. He honored their agreement for a couple of years, working several jobs to make ends meet. The PI business was still in its infancy, so he worked as a security guard at a mall and as a doorman for a dance club.

But then the restlessness took over again.

He stopped sending money to her and fell behind on his child support payments. He vowed to pay her in full, but things always got in the way.

"So, what brings you down here?" Patti asked, crossing her arms under her chest.

Callaway shrugged. "I was in the neighborhood, and I thought I'd drop by and see you and Nina."

She gave him the same look she always did when she knew he was lying. "Really? Or are you here to grab your stuff?"

After Callaway was booted out of the last place he was staying, he begged Patti to let him store his personal belongings in the garage and shed. He promised to pay her rent for the storage, but he never did.

Callaway pulled an envelope out of his pants pocket. "No, I actually came to give you this."

He handed Patti the envelope. She squinted. "What's this?"

"It's three thousand dollars."

She quickly grabbed the envelope, as if her ex-husband might suddenly change his mind and try to keep the money. She looked inside the envelope and saw a stack of hundred-dollar bills.

"Where did you get it?" she asked.

"A job."

"You sure you didn't rob a bank or something?"

"I can't believe you would even think that." He feigned disappointment. "I used to be on the side of the law."

"You used to also have a stable job, a house, a family, but you threw all that away."

He grimaced. "Ouch. You made your point."

She stared at the money as if it was not real.

"I know the house needs a bit of fixing up, so I thought I'd help out."

Patti worked long shifts at the local hospital. She made enough to pay the mortgage and cover most of the bills. He found out through Nina that the roof had started to leak, and Patti was struggling to raise the money needed for the repairs.

Patti was a great mom to Nina. She made sure their daughter was never without anything. She gave her as much love as two parents. Callaway had a million faults, but he always appreciated what Patti had done in raising Nina.

"Why're you suddenly so generous? It's not like you," Patti asked.

Callaway shrugged. She was right. It was not like him. Whenever he had two cents to rub together, he would spend it on some get-rich-quick scheme. There was something bothering him, though. Was it Kyla Gardener's murder? Her father was charged with killing his daughter, but Callaway had seen the pain and anguish in his eyes. Paul's feelings were genuine, not fake. Callaway could not imagine any harm coming to his little girl, especially not at his hands.

I guess I'm feeling guilty about what a lout I've been, he thought.

"Where's Nina?" he asked.

"If you were more involved, you would know she is at school."

Right.

"Do you mind if I pick her up?" he asked.

She stared at him. "Sure. It'll give me a chance to run some errands."

She was about to shut the door when he said, "Hey, I was thinking, one of these days, why don't I take you and Nina out to a nice restaurant or just a simple place to grab a bite to eat?"

Patti sighed. "Okay, fine, whatever, but don't make any promises to Nina. You always end up disappointing her."

Can't argue with that, Callaway thought.

THIRTY-NINE

The bar and restaurant was not far from where Pedro lived. The weather was nice, and the bar's patio was jam-packed. People drank, ate, chatted, and smoked as waiters moved around the tables, bringing them their orders.

Holt and Fisher asked a waiter about the employee they were seeking. He pointed to a girl at the far end of the patio. They approached her.

"Martina Delacruz?" Holt said.

"Yes."

Martina had olive skin, dirty blonde hair, and full lips painted red. Her eyes were hazel, and they were covered in heavy mascara. When she turned her head, a large tattoo of a cross could be seen on the back of her neck.

Holt and Fisher flashed their badges.

"What do you guys want?" Martina asked.

"We're looking for Pedro," he said.

"I haven't seen him in weeks."

"Isn't he your boyfriend?"

"He used to be until we broke up."

Holt looked over at Fisher. She, too, was thinking the same thing. This was a dead end.

"Listen," Martina said. "This is the time I make most of my tips for the day. If you guys come back later, I'll answer your questions."

Some patrons left the patio. "Why don't we get a bite to eat?" Fisher suggested, gesturing at the empty table. "I'm kind of hungry."

Holt understood. She did not want to go back empty-handed. He did not want to either.

Martina took them over to the table and handed them menus. "You guys want anything to drink? We have a special on tap," she said.

"We're on duty," Holt said. "Water for me."

"I'll have an iced tea."

"Coming right up."

Once they had their drinks, Holt ordered a chicken breast sandwich with fries on the side. Fisher ordered pasta and a Caesar salad.

While they ate, they watched as Martina moved around the patio, serving the patrons that came and went.

Almost an hour later, with their plates empty and the restaurant less busy, Martina came over to them with their bill.

"Do you mind talking to us now?" Holt asked.

"It depends if you guys give me a nice tip," Martina replied.

Holt almost laughed. *She sounds like a paid informant*, he thought. "Sure, why not," he said.

Martina pulled up a chair and sat down next to the detectives. "So, what do you want to know about Pedro?"

"We're looking for him," Holt replied.

"As I told you, I haven't seen him in at least a week or two."

"You said you guys broke up. Why?"

"He was acting weird and stuff."

"Weird? How?'

"Whenever we were together, he was always on the phone. He was distracted all the time. He would get upset and angry for nothing. I think it was that bitch…" Martina caught herself. "Sorry."

"Who?"

"The one who got killed."

Holt sat up straight. "Kyla Gardener?"

"Yeah. Pedro was always calling her, or she was calling him. I asked him about it, and he would always say they were friends, but I got the feeling that he liked her. I mean, she was white, and she had money, so I get it, right?"

Holt and Fisher did not know how to respond to that.

"I got me a white boy too. He's sweet, and he takes care of me," Martina said.

"Did Pedro and Kyla ever get into a fight?" Fisher asked.

Martina shrugged. "I dunno. Pedro didn't like talking about her with me. Whenever I brought her name up, he would get quiet. I think he was sleeping with her."

"Are you sure about that?" Fisher asked.

Martina gave her a look. "A woman knows when her man is cheating on her."

"Did Pedro ever talk about Kyla's father?" Fisher asked, getting Martina back on track.

She thought a moment. "Yeah, he mentioned him a few times."

"What did he say?"

"He was a nice guy, and Pedro liked him."

"Anything else?"

Martina shook her head and got up. "I gotta go. My boss is staring at me."

She grabbed the bill and smiled at the size of the tip. "I thought cops were cheap asses, but you guys are okay."

"Glad to know," Holt replied.

FORTY

The school was only a couple of blocks from Patti's house. Even then, Patti never let Nina walk home alone. If she was off work, she would pick up Nina herself. If she was working, she would ask a neighbor or another parent to take Nina home. Nina was also enrolled in a lot of extracurricular activities, from music classes to dance classes to art classes. By the time Nina was done with one of those, Patti was there to pick her up. Things would be easier if Callaway shared duties as a parent, but he did not. He tried, but there were too many times he left Nina waiting at the school's front steps. Luckily, a teacher or concerned parent would notify the school or Patti. His ex-wife would be furious at Callaway's irresponsible behavior. She would forbid him from seeing Nina. Eventually, she would let him back in, only for Nina's sake. A girl needed a father, even if he was a cad.

Patti was far more mature than Callaway would ever be, although her decision to marry him may have been most unwise in many ways. Regardless, she knew if she cut Callaway off from Nina's life completely, the man would just move on to something else. It was better if he was always reminded he had a child who needed him every once in a while.

Callaway would be the first to admit he was not always there for his daughter. It was not that he did not love or care for her; his situation was just… well, *complicated*.

The birth of his only child was the happiest day of his life. He broke down in tears when he laid eyes on her. He felt overwhelming joy when he held her in his arms. He stayed up all night staring at her.

Callaway never imagined that at this stage of his life, he would be divorced from a woman who was better than him in every way, would hardly see his daughter, would always be struggling for money, and would be sleeping at a stranger's house. But certain events led him to where he was. He had no one to blame but himself.

There was a bigger reason why he was not always available to his daughter. There were times he felt like a loser, as if he was not worthy of his daughter's love. The other parents had cool jobs, incomes in the six-figures, drove fancy cars, and lived in nice neighborhoods. He barely eked out a living. He later realized Nina did not need anything from him except his time and his unconditional love. He vowed to give her that, but he kept coming up short.

He spotted her standing by the school's steps. Nina had dark hair like her mother, albeit longer, almost reaching her lower back. Her eyes were emerald green, like his, but her smile was again like her mother's. She looked like a mini version of Patti. He was glad his daughter got her mother's beauty.

He waved at her, but she did not wave back. A woman was standing next to her. Nina turned and said something to the woman. Callaway recognized her as one of Nina's teachers. The teacher scowled as Callaway approached. He just smiled back at her.

"Are you sure you'll be okay?" the teacher asked, ignoring Callaway completely.

My reputation precedes me, Callaway thought.

"I'll be fine, Mrs. Jennings," Nina said.

"She'll be fine," Callaway said.

The scowl on the teacher's face did not disappear.

He held out his hand and she reluctantly took it. She did not want to come across as rude in front of her students.

Screw you, Mrs. Jennings, he thought. *I'll get you with my kindness.*

As Nina and Callaway walked back to Patti's house, he said, "So, how's my princess doing?"

"I'm almost ten, dad. Please don't call me 'princess.'"

"You'll always be my princess."

She rolled her eyes. "Whatever."

"How's school?" he asked.

"Good."

"You like it?"

She shrugged. "It's okay, but if I want to be successful when I'm older, I need an education."

"That's right. Or else you'll end up like me."

"Broke and homeless."

"Hey, did your mom tell you that?"

"Are you?"

He stared at her. Even though she had his eyes, they were great lie detectors, just like her mother's.

"Okay, next question," he said, trying to change the subject. "Do you have a boyfriend?"

She made a face. "If I did, I wouldn't tell you. I would tell mom first."

"So, you *do* have a boyfriend?" He started jumping up and down. "Nina's got a boyfriend. Nina's got a boyfriend."

Nina rolled her eyes. "Dad, you're embarrassing me. And no, I don't have a boyfriend."

"Good," he said, stopping. "Or else I'd beat him up."

"Whatever," she said, and they continued walking. "You gave mom some money, right?"

He frowned. "How did you know that?"

"Did she give you a hard time about seeing me?"

"No."

"Then you must have given her money," she said.

"Maybe I came all the way just to see you."

"Dad, I'm not a child anymore. I know when you come to visit."

"Okay, when do I come?"

"When you have something for her. Or else, if you came empty-handed, she would have yelled at you by now."

"Then how did you know I gave her money?"

She let out a dramatic sigh as only a young person could. "Dad, you're not so bright, are you? If you didn't give mom money, she wouldn't have let you pick me up. Don't you see that?"

She not only looked like her mother, but she was also just as whip-smart.

God help me, Callaway thought.

"On my way here, I saw an ice cream shop. What do you say we get some right now?" he suggested

"Before dinner?" Nina asked with a raised eyebrow.

"Why not?"

"And you're okay with explaining this to mom?"

"Okay, never mind." He was suddenly disappointed. He wanted to do something for his little girl and he couldn't even do that. His irresponsible behavior had stripped him of that right.

She squeezed his hand and said, "I still love you, dad."

He smiled at her. "I love you too, baby."

FORTY-ONE

Holt and Fisher were at the DA's office. Barrows was behind her desk, looking disappointed. "As you know," she said, "the defense always has more resources than we do. They are being paid by clients who, at times, are quite wealthy, while we at the DA's office are at the mercy of elected officials for our annual budget. We were fortunate the current governor has allocated extra funding to our department. This has allowed us to level the playing field somewhat against the criminal defense lawyers and their heavy bank accounts."

Where are you going with this? Holt thought. He glanced at Fisher. He could tell she was thinking the same thing.

Barrows saw the look on their faces and said, "I hired a private company to conduct a blind survey of citizens of this city. I've heard of defense lawyers investing in such a study, so I wanted to gauge public opinion before we went to trial. We gave them a case that was exactly like Gardener's, minus the names, of course. We asked them if they would give a verdict of guilty or not guilty if they were members of a jury, based on the evidence presented.

Holt's back arched. He was suddenly eager to know the answer.

Barrows said, "Overwhelmingly, the majority said *not* guilty."

"What?" Holt jumped up from his chair. "That's bullshit."

Barrows was not the least bit offended by the profanity. She had heard far worse while in court. Holt began to pace the room like he normally did. He was like a bull who wanted to let off steam. Barrows gave him a moment to compose himself.

Fisher asked, "What was their reason for giving such a verdict?"

"In order to convict, they have to believe without a shadow of a doubt that Paul Gardener murdered his daughter. And they did not."

"What about the blood on his shirt?" Holt asked. "How can that not be conclusive?"

"We are still waiting for the report to confirm whether it's the victim's blood on his shirt or not."

"It is," Holt said firmly. "Paul Gardener was not bleeding anywhere on his body."

"I agree, and those surveyed were never told whether the blood was his or the daughter's. Their concern was—and I'm going to relate it to the Gardener case—if Paul Gardener did indeed murder his daughter, then why did he not dispose of the shirt with the evidence on it?"

"Maybe he didn't realize there was any blood on him," Fisher suggested.

"It was easy for you guys to spot, so why not by him?"

"Maybe it was dark, and he didn't see it."

Holt jumped in. "Maybe while in a state of panic at what he had done, he got careless. That's known to happen in cases like these."

Barrows said, "There was blood on the victim, on the bed, everywhere. Surely, he would have known some of it was on him."

"Maybe he was too drunk and didn't realize it was."

"Apparently, he was not too drunk to go out to his car and hide the murder weapon in the glove compartment," Barrows said. "That tells us he was aware of his actions and their consequences."

"But remember, he went back inside the guesthouse to sleep off the alcohol," Holt said.

Barrows frowned. "That's another thing the people surveyed found questionable."

"What?"

"Why would someone not leave the scene of the crime? They must have known that the victim's body would be found by someone."

"Maybe he hoped that by morning he would be clearheaded. He would then conceive a plan to get rid of the body and the evidence."

"At the moment, it's all conjecture and not sufficient enough to convict. If it was premeditated murder, then the onus is on us to prove the killing was motivated. So far, we don't have that."

"Sure we do," Holt said. "We have the text messages between the suspect and his daughter.'"

"That exchange could simply have happened during the heat of the moment. How many times have we said something to our parents in anger only to regret it later?"

"The victim wanted to get married; her father disagreed. They got into an argument, and he killed her," Holt insisted.

"That very well may be the case. But based on the facts at hand, we may not win this case, or we may end up with a hung jury. Neither of those options looks very appealing to me."

Fisher jumped in. "Are you saying we should drop the charges?"

"Of course not," Barrows replied. "What I'm saying is you need to get me something that will persuade a jury without a shadow of a doubt that Paul Gardener did murder his only child."

FORTY-TWO

Callaway returned to his office with a far lighter wallet. He had stopped by the noodle shop and handed over the last two months' worth of rent. The landlady had been after him for so long that on some days, he considered not coming to his office.

On his last trip to his office, he knew his landlady was out of town visiting a relative, so there was no way he would run into her. Sometimes he would show up at odd hours to avoid her, like early in the morning or in the middle of the night. He hated hiding like a criminal, but when you do not have money, you make yourself scarce.

He could have given Patti less money, but the longer the money was in his pocket, the more tempted he would have become. He would have gone straight to a casino or a bookie and tried his luck. Over the years, he had won some serious money, but he had lost it too. That was how it was with gambling, although in his experience, he lost more than he won.

Callaway also believed in always clearing up his debt, no matter who it was to. The money he gave to Patti was well overdue. She was raising Nina on a single income, which was not easy. And with Callaway hardly there to help out physically, the very least he could do was help out financially.

As for the landlady, she had expenses relating to the restaurant and the building. She did not need someone like Callaway taking advantage of her.

The situation reminded him of a saying his high school Economics teacher would say: *There's no such thing as a free lunch. Even if it was free to you, someone is paying for it, and they hope to earn back the cost sometime down the line.*

The landlady was getting no benefit from letting him squat, which was, after all, what he was doing by not paying rent.

He sat down behind his laptop and began to go through his emails. He was surprised by the number of people who found him through his website. In fact, right after solving the Hotel Murders in Fairview, he was certain his business would explode. And it did, but for all the wrong reasons.

A potential client had said Foo Foo, his pet cat, had run away and he wanted Callaway to bring her home. *It's an animal*, he thought. *It was probably sick and tired of its owners.*

Two other potential clients, the parents of a teenage girl, said her boyfriend stopped returning her calls, and they wanted Callaway to find out what happened. Unless there was a missing persons report filed by the boyfriend's family with the police, the boyfriend probably moved on with someone else.

One man had the gall to contact him about a particular job, which involved scoping out a bank for info that could be useful in a robbery. Callaway was furious and dumfounded at the offer. Did the guy not realize what he was asking him to do was illegal? That moron had no idea the client/PI relationship was not protected by the courts like the doctor/patient relationship was. Callaway had forwarded the email to the Milton police.

Then there were jobs he turned down because the outcome could end up being dangerous. He had stalkers reach out to him to locate celebrities or people they were infatuated with. He had one disturbed person ask him to follow a congresswoman because he did not like her policies.

Callaway did, however, take on jobs that involved finding dirt on a client's colleague or supervisor so the client could wrangle a promotion. He also took jobs from companies who hired him to ferret out the secrets of their competitors, like when they were launching their next product, or what products they were currently developing. Such snooping might be unethical, but he figured if no one was physically harmed in the process, then it was okay. Plus, the individuals and companies who hired him always paid on time, or they always sweetened the fee if the outcome was favorable to them.

Callaway began going through his emails, hoping he would find more of those types of cases to work on.

FORTY-THREE

Outside the DA's office, Fisher said, "We need to find Pedro."

"No, we need to find more evidence against Paul Gardener," Holt shot back.

"What if Pedro murdered Kyla and now he's disappeared?" she asked.

"I don't buy it."

"Kyla did call Pedro on the day she died."

"But she also called other people," Holt said.

"Yes, but none of those people have suddenly gone missing."

"Okay. What about the unknown number?"

"What about it?'

"That's exactly my point," he said. "It could be someone of no consequence, or it could be someone relevant to the case."

Fisher shook her head. Holt was stubborn. He was like a hound who had his eyes on only one fox.

"Paul Gardener is our man," he said. "If we start broadening the scope of our investigation, it will only distract us from the real killer."

"If we broaden our scope, and we do a good job of eliminating all suspects and possibilities, then I'm sure it will lead us back to Paul Gardener," Fisher replied.

"Why bother when we already know he did it?" Holt asked.

"Do we?"

He stared at her. "You don't believe he did?"

"I'm not so sure."

Holt sighed. "I can't believe you're siding with Barrows."

Fisher frowned. "I'm not."

"You are," he insisted. "I can see where she's coming from, but not you."

Fisher's face hardened. "Please do explain?"

"All she cares about is winning the case, but I'm not sure what your angle is here."

"I care about putting a guilty man away," Fisher said. "Not an innocent man."

Holt scowled. "Paul Gardener is not innocent."

"How do you know that with certainty?"

Holt stomped over to his car and removed a folder from the backseat. "I had someone at the department dig up Gardener's financial records. The house that he and his wife bought with his father-in-law's gift was recently re-mortgaged. His business is bleeding cash, and he has tried to sell it, with no takers. The bills are piling up, and he is drowning in debt. I believe he saw his daughter as the only way out."

"How?" Fisher asked, confused.

"The text messages," Holt replied. "The victim was going to inherit a million dollars when she turned twenty-one, which was only a few months away. That would have been enough to get Gardener out of the mess he was in."

"Okay, but the victim did say she would help her father out, so why kill her?"

"Maybe at the time they texted, she agreed to do it. What if she changed her mind, and Gardener was so overcome with rage, he attacked her?"

Fisher did not look convinced.

"Remember," Holt said, "the victim was also considering getting married. Who do you think would lose out if she did? Paul Gardener."

FORTY-FOUR

Callaway came to the end of his emails and frowned. There were none that stuck out to him. Most were from people who had a story to tell, but they were not sure if they needed a private investigator. If Callaway had to convince someone they needed his services, then he did not want them as a client. They would always question his fees, the duties performed, and the end result of the work. The situation reminded him of people who always griped about the fees accountants charged for preparing their tax returns. They considered filing returns a simple job, one that should not cost much. It was only when the IRS came knocking on their doors that they were willing to pay just about anything to make the problem go away.

People did not value what private investigators did for them. They took for granted all the grunt work that was needed to perhaps get photos of a cheating husband, or get information on someone who had disappeared, or get names of people who had caused them harm. People who genuinely needed him made the best clients. They knew they had nowhere else to turn, and so they were willing to open their checkbooks with little hesitation.

Callaway logged out of his email account. He would have to go door to door and drop off his business cards to drum up more business. He did not have the money to pay for newspaper or television ads. The website was built for him, courtesy of a client, but he still had to promote the site. *Maybe I should invest some time in this* AdWords *I keep hearing about*, Callaway thought.

He heard a noise outside. He stopped and listened. It sounded like someone was walking up the metal steps.

He was not expecting anyone. He reached for his belt to draw his gun before he realized it was still locked up at the beach house.

Damn. Must be Baxter. I guess Mason figured it out.

He was cornered.

He saw a shadow in the doorway.

He held his breath.

The stranger knocked on the door.

Callaway slowly got up to check.

A man stood at the entrance. He had coiffed hair, smooth skin, and perfect teeth. He wore a white suit with a pink shirt and black dress shoes. Everything about him said expensive, which made him stick out in this neighborhood.

The man also had a bandage on one hand.

No, it's not Baxter, Callaway thought. *Maybe he's one of those cheating husbands I busted? He doesn't look familiar, though.*

Callaway opened the door.

"Lee Callaway?" the man asked.

"Can I help you?" Callaway replied hesitantly.

"My name is Dr. Richard Lester."

Callaway just looked at him.

"I am Sharon Gardener's brother," Dr. Lester said.

"Oh," Callaway said. "So that would make Kyla Gardener your niece?"

"Yes," Dr. Lester replied.

Callaway wanted to invite him inside for a seat, but his office did not give off the best impression. "What can I do for you?" he asked as he stepped out and closed the door behind him.

"I know you're a busy man, so I won't take too much of your time."

"Okay," Callaway said. *Nice he thinks I'm busy as a bee*, Callaway thought, *but I've got all the time in the world.*

Dr. Lester cleared his throat. "I'm here about the photos you took for my brother-in-law, Paul."

Callaway squinted. "What about them?"

"I'm interested to know what's in those photos."

"I'm sorry, but that's privileged information. I cannot tell you what's in those photos without Mr. Gardener's okay."

Dr. Lester did not seem offended by Callaway's direct response. "My sister was very upset that her activities on that particular night were made public," he said. "We don't want the actual photos to get out either."

"I understand your concern, but my client hired me to take them. Whatever he does with them is his choice. If I were you, I'd speak to him," Callaway said.

"I would, but right now, due to tragic circumstances, we are not on speaking terms."

"So I heard," Callaway said. *Nice family, abandoning an in-law to sink or swim*, he thought.

"I would be willing to buy them off you. Name your price, Mr. Callaway," Dr. Lester said.

Callaway grimaced. *Sure I need the bucks*, he thought, *but client confidentiality is set in stone for me.* "I'm sorry you wasted your time coming here," he said, "but those photos are not for sale."

Dr. Lester was unfazed. He put his hand inside his pants pocket and pulled out a business card. "Well, if you change your mind, I'll make it worth your while."

FORTY-FIVE

Roth was once again seated across from Paul in his mother's house. Roth was preparing for another case when Paul called him. He sounded hysterical and upset, constantly wailing, "I want this nightmare to end!" Roth worried his client was going to do something stupid, so he rushed over.

Fortunately, Paul was composed when he arrived at the door. His mother had given him one of her anxiety medications to calm him down.

As he stared at him, Roth could not help but see a man who looked more like a scared boy. Paul wore a t-shirt, and his track pants were white, but Roth could see coffee stains on them. He had stubble on his cheeks, and his hair was sprouting in all directions. Roth would have to clean him up before he presented him to the jury. There was no way he would let anyone see him like this.

Paul rubbed his hands together. He avoided making eye contact, but Roth could see his pupils were dilated. Maybe it was the effects of the medication, or maybe it was the medication combined with the alcohol that was causing his eyes to look that way.

Paul reeked of booze. There was no telling how many bottles he had consumed. Roth would have to ask his mother.

"I'm sorry that you had to drive over here because of me," Paul said.

"I'm here whenever you need me," Roth replied. *It's all billable hours*, he thought.

Paul nodded.

Roth said, "You told me on the phone that you wanted this nightmare to end. What did you mean by that?"

"My daughter is dead. My wife has abandoned me. My reputation is in tatters. My life is destroyed."

"It can all be redeemed once you are found not guilty."

"How long will that take?" Paul asked, finally looking at him. "I can't go back to my own house because of all the attention. I can't even leave my mom's house without reporters following me. Even my mom is constantly being harassed by them."

"I can ask the Milton PD to make them stop bothering her."

"Why can't you make them leave *me* alone too?"

"The media wants a story, and you are a person of interest in a horrible crime. Your mom, on the other hand, has nothing to do with what happened. They can't force her to talk to them."

They were silent a moment.

Paul said, "When can I see my daughter's body?"

"I put in a request, but your wife, as the next of kin, won't allow it."

"I'm her father. I'm also her next of kin."

"Yes, but you are charged with murdering her."

Paul shook his head. "This is not right. I may be charged, but I haven't been found guilty. Can't we get a judge to grant me access to see my daughter?"

"We can try, but in my opinion, it would be a waste of time. Even if we went ahead with it, I could almost guarantee a judge will side with your wife. She's also a victim in all of this."

Paul blinked. "A victim?"

"Let me rephrase that. She is the victim's mother. I can bet the prosecution will use her against you, to show that you were a horrible father, that you never got along with your daughter, and that you had a motive to kill her."

"I didn't," Paul said.

"Regardless, when a jury sees a grieving mother on the stand, weeping about the loss of her child—an only child, I might add—they will sympathize with her pain. And to make matters worse, you and she were on the verge of separation, so I highly doubt she'd hold back any vitriol against you."

Paul's head fell to his chest.

"My advice to you is to stop watching the news, to stay indoors as much as possible, and to keep your mind occupied with things other than what happened. It's going to be some time before we go to trial, and I can't have you falling apart. And trust me, the media will be bored of you the moment something else catches their attention."

FORTY-SIX

After the visit from Dr. Lester, Callaway decided to leave his office and walk down to the bar around the corner. He was still thinking about the offer Lester had made him. The doctor would have paid far more than what Paul had given him, but it came down to principle. Paul was his client, and his loyalty was to him and no one else.

There were many times when cheating spouses of his clients had tried to buy him out. They would make personal visits or go through their lawyers. Their main objective was to make sure the information did not become public, or that the information did not make it into the hands of their spouses. Their offer would be double or even triple what he received from his clients. The more damning the evidence, the more money they were willing to throw at him.

Callaway was not a blackmailer. He despised even being referred to as one. Right after he was hired for a job, he usually had no idea what he would dig up. And when he did, he forwarded that information to his client. If that client used it to blackmail their husband or wife, that was up to them. It did not change the price Callaway charged for his services. Now, if the client was gracious to give him a bonus or let him stay at her beach house rent-free, that was something extra. He never demanded free perks.

There were a couple of times where Callaway had to return the money because he did not feel compelled to finish the job. Once, a woman came to him and said she was certain her husband had another family she was not aware of. Callaway took on the case and followed the husband. He discovered the husband was indeed meeting another woman, but she turned out to be his half-sister. They had found each other through social media. The husband was embarrassed that his deceased father had a child out of wedlock, so he hid his half-sister's existence from his wife. He also feared that if his wife found out, she would tell *his* mother, whom she did not get along with. His mother, a cancer survivor, would be devastated that his father had been unfaithful in their marriage. The husband was waiting for the right time to break the news to his mother. Callaway decided to keep the information to himself and refunded the wife.

He walked into the restaurant and headed straight to the bar. He ordered a drink, and he spotted someone familiar in a booth by the window.

He grabbed his glass and went over. "Mind if I join you?" he asked.

Fisher looked at him. "What if I said no?"

"I would still sit down, but then it would be very awkward."

She smiled and took a sip from her drink.

"Aren't you still on duty?" he asked.

"It's cranberry juice," she replied.

"Mine is four percent alcohol," he said, holding up his glass.

"Glad to know," she said.

He looked around. "What brings you all the way here? I'm sure there are nicer places to get a drink near the Milton PD."

"I just wanted to get away."

"From Holt?" he said. "I don't blame you. The man is anal as they come."

"He's not so bad," she said. "He's actually a very good detective. I've learned a lot from him."

Callaway grinned. "And what have you learned from me?"

"To stay away from guys like you."

"And what's wrong with guys like me?"

"They think they can do whatever they want in life and that it doesn't have any repercussions."

"What have I done?" he asked, feigning surprise.

She shook her head and took another sip from her glass.

"Is this about Patti?" he asked.

Fisher had a theory that Callaway was still in love with his ex-wife. She believed he did not feel worthy of a woman like her and that was why he was jumping from one relationship to another. "How's Nina?" Fisher asked instead of replying to Callaway's question. "Have you gone to see her yet?"

"As a matter of fact, I did, and we had ice cream."

"How is she?"

"Growing up fast."

"They do when you don't pay too much attention."

"Okay, I got your point."

There was a pause.

"How's the investigation going?" he asked.

"Which one?"

"The Gardener case?"

"It's coming along."

"That's not what I heard."

"What have you heard?"

"I heard you guys don't have enough evidence to send him to prison for a very long time."

"And where did you hear that?"

"I read it online."

"Don't believe everything you read, especially online," she said.

"Is it true or not?"

She stared at him and decided to come clean. "We don't have enough yet, but we'll find it. Holt won't stop until he does."

"He is convinced Paul Gardener is guilty?" Callaway asked.

She nodded.

"And what about you?" he asked. "Do you think he's guilty?"

She shrugged. "So far, all signs point to him, and until I see something otherwise, I'm inclined to think so too."

"Do you mind letting me see what you got on him?" he asked.

She laughed. "You know I can't do that. We are only supposed to let Gardener's defense see what we have against him. If you are so inclined, you can ask his lawyer. By the way, why are you suddenly so interested? I thought you completed the job he hired you for?"

"I did. It's just that he doesn't come across as a killer to me."

"They never do until they end up committing the crime."

Callaway could not argue with that.

FORTY-SEVEN

Fisher returned to the Milton PD. She found Holt waiting at her desk. He had a smile on his face.

"What's up?" she asked.

"Where have you been? I called you several times."

She checked her phone and saw she had many missed calls. "I had to meet a friend."

"Was it Lee Callaway?" he asked.

"How'd you know?"

"Call it a wild guess. I thought you were done with him?"

"I am, but still, how did you know I met him?"

"You said you were driving to Chinatown, I know his office is around there. I figured you'd run into him."

"I did."

"You should be careful with him," Holt warned her. "He screwed us when he took those photos of Sharon Gardener."

"No. He just gave us proof that she was lying to us."

Holt scowled. "Because of those photos, Gardener got bail."

"He would have gotten bail regardless. His lawyer would have seen to it," Fisher shot back.

"I don't know about that."

"Roth gets big bucks for keeping his client out of jail. He would have pulled a lot of strings to make sure Gardener didn't spend another minute in a cell."

Holt pondered her words. "All I'm saying is that Callaway was instrumental in the outcome. He works for our suspect, so that makes him our enemy."

Fisher laughed. "No, it doesn't. Gardener hired him for a job, and he did it. He doesn't work for him anymore."

"Okay, sure," he said, not believing her.

"Why were you smiling when I came in?" she asked.

The smile reappeared on his face. He held out an envelope for her. "The fingerprint analysis came back from the lab."

Fisher grabbed it, pulled out a sheet of paper, and read the report. Her eyes suddenly widened in astonishment.

Holt was now grinning from ear to ear. "Gardener's prints are on the knife that was found in his Audi. On top of that…"

"The blood on the knife matched the victim's," Fisher said, completing his sentence.

"Bingo."

Fisher stared at the report.

"You look disappointed," Holt said.

"I'm not," she replied. "I just figured Gardener would be smarter than that."

"What do you mean?"

"We found no blood anywhere in the house except for Kyla's bedroom. It's reasonable to assume that he may have wiped the house clean of any evidence."

"So?"

"So why didn't he wipe the knife after he hid it?"

"Maybe he never expected anyone to find it."

"But there was blood on the door of the Audi, which lead us to the knife in the first place."

Holt shrugged. "Maybe he got careless."

Something still doesn't feel right, Fisher thought. *I can't argue with a lab report, though.*

Holt picked up the phone and punched in a number.

"You're calling the DA?"

"I already told her. Barrows is beyond ecstatic. But I think we need to turn up the heat on Gardener."

"So, who are you calling?"

"*The Milton Inquirer.*"

She was surprised. "Why?"

"Even with the knife in our possession, Gardener refused a plea deal. He had to have known we would eventually match his prints. And the blood on the knife could only have come from the victim. I bet he knows something we don't. He must have an ace up his sleeve."

Fisher sighed. "You're giving him too much credit."

"He is far more cunning than he looks," Holt said. "I have a contact at *The Milton Inquirer*. He will relay the fingerprints report to the press as an anonymous tip. Let's see how Gardener handles it when the entire city knows he did it."

FORTY-EIGHT

Callaway was back at his office when he checked his voicemail. There was a message from Mike Grabonsky.

Mike had secured a buyer for his investment property. The price was not as high as he had hoped, but with creditors on his back, Mike was grateful to unload the property. He felt an obligation to tell Callaway and was grateful for what he had done for him. Callaway felt it should be him thanking Mike. The five thousand dollars went a long way in helping him clear up his debts too. Sometimes, his job enabled him to do some good for a change. There were only so many cheaters he could follow.

Mike was a decent person who got caught in a situation he did not know how to get out of. When Baxter came looking for him, his primal instincts of fight or flight kicked in. He chose the latter option. Neither made for a good choice. Mike could never have taken on Baxter if he chose to fight him, and sooner or later, Baxter would have found him anyway. The best option, the one Callaway took, was to go back and work out a deal that was beneficial to everyone. It required some clever maneuvering, but Mason got his money, Callaway got his fee, and Mike got back to his family in one piece.

Callaway turned on the TV.

He froze when he saw who was on the screen.

Sharon Gardener stood in front of a large house. Callaway recognized it as her brother's. Next to Sharon was Senator Barron Lester, her father. He had his arm around her shoulders. Microphones and tape recorders were pushed in front of her.

What the hell? Callaway thought as he turned up the volume.

Senator Lester spoke first. "We were just informed of new information that has surfaced regarding the death of my granddaughter, Kyla. We have further confirmed this information with the Milton Police Department, and I have to say it is true. My son-in-law Paul's fingerprints were found on the knife used to murder Kyla."

Callaway grimaced.

Sharon Gardener spoke. "Paul, if you are watching this, we want this ordeal to be over for us. We just want to bury Kyla in peace."

She broke down in tears and disappeared from view.

Senator Lester took the microphone again. "As you can see, this is a devastating time for our family."

Wasn't Paul a member of your family too? Callaway thought. *Now you are no longer leaving him to sink or swim. You are leaving him for the sharks to feed on.*

"We never thought in our wildest dreams that something like this could happen to us. We have issued our statement, and in doing so, we ask the media to respect our privacy. Thank you for coming."

Senator Lester moved away from the cameras as reporters began shouting questions. "Do you intend to keep running for re-election?" one reporter asked.

Senator Lester turned and said, "Even though this is a tough time for us as a family, I will continue to fight for the people of this state. I know there are families who are going through worse times than us. They have lost loved ones to gun violence, gang violence, and many other forms of violence. With health care being underfunded, threats to reduce social security, and taxes for the rich being cut, there is still so much work to be done. I won't stop—"

Callaway shut the TV off. *I'm in no mood for a campaign speech*, he thought.

FORTY-NINE

Roth had watched the impromptu statement from the Lester family with a scowl on his face. They were trying to distance themselves from Paul. Even Sharon's last name at the bottom of the screen did not read *Gardener* but *Lester,* her maiden name.

After the family's statement ended, he immediately called Barrows and gave her a piece of his mind. She denied any involvement, but he did not believe her. It was a tactic he would have used if he were in her place.

They were pushing Paul into a corner so that he would confess to the crime. Even if he refused, the media would jump on the recent development and roll with it. The jury pool was now tainted because the bias against Paul was going to rise quickly. Roth would have to file a formal request for the judge to move the trial to another city, far away from Milton.

In case the judge denied his request, he had to find a way to mitigate the damage that had been done. The first thing he did was call the producer of a local news program. Roth had represented the producer in a sexual harassment case involving him and a female colleague. Roth was able to work out a settlement that satisfied both parties. After speaking to him, the producer was more than willing to accommodate Roth on such short notice.

As Roth was hooked up to a microphone, the program host, a woman in her mid-thirties with blonde hair and long legs, said, "We didn't have time to prepare cue cards, so I'll let you do most of the talking."

Roth gave her a smile. "That's perfectly fine by me."

He had come with a prepared statement, and he did not want some eager host to contradict him. The pre-recorded segment would appear later in the day when the program aired in its allotted time slot. It would not be a live rebuttal to the family's statements, but it would still have an impact.

When the cameraman gave the signal, the host introduced herself and then Roth. She then turned to him. "Thank you for giving me this opportunity," he said. "I wanted to speak for my client, Paul Gardener, in order to clear up some misconceptions that have been blatantly distributed to the media. My client is innocent of the crime he has been accused of. Contrary to what the prosecution or anyone else says, he loved his daughter, and he had no motive to harm her. The truth is that the facts don't add up. The prints on the knife found at the scene may belong to my client, but it still does not mean he committed the crime."

"Doesn't it?" the host asked.

Roth smiled. He had given her an opening and she took it. "Of course not. It doesn't make sense for my client to kill his daughter in cold blood, then place the murder weapon in his car, and then go back inside his house and take a nap. If he did it, he would be scrambling to clean the crime scene of any evidence that might incriminate him, not be concerned about catching up on his sleep. This speaks volumes about his innocence."

"What about the fact that your client was intoxicated when he committed the crime?" she asked.

Another easy question, he thought.

"If he was drunk, as they have repeatedly said in the media, then how did he have the presence of mind to know he needed to hide the murder weapon? Also, if the crime was committed in a drunken rage, there would have been more blood at the scene. The fact that no drops of blood were found anywhere else in the house also supports my client's innocence."

"Do you think, perhaps, that your client might have been set up?" the host asked.

Roth paused. *I never considered that before*, he thought. *She might be onto something.* "That's a strong possibility," he said, casually. "We will definitely look into this as time goes on."

"Before we end our segment, is there anything you would like to add?" the host asked.

Roth looked into the camera. "I would like to say that Mrs. Sharon *Gardener*," he said, emphasizing her last name, as she was still married, "has gone on TV and accused my client of committing this terrible crime. I would like to ask her this: Where were you on the night your daughter was murdered? Why did you turn off the security cameras that would have shown the real killer and made sure this *ordeal* could be over for my client so he can be involved in his daughter's burial?"

The host smiled. "Thank you, Mr. Roth, for speaking to us."

Roth smiled back. "Thank you for having me."

The prosecution had served him a fastball, and he had hit it out of the park.

FIFTY

Callaway frowned in dismay. Reporters had staked out Paul's mother's house, and it looked like they were going to be there for a while. They had brought tents, lawn chairs, and even a Winnebago.

After the news broke about his fingerprints being on the knife, the press had descended like vultures. They wanted a glimpse of Paul Gardener, whom they had dubbed "The Baby Killer." Callaway thought that was an odd moniker, given Kyla was close to the Minimum Legal Drinking Age. But if he thought about it, she was once Paul's baby. And the name given to him was sensational and sure to sell loads of newspapers and magazines. Even the local news channel had been repeating the Gardener story nonstop for the last couple of hours.

There was no way Callaway could go through the front door. The press would go ballistic. He was surprised that, so far, his name had not appeared anywhere, even though he was the one who discovered Sharon Gardener's infidelities. If he was seen meeting with Paul, he would definitely make the six o'clock news. While he believed all publicity was good publicity, Paul's case was an exception. Being associated with "The Baby Killer" was career suicide.

He decided to find another way in. The back of the house had a throng of reporters gathered behind the fence surrounding the property, so the only other option available was the neighboring houses on each side.

The one on the left had a large *Beware of Dog* sign on the front lawn. Callaway could not risk getting bitten or having the dog bark, betraying his whereabouts.

He chose the house on the right, but instead of going through there, he went through the house next to it. In a single leap, Callaway was up and over the fence gate that led to the backyard. He then hopped the fence and into the next neighbor's yard. He looked around, in case anyone was looking, and hopped the next fence too. He was now in Paul's mother's backyard. He approached the house and knocked on the back door.

Paul's mother appeared in the kitchen. She saw him and immediately put her hand over her mouth to stifle a scream. Callaway waved at her and smiled. Still horrified, she was reaching for the phone when, to Callaway's relief, Paul appeared behind her.

He spotted Callaway and took the phone away from his mother. He said something to her, which calmed her nerves. Paul then let Callaway in.

Once seated in the living room, Callaway waited as Paul's mother made coffee. She thought he was a reporter, and she was about to call 9-1-1. "I'm so sorry," she had said to Callaway. "Can I get you something to drink?"

"Coffee would be good," Callaway had replied.

Callaway watched as Paul stood by the window. Every so often, he would pull the blind aside an inch and peek out at the people trespassing on his mother's front lawn.

"We've called the police many times," he said. "They would come, push the press off our property, but the moment the cops leave, the reporters would take up position again. Why can't they just leave me alone?"

"You're the man of the hour, I'm afraid," Callaway replied.

His mother brought Callaway a steaming cup and placed it on the coffee table before him. She also placed a plate filled with cookies. Even with everything happening around her, she was still a good host.

When his mother had left the room, Paul turned to him and said, "Why are you here, Mr. Callaway?"

"I came to give you this," Callaway said, holding out a USB drive.

"What is it?" Paul asked.

"They are the images I took of your wife leaving the house. I couldn't give it to you when you were in jail, or else the guards would have taken it," Callaway replied.

Callaway preferred film over digital because the images could not be altered. He used to pay a guy to use his darkroom at a film-developing studio. Callaway could not trust anyone to do it for him. The images were too sensitive and were for his client's eyes only. But with the advent of digital photography, the guy went out of business. Callaway had to resort to creating his very own darkroom in the bathtub of his apartment, but then he got evicted and that was no longer an option either. He turned to digital photography out of necessity.

Paul looked at the USB. "Didn't you already give them to my lawyer?"

"I only gave him some. These are the rest of the photos."

Paul shook his head. "They are of no use to me now."

"I figured I should give them to their rightful owner."

"And also get paid, correct?"

Callaway looked away. He suddenly felt sheepish.

"Don't feel bad for me," Paul said with a short smile. "This isn't your fault. I probably wouldn't be out on bail had it not been for those photos you took. The judge considered my wife's testimony—to be more precise, her forever changing testimony—in releasing me."

Paul left the room and returned with an envelope. "It was five hundred, right?"

Callaway nodded and placed the envelope in his pocket without counting the money. He stood up and said, "Your brother-in-law dropped by my office, and he offered me a nice sum for them."

"Richard?" Paul asked, surprised.

"Yes."

"He's far more dangerous than my wife."

Callaway waited for him to explain.

"My wife's brother and her father run everything for the family. The father and son are very close. They always have been, ever since I've known them. Sharon is spoiled and naive, but Richard and Barron are calculating and ruthless. They will do anything if it benefits the family. The whole thing on TV with Sharon and Barron was most likely Richard's doing. They wanted the public to see me as the bad guy and the family as the victim. I'm just collateral damage in their PR campaign."

"Your daughter is the real victim here," Callaway said.

Paul's eyes welled up with tears. "Yes, you're right. I can't complain about myself when she is gone forever."

FIFTY-ONE

Callaway left through the back door, twice hopped over the neighbors' fences, then walked down the street to where his car was parked.

He felt sorry for Paul. He was a prisoner in his mother's house. Callaway almost wondered if being out on bail was such a good idea. At least in prison, you could shut out the noise from the outside.

He was approaching his car when a large shadow fell over him. He turned and was face-to-face with Detective Greg Holt.

"Oh, it's only you," Callaway said, relieved. "I thought it was a reporter."

"What are you doing here?" Holt growled.

"I could ask you the same thing."

"I am keeping an eye on a suspect."

"Paul Gardener?"

"Good deduction."

"Well, you're wasting your time. He isn't going anywhere. Those reporters outside his house will make sure of that."

Callaway squinted as something occurred to him. "Let me guess, it was *you* who went to the press about the knife."

"I won't confirm anything."

"You do not deny it either."

"I heard Gardener was no longer a client of yours," Holt said.

"He's not."

"In that case, I would advise that you stay away from him."

"Why is that?"

"He's going down for murder, and you don't want to be too close when he does."

"How can you be so certain he did it?"

"The facts speak for themselves."

Callaway scowled. "I don't know about the facts, but have you spoken to *him*?"

"Of course, we had to get a statement from him."

"And in it, he said he didn't do it."

Holt snorted. "They all do until they are found guilty. You ask any convicted felon and he'll tell you he is innocent."

"Okay, let me ask you this. When you spoke to him, did he come across as a smart person?"

Holt eyed him. "Okay, I'll bite. He seemed smart enough."

"Well, he had to be. He built a business that was worth close to ten million dollars at one point."

"It's not worth that much anymore. In fact, from what I read, it's bleeding cash."

"It's not his fault the economy turned on him."

"What's your point in all of this?" Holt asked.

"For a person who seemed smart enough, as you just said, why would he not hide the knife where it can never be found?" Callaway replied.

"Simple," Holt said. "He never expected he would be caught."

Callaway frowned. "I doubt that. His wife lived in the very house he supposedly murdered his daughter in. The chance of his crime being discovered was very high."

"In my years of experience, sometimes even geniuses do very dumb things," Holt shot back.

They were silent a moment.

Holt said, "There is something else you failed to consider."

"And what is that?" Callaway said.

"What if he wanted to be caught?"

"Why would he want that?"

"Guilt," Holt said slowly. "He knew what he had done, and he wanted us to catch him."

"Then why not just plead guilty and pay for his crimes?" Callaway asked.

"He might have changed his mind when he saw how long he would end up spending time behind bars. Or his lawyer might have talked him out of it."

"I doubt that very much," Callaway said.

"Why would you say that?"

"I know people like Evan Roth. They only care about winning. If he knew he didn't have a case, he would have convinced his client to take the deal."

"Give us time, Callaway," Holt said. "We're still building a case against him. Sooner or later, we'll find that one thing that'll convince you and everyone else that Gardener is guilty of murdering his daughter."

FIFTY-TWO

Stan Waterson took a sip from his thermos and then placed it back in the garbage truck cab's cupholder. Stan was fifty-two, married, and the father of two teenage daughters. His wife and kids were his life. He would do anything to provide a good life for them, including picking up garbage in the middle of the night and hauling it to a waste facility.

Stan never got a formal education, something he regretted in his life. He dropped out in tenth grade to work for a logging company. He learned to cut trees and then moved on to managing a shift in the company's manufacturing plant. With China's economy exploding, there was a huge demand for lumber. Construction projects were sprouting up all over the country, and Stan's company could not keep up fast enough. They hired more and more labor, and they expanded at a rapid pace. Then the Chinese economy began to falter, and demand quickly fell off. Projects were being abandoned left, right, and center. The impact was felt as far as Stan's company. They had taken on too much debt, and with companies defaulting, they were left with unpaid invoices. They went into receivership and were bought out by a German company. They decided to lay off half the workforce in order to restructure the company and make it profitable again. Stan became a casualty of this. He even lost his pension when the company refused to pay it out. His union took them to court but lost, as the company was not obligated to continue the plan as part of the takeover. After kissing his dreams of retiring from the lumber company goodbye, Stan, now in his mid-thirties, began looking for work again. He drove a taxi, a grocery truck, an excavator for a construction firm, anything to put food on the table. His wife even went back to work during the months Stan could not find employment. He then landed a job with his current employer.

PWM, Professional Waste Management Inc., specialized in collecting bulk waste and non-hazardous materials, which included recyclable and organic material. Their customers included retail stores, shopping centers, schools, and hospitals. After ten years with PWM, Stan hoped the company would be his last stop before he retired. He did not want to start knocking on doors again at his age.

Stan's route included strip malls and plazas. He had driven the route so many times, he knew it like the back of his hand.

He took another sip from the thermos. The coffee was still hot and strong, helping to jolt his senses. He needed it this early in the morning. He could not risk falling asleep at the wheel.

Next to the thermos was a plastic bag that held his bagel. He grabbed the bagel and took a bite. He should not be eating in his truck, but who would find out?

Three bites later, the bagel was gone.

He entered the back of a strip mall that contained two restaurants, one pharmacy, an optician, and a convenience store. From past experience, he knew the dumpster would not be overloaded with garbage bags. Except for the restaurants, the other three businesses hardly produced garbage.

Stan carefully got the dumpster onto the forks and lifted it up to dump its contents into the truck.

As the waste emptied, he heard a sound that caught his attention. It did not sound like anything he had heard before. *I'm not sure what that was*, he thought. *Gosh, I hope somebody did not toss out something you shouldn't put in a dumpster.*

He had found rubber tires, paint cans, and even propane gas tanks in the dumpsters. If crushed, these items would contaminate the other garbage and take a ton of work to remove at the processing plant. And in the case of the gas tanks, there was the risk of an explosion.

He lowered the dumpster. He got out of the truck's cab and moved to the back of the truck. He grabbed the top ledge of the hopper and pulled himself up.

He took a peek inside.

Bile rose in the back of his throat.

He threw up the bagel.

FIFTY-THREE

Holt was at the scene the moment he received the call. He spotted Fisher talking to the garbage truck driver. The man looked visibly ill.

The body was identified as belonging to Pedro Catano. He lay among the garbage in the back of the truck, resting at an awkward angle. His legs were spread apart, and his arms were twisted to the sides. His eyes were closed, but his mouth was open. Blood had caked the right side of his face. Holt believed the bullet must have gone through the left and come out the right.

As he leaned into the hopper, he noticed something on Pedro's body.

"It's the driver's breakfast," Fisher said, coming up next to him. "The moment he saw the body, he threw up."

"Is that bagel?" Holt asked.

"Yep."

"Why don't people chew properly like they taught us back in school?" he griped.

"Don't tell me you chew like thirty times?"

"Maybe not that much, but I most certainly don't swallow my food whole."

They stared at Pedro's body in silence. His father would be devastated when they broke the news to him.

Holt said, "How did you know it was Pedro? I don't see any ID on him unless you went inside the hopper."

"There's no way I went in there," she said. "There's no telling what people throw out in their garbage."

"Then how?"

"Simple. I did an online search, and several photos came up belonging to a Pedro Catano. I matched one to the body."

That was *simple, so why didn't I think of it?* Holt wondered. "What did the driver tell you?" he asked.

"He said he picks up the garbage three times a week."

"When was the last pickup?" Holt asked.

"Two days ago."

A light went on in his head. "That's the day Kyla Gardener was found murdered."

"Exactly."

"But if the body has been here two days, why didn't anyone notice it?"

"I was thinking the same thing, and I have a theory that might answer it. The garbage truck driver must have emptied the dumpster right before the killer arrived and left Pedro's body. The container is almost six feet in height, which makes it very deep. No one would know his body was in the container unless they climbed up the side and took a peek inside. Over the next two days, people just threw garbage into the dumpster, covering Pedro's body in the process."

"What about the smell? The odor is unmistakable."

Fisher grimaced. "It's a dumpster. What else is it supposed to smell like, roses?"

She's got a point, Holt thought.

Fisher said, "I think the timing can't be a coincidence either."

"Timing?" Holt asked.

"The garbage truck driver emptied the container around one A.M., which is what he said was his usual pick up time. We think Kyla was murdered between eleven-thirty P.M. and two-thirty A.M., give or take a couple of minutes. The drive over here is less than twenty minutes, which means…"

Holt's eyes widened. He now understood what she was getting at. "It means whoever murdered Kyla could have also murdered Pedro."

FIFTY-FOUR

The press arrived as soon as news broke of another dead body. Cameramen tried to capture the scene as it unfolded before them. They wanted enough footage for the early morning broadcasts. One man approached Holt and aimed the camera directly in his face. Holt glared at him, and he quickly moved away. Holt had no personal issues with the media in general, but at the moment, he just was not in the mood for a close-up. He had not had any sleep, the adrenaline was wearing off, and lethargy was taking over. He worried he might say something on camera he would later regret.

The sun had risen over the horizon, and soon there would be light. *That's good*, he thought. *Daylight will help clear my head*.

His walk around the strip mall answered one question that had been nagging him since the moment he arrived. Why did the killer choose to dump Pedro's body here and not someplace else?

There were no CCTV cameras anywhere on the property. The tenants in the mall may have their own security, but it likely only covered their business.

What transpired behind the mall, including the area where the dumpster was situated, would never be known.

He spotted Fisher coming his way. She was holding two cups in her hand.

"It's hot and just the way you like it," she said.

He took a sip of the coffee. It was cream, no sugar. His senses suddenly came alive. He took another sip.

"They're waiting for a statement," Fisher said, nodding in the direction of the press gathered behind the yellow police tape.

"We should tell them something."

"We should," she agreed.

They sipped coffee in silence. Neither had the energy to speak to the press.

"I have a theory," Holt said. "And I know you won't like it."

"I have a feeling I know where you're going with this."

"Paul Gardener killed Pedro Catano," he said.

She shook her head. "Isn't that a bit of a stretch?"

"Just think about it. Kyla told her father she wanted to get married, and he was fervently opposed to it. Pedro's ex-girlfriend believed Pedro was in love with Kyla. What if Kyla wanted to marry Pedro, and Gardener couldn't accept that his daughter would marry an employee of the family?"

"Employee?"

"Pedro's father has been the family's gardener for decades. Pedro and Kyla grew up together."

"I don't know if they grew up together," Fisher said.

"Okay, but they played together as kids. Luiz said while he worked, Pedro would spend time with Kyla."

"Let's say I somewhat agree with you, but I don't think Gardener would kill his daughter for wanting to marry the son of a gardener. He himself came from humble beginnings."

"Yes, but you forget one crucial thing," Holt said with a smile.

"And what is that?"

"Kyla was in line to receive a substantial inheritance when she turned twenty-one, which was only a few months away. And she had promised her father that she would help him out because he was under a lot of financial pressure. Gardener might have feared that she would renege on her promise if she married Pedro. Or, Pedro was only marrying her for her money, and Gardener wanted to stop that from happening."

"There's a big flaw in your theory," Fisher said.

"How?"

"Kyla was stabbed and Pedro was shot. If Gardener did it, why stab one and shoot the other?"

"Maybe he didn't want the crimes to be linked. Maybe he killed Kyla by accident. Remember, she was strangled first and then stabbed later. And to tie up loose ends, he shot Pedro because, unlike Kyla, he couldn't overpower Pedro, who was taller and younger than him. Shooting him was the easiest way to get rid of him."

Fisher opened her mouth but then shut it. She hated to admit it, but Holt was beginning to make sense.

FIFTY-FIVE

Holt and Fisher looked inside the hopper as Andrea Wakefield examined the body. The medical examiner had run through a series of tests that gave her an indication of the cause of death, time of death, and place of death.

"The victim definitely died from a gunshot wound to the head," she said. "It was most likely at close range; perhaps the assailant was a foot or two away. The bullet went through the left side of the head and is still lodged in the skull."

"Are you saying the bullet did not exit?" Holt asked. He was certain that it had.

"I can't say with complete accuracy until I open the skull and take a look," Wakefield replied. "But, I didn't see an exit wound during my initial observation."

"What about the blood on the right side of his head?" Holt asked.

"The force of the bullet was so strong that the impact caused the side of the skull to tear open, causing blood to drain out. If the bullet had exited, you would also see brain tissue."

"What about the time of death?" Fisher asked. She wanted to move on from the gory details.

"Rigor mortis can last up to seventy-two hours," Andrea replied. "But decomposition has started to take effect. It could be due to the environment the body was under." She turned to Holt. "You said you believe the victim was covered in garbage bags?"

"I did," Fisher replied. "The driver explained that he only heard the body after some of the garbage and debris was in the hopper. We believe whoever left him here did so after the driver had previously picked up garbage. So the body was at the bottom, and the tenants of the strip mall, unbeknownst to them, kept throwing garbage on it. When the container was flipped over to be emptied, the body ended up on top. I strongly believe if the body was at the top of the garbage, the driver may not have heard the 'odd noise,' as he kept calling it, and would have crushed the body with the compactor."

"Thank you, Detective, that explains a lot," Wakefield said. "So to answer your question, I believe the time of death to be between forty-eight hours and seventy-two hours."

Holt looked over at Fisher. He knew she was thinking the same thing: *Pedro was indeed murdered the same night Kyla was.*

"And place of death?" Fisher asked.

"I took a quick look at the dumpster," Wakefield replied. "I did not see any blood, which leads me to believe the victim could not have been shot where his body was eventually discovered."

"So, he was shot someplace else and dumped here?" Holt said.

"That would seem like it."

"So, I guess when we search the hopper, we won't find the murder weapon?" he said, more as a statement than a question.

"Unless the killer became impatient and left both the body and gun behind for you to find," Wakefield suggested.

Not likely, Holt thought.

FIFTY-SIX

Roth slowed down. He looked around and saw no reporters on the front lawn. Dawn was still breaking, but soon they would be back to resume their positions.

Roth was annoyed at being awoken in the middle of a dream. He could not remember what the dream was, but he still did not like having it broken.

Roth had contacts at various newspaper outlets. If there was news he needed leaked to the public, he would use them. The reporters got an exclusive breaking story, and he was able to disseminate information without it tracing back to him. This was extremely useful when a judge imposed a gag order that restricted lawyers, prosecutors, law enforcement officials, witnesses, and the jury from talking to the press. Anyone who disobeyed this could be found in contempt. Roth did not like getting on the wrong side of a judge. He saw no real advantage in that, but it still did not prevent him from being found in contempt of court over the years.

What the caller told him made Roth jump up in bed. He quickly called Paul, but when there was no answer, he decided to get dressed and drive over. This personal visit would be billed to Paul at a premium rate.

Roth rang the doorbell and waited. A few minutes later, a weary-eyed Paul answered the door. He was wearing a robe and no shoes.

He squinted and said, "Evan, what are you doing here so early?"

"Why don't you pick up your phone?" Roth asked, pushing past him as he stormed inside.

In the living room, Roth placed his briefcase on the coffee table and took a seat.

"What's going on?" Paul asked, rubbing his eyes.

"Do you know a person by the name of Pedro Catano?"

"Yes, he's our gardener's son."

"He's dead."

Paul's face turned pale.

"His body was found in a dumpster behind a strip mall," Roth said matter-of-factly.

Paul dropped to the sofa, holding his head.

"If there is something you want to tell me," Roth said, "this would be the right time."

Paul looked up. "Like what?"

"My contact at one of the newspapers said there is a chance the police will pin Pedro's murder on you."

Paul's eyes widened in disbelief. "What?"

"She overheard two detectives discussing this. I bet it must be Holt and Fisher."

"They're out to bury me," Paul said. "I saw Detective Holt outside my house."

Roth's eyes narrowed. "He's following you?"

"I think so."

"Make a note of how many times you see him. I can file a harassment case against him and the department."

"I can't believe Pedro is dead," Paul said, shaking his head. "He was friends with Kyla."

"They were?" Roth asked.

"Yes. Luiz Catano, Pedro's dad, has been the Lester's family gardener for a long time, way before I came into the family. When they were kids, I used to see Pedro and Kyla running in our backyard."

A thought occurred to Roth. He snapped open his briefcase and rummaged inside. "Didn't your daughter call Pedro on the day she was murdered?"

"Yes, why?"

"What if he met your daughter that night, they had a disagreement, he killed your daughter, and then he committed suicide?"

"Didn't you say his body was found behind a strip mall?"

"So?"

"You mean, he shot himself in the dumpster? That doesn't make sense."

"Let the prosecution tear our theory apart. Our job is to place doubt in the jury's mind regarding your guilt."

"I thought your job was to prove my innocence?"

Roth smiled. "That's where you're wrong. In the eyes of the law, you are innocent until proven guilty. And if the case goes to trial, we're not interested if the jury thinks you are innocent. We only care that they find you *not* guilty."

FIFTY-SEVEN

Callaway was awake even before the sun was up. He was not sure why, but he had a fitful night. He was a sound sleeper. No matter what was going on around him, he would be passed out like a drunken sailor.

There was something bothering him, but he could not put his finger on what it was.

He tried to go over the events of the past couple of days, but there was nothing that required his attention. Maybe he had neglected to do something. He could not think of anything. He completed the task he had been hired to do by Paul Gardener. He helped Mike Grabonsky out of a bad situation. He was able to make extra cash without Mason and Baxter coming after him. He provided Patti with much-needed funds. He even spent time with Nina. All in all, he had a positive, productive past few days. These kinds of days did not come very often, but when they did, he tried to take full advantage of them.

Most of his days were spent waiting for a client to appear with a job that would cover his monthly expenses. They often did not, but that was the nature of the job. In times of great stress, when bills were piling up and he had gone without a client for months, he would resort to finding work outside his profession.

The worst was wearing a giant mattress costume and waving at cars that drove by. The store that hired him was having a mattress sale, and they needed a gimmick to attract customers. He was on his last penny and desperate.

He shivered at the thought of doing something like that again. It was embarrassing on all levels. He had gone from being a deputy sheriff to being laughed and honked at by drivers. At first, he did not understand the reason for their derision until he spotted a yellow stain on the back of the costume. It looked like someone had peed on it. Callaway had a suspicion it was the store owner's Rottweiler who had done the deed.

He hoped he would not have to do something like that ever again. He still had some money left over from Mike's job. Plus, the five hundred Paul had given him would keep him on his feet for some time.

However, if the client whose beach house he was staying at decided to return unexpectedly, he would have to find other accommodations fast.

What he needed was a permanent solution to his financial problems, not to be reliant on the kindness of his clients.

When he could not go back to sleep, he got up and made coffee. With a hot cup in his hand, he strolled to the water. The weather was cool and a bit chilly this early in the morning. He shivered and returned to the beach house, where he found a spot on the deck where the sun was beating down strong.

He took a sip of coffee and closed his eyes.

He would go and sit in his office in case a client showed up. True, he had his telephone number on the front door, but sometimes, people were hesitant to speak on the phone. When they arrived at his doorstep, they were desperate, or in some cases, paranoid. They worried their telephone was bugged and their spouse might be listening in on them. They wanted to speak in person. And if he was not there, they would leave.

Once I'm finished with this cup, he thought, *I'll head straight there.*

FIFTY-EIGHT

Holt and Fisher were at a diner across from the strip mall. Holt stuffed eggs, hash browns, and toast down his gullet so fast, his cheeks looked like they were blowing air.

"You're disgusting, you know that?" Fisher said. "I can't believe you are married."

"Neither can I, but I've been up all night, and I'm starving." He paused and said, "Why aren't you eating?"

"Just by watching you, I've lost my appetite."

"You shouldn't have too much coffee on an empty stomach," he said.

She stared down at her cup. It was her fourth since she was awoken by a report of a dead body. She needed the caffeine to keep functioning, or else she would crash. There was also the half-digested bagel the garbage truck driver had thrown up. She could not get the sight out of her head.

Fisher took a sip.

The medical examiner had taken Pedro's body to the morgue. She would conduct an autopsy and let them know what she found. Fisher doubted the autopsy would contradict what they already knew.

The crime scene unit had combed through the hopper but found no murder weapon. She didn't expect they would unless the killer figured the garbage truck would end up crushing the body and the gun with it.

Whoever was behind this was fully aware of their actions. They chose a spot where there would be no CCTV cameras. The alley that led from the front of the strip mall to the back was off to one side, away from the prying eyes of the tenants' security.

Holt and Fisher had provided a brief statement to the press. They did not take any questions: one, because they were tired from an all-nighter, and two, they found out the press had gotten a whiff of their theory.

Fisher said, "You don't seriously believe Gardener could have killed Kyla and Pedro on the *same* night. It's just not possible."

"Didn't your friend Callaway have a case in Fairview where the murder victim was seen entering a hotel but was never seen leaving, even though her body was later discovered under a bridge?"

"I asked him about it, and even he agreed that it was a bizarre one."

"It seemed impossible, but it happened."

Fisher said, "Okay, sure, but what you are essentially saying is that Gardener knew his wife was going to leave the house that night. He also knew exactly how long she would be gone and that the cameras would be off, which would allow him enough time to kill his daughter and her lover, and also dump the lover's body far away from the house."

Holt swallowed slowly, but he said nothing.

"There is also something else you forgot," she said.

"And what's that?"

"How did he pull this off while intoxicated? Someone would have reported a drunk on the road in the middle of the night, would they not?"

Holt blinked. "Are you sure you're not working for the defense? That's exactly what you sound like right now."

"I sound like someone who's not trying to fit a square peg in a round hole."

"I never said my theory was without errors. I'm only going based on the facts. Gardener had a fight with his daughter on the day she was murdered. The text messages prove that. She had called Pedro that same day, and both she and Pedro were murdered on the same night. The times of death support this. You don't have to be Einstein to put two and two together."

"I still think we are pinning all our theories on one person."

"Do you think there are two killers out there?" Holt asked.

Fisher was about to say something in reply, but then she thought better of it.

Holt went back to finishing his breakfast, and she went back to emptying her cup.

A man approached them. He was wearing a stained apron. "Are you the detectives investigating what happened across the road?" he asked.

"We are," Holt replied.

"My name is Josh. I'm the diner's cook," he said.

"Okay. What can we do for you?" Holt said.

"I'm not sure if this is important, but I was at the diner a couple of nights ago."

Holt dropped his fork and said, "Go on."

"The kitchen stove had stopped working, and I figured I could try to fix it. It took longer than I expected, and by the time I left, it was really late at night. I remember when I was locking up, I saw a car pull out from the back of the strip mall. The only reason it caught my attention was the way the car sped away like it was in a hurry or something. I could hear the squealing of tires."

"What did it look like?" Holt asked.

"It was a black sedan."

"Did you get the license plate number?"

He shook his head. "It took off fast, and I was too tired to pay much attention to it."

Holt turned to Fisher. "What car does Gardener drive?"

She knew where he was going with this. "A black Audi," she replied.

Holt smiled and turned to Josh. "Thanks for your help. By the way, the food was excellent."

FIFTY-NINE

Before heading to his office, Callaway decided to check his emails in case a potential client had contacted him. This way, he could go straight to the client instead of making a stop at the office, wasting time and gas.

He turned on his laptop and quickly browsed through the unread messages. Most were spam and went straight to the junk folder. Some were downright bizarre and got deleted. One or two held potential. He jotted the information down. He checked his watch. It was still a bit early. He would contact them later in the morning.

He then checked the news online. The breaking news revolved around a body being discovered in a dumpster behind a strip mall. The body was identified as belonging to a Pedro Catano. The name did not mean anything to Callaway. He was about to move on to the next headline when he sat up straight. The reporter stated that Catano and Kyla Gardener knew each other and their deaths may be linked. The reporter did not mention any names, but Callaway had a feeling she might be referring to Paul.

Callaway got up and moved to the bedroom. Right above the bed was an air vent. He pulled out the metal cover and shoved his hand inside. He pulled out a small box. He used to keep the box in his office, but when he fell behind on his rent, he feared his landlady would change the lock on the front door. He started carrying the box with him wherever he went.

The box contained DVDs of all the cases he had worked on.

He always told his clients he never kept any relevant information on him. The hard drive on his laptop was empty. Anyone who accessed it without his permission would find nothing. He did not want to be held responsible in case anything happened to him or the client's information. He made sure to burn a copy for safekeeping, however. It was more of an insurance policy than anything else.

He once gave photos to a client that showed an affair his wife was having. The client wanted him to destroy all the copies he had. Callaway agreed, but something did not feel right. It turned out the client was planning to murder his wife and blame it on Callaway, as he was seen following her around the previous week. Callaway alerted the authorities before the client was able to take any action. The photos he took proved he had been hired by the client for a surveillance job and nothing else.

This was why Callaway had gone straight to Paul after he found out Paul was a murder suspect. Callaway was at the scene on the night of the crime. He did not want Holt or someone else from the Milton PD. knocking on his door. He wanted to be proactive rather than reactive. This way, they could not point any fingers in his direction.

Even though the authorities could compel him to hand over a client's information, and some did take him to court, the judge always sided with him. The judge wanted the detectives to build their own case and not rely on information from a third party. The underlying reason was that the information provided by the private investigator might not be complete, and the detectives should not make assumptions based on a few photos taken at different times.

When it came to a serious offense such as murder, Callaway took no chances. Judge or no judge, he would make sure nothing ever led back to him.

Callaway searched through the box and pulled out a DVD with the name *Paul G* written across it in black marker.

SIXTY

On the night I was at the Gardener residence, did I see something that could be crucial now? Callaway thought. This was something he had asked himself the moment he found out Paul had been charged with murdering his daughter. Callaway was not convinced Paul was guilty, but he was not convinced of his innocence either. The evidence against him was stacking up fast. Callaway strongly believed the link between Pedro and Kyla could have only come from Holt. He wanted an airtight case, something the prosecutor could use to get a verdict in the state's favor.

Anytime a jury was faced with doubt as to the guilt of the accused, they always ruled against the prosecution. They would rather let a killer go free than let an innocent person rot in prison.

Callaway had seen all types of people in his profession. From liars to cheaters to sadists, and Paul did not come across as any of them. He could turn out to be a manipulative sociopath, but Callaway had a feeling he was not.

At least, he hoped not.

In order to satisfy his own intuition, he wanted to do his due diligence and make sure he had not missed anything.

If Paul was guilty, he would pay for his crime. The detectives and the DA's office would make sure of that. But if he was innocent, Callaway wanted to clear his conscience and say that he did everything he could to help him.

He stuck the DVD in the laptop and pulled up the photos from that night. The first image was the front of the Gardener residence. Callaway was parked across the street, so he had a clear view. There were no cars parked in the driveway. The lights in the entire house were off.

He moved to the second photo. It showed a Lexus parked on the driveway, and Sharon was removing grocery bags from the trunk. The third photo showed Paul getting out of his Audi with a briefcase in his hand. The fourth photo was of the house again. This time, the lights were on, but only on the main floor. The second floor was dark. Kyla's bedroom was on the second floor. He was not sure if it faced the front of the house or the back. He could not be sure if she went to sleep or not.

The next photo showed Sharon leaving the house in the middle of the night. Callaway was up all night. He had dozed off at one point, but the headlights from Sharon's car had awoken him. He was lucky to snap a photo of her driving away before he tailed her.

He clicked on another photo. It showed her parking behind an apartment building. She then got out and disappeared inside the building. A couple of hours later, he snapped her leaving the building with a man. The man escorted her to her car, where they kissed before she drove away. The man left the parking lot a moment later. Callaway snapped a picture of the man's license plate in case Paul wanted to know who he was. Callaway later found out the man was Sharon's yoga instructor, Kenny Goldman.

Callaway had then driven to the beach house, only to find out the next morning that something terrible had happened at the Gardener residence.

SIXTY-ONE

Fisher tossed and turned on the sofa. She was in the breakroom of the Milton PD. After an all-nighter spent gathering evidence from the scene of Pedro's murder, she decided to close her eyes. She did not want to drive all the way home. She figured she could get some sleep here, although she could have used a shower. Going through the hopper had left a strong odor on her. But she was used to foul smells.

As a law enforcement officer, she was often confronted with all kinds of situations. Homeless people who had not bathed in weeks needing to be escorted out of a building. Finding an unconscious man in his apartment who had soiled himself after consuming too much alcohol. Examining a dead body that had been discovered after several days. For her, the latter was the worst of all.

A dead person's organs stopped working, and the body began to release all forms of liquids. And if decomposition took over, the smell was downright unbearable. To make matters worse, the smell of death lingered with you for a very long time.

Fisher changed her position on the sofa in order to get more comfortable. It was a futile attempt. The sofa was over ten years old. The coils had begun to poke out of the fabric, and the sofa had a stale odor.

Holt would not be caught dead sleeping on a sofa such as this one. He much preferred his own bed. Fortunately for him, he lived only twenty minutes away from the police department. He easily popped in and out whenever he wanted. Also, he needed to see Nancy.

Whenever Fisher would fall asleep, something would stir her up. After a few tries, she finally got up. She checked the time. She had been on the sofa for a couple of hours. Even though her sleep was interrupted, it was enough to get her through the day. She could always go home and catch up later.

She headed to the ladies' bathroom. She splashed cold water over her face. Whatever lethargy she was feeling was suddenly washed away. After freshening up, she moved to the kitchen. Someone had left the coffee to brew. The aroma was inviting as she waited for the coffee pot to fill. She poured herself a hot steaming cup and then walked to her desk in the corner.

She was surprised to see Holt seated at his desk. "I thought you'd be in your bed, snoozing away."

"I couldn't sleep," he said. "What about you?"

"I couldn't sleep either." She took a sip from her cup. She waited until the caffeine coursed through her body before she said, "What're you looking at?"

Holt was staring at a stack of paper. It was stapled together at the top corner. He had a tiny smile on his lips.

"What's so funny now?" she asked. "You found actual evidence that Pedro Catano was having an affair with Kyla Gardener?"

"Even better."

She stared at him.

"The blood found on Paul Gardener's shirt matched the victim's."

"And you were surprised by that?" she said. "I could've told you that just by looking at it."

"No, that's not what I was surprised by. It was something else."

"What?"

"When we arrested Gardener, we took a swab of his saliva. Well, the DNA test came back."

"Okay."

"Paul Gardener is not Kyla Gardener's biological father."

Fisher blinked. "Excuse me?"

"She's not his daughter."

"Wow. I didn't see that coming."

"And it gets better."

"How?"

"Kyla Gardener was nine weeks pregnant."

Fisher almost dropped her cup. "She was?"

Holt's smile widened. "She sure was. I have the tests right here to prove it."

Fisher pondered this new development. "Okay, but why are you smiling?"

"It's simple. Kyla wanted to marry Pedro because she was carrying his child. When Gardener found out about it, he went into a rage, and he killed Kyla and then Pedro. He knew if Pedro married Kyla, Pedro would also be in line to get the money. Gardener must have also known Kyla wasn't his biological child. This made getting rid of her easier."

Fisher stared at her cup in silence.

Holt said, "You know what this means, don't you?"

"What?"

"We have the motive we were searching for all along."

SIXTY-TWO

Callaway parked the car across from the apartment building. It looked different in daylight. The exterior was gray, and the main doors were white.

The last time he was here was at night. There was hardly anyone he saw. Every once in a while, a car would enter the property and disappear around the back. He figured that was where the tenant parking was.

It was an entirely different scenario than before. Several cars were lined up by the apartment's front entrance. They were waiting to drop off or pick up passengers. Even the visitor's parking lot was full.

He had driven by the Gardener residence on his way here. There was still yellow police tape across the front door. On the front lawn was a makeshift memorial for Kyla. Someone had stuck a piece of four-by-four on the ground with her photo taped on it. Around it were flowers, cards, even teddy bears that neighbors, friends, and strangers had left behind.

He had wanted to go inside the house and see the crime scene for himself. He was not sure what he would find if he did, but curiosity was getting the better of him.

He watched as people walked in and out of the apartment's front lobby.

I shouldn't be here wasting my time, he thought. *I should be in my office, drumming up more business.*

Somehow, it felt like his assignment from Paul was incomplete, as if there was still more he had to dig up. But what? Paul's lawyer and the prosecutor had his photos. If there was anything relevant in them, they would have followed up on it by now.

Why haven't they? he wondered.

Maybe neither of them cared what Sharon was up to that night. They were more focused on Paul and what happened at the Gardeners' home. If his wife was unfaithful, that was a personal matter between a husband and wife, not related to the crime itself.

Callaway did not entirely agree with that. Every action had a reaction. What if Sharon had not left her home that night? Would Kyla still be alive? Callaway had to believe the answer was yes.

Sharon would have prevented her husband from hurting their daughter. Even if she was under the influence of sleeping pills and had no idea what was happening in the room next to her, the alarm system would have still been operational. That would have deterred Paul from doing anything rash out of fear the cameras would capture something. He could disable the security if he wanted to, of course, but that would mean Paul was not intoxicated and had the presence of mind to plan the entire crime.

There were so many what-ifs, but none of them changed the fact a young woman was brutally murdered.

He started the car, but instead of driving away, he pulled into the building's visitor parking lot. He found a spot and got out. He walked to the main doors, wondering how he could get into the building.

He spotted a girl holding the door for her mom. The mom was pushing a baby stroller. Callaway rushed over and helped the girl with the door. He smiled and the girl smiled back. He watched as the mother and daughter walked to a waiting car.

He went inside and scanned the lobby directory. He did not see a name he recognized. He was about to leave when his eyes caught a stack of mail sitting on a ledge below the directory. He was not sure why, but he reached for it. There were about a dozen envelopes.

He flipped through the envelopes, wondering what he was looking for.

When he saw the name on one of the envelopes, he stopped.

Dr. Richard Lester.

Callaway's eyes widened. *So that's why he paid me a visit*, he thought. *He wanted to buy the photos to spare* him *embarrassment, not his sister, because the photos would reveal she used his apartment as the place to meet her lover the night her daughter was murdered.*

SIXTY-THREE

Paul's hands shook as he wiped his eyes with a tissue. Roth had just broken the news to him. He wanted to do it in person, and so he had a taxi pick him up and bring him to his office. Roth did not want to go through the press that was waiting outside Paul's mother's house. By now, the news would be spreading like wildfire, and the questions would be unrelenting.

When Roth had received the call from Barrows, he did not believe it at first. It was when she sent him a copy of the lab report of the blood and DNA tests that he was able to confirm it. She did not have to inform him of the lab results. She said she was doing it out of professional courtesy.

Roth knew she was not.

Barrows wanted him to know that her case was strengthened by the new discoveries. The prosecution might even consider going for the death penalty unless Roth was able to convince his client to plead guilty, which he had no intention of doing. Until now.

But there were a few things he wanted to clear up first. "Paul," he said, starting gently, "Did you know Kyla was not your daughter?"

Paul looked up. His eyes were red. "I had no idea. I swear. Maybe I should have sensed something was wrong when Sharon wanted to get married the moment she broke the news to me that she was pregnant. I didn't ask a lot of questions. We had only been intimate once. But I didn't care. I was over the moon with excitement. I was going to be a father, and guys like me don't marry girls like Sharon. She was beautiful, confident, and she came from a family with money. I was struggling to pay my bills and my student loans. I remember it being the happiest time of my life." His chin dropped to his chest. "I had no idea she only wanted to get married because the baby she was carrying was someone else's. I need to speak to Sharon. I need to speak to my wife right now."

"Your *ex*-wife."

Paul looked at him, confused.

"Sharon's filed for divorce. I was going to tell you when the time was right. You already had a lot on your plate."

Paul was silent. He stared at nothing in particular. A few minutes passed before he lifted his head and said, "Then I need to talk to my ex-wife. I need answers. I'm owed that much, at least."

"She doesn't want to talk to you, Paul. The documents were delivered to my office, not your mother's residence. I think she is hoping to use me as an intermediary, as I am currently your lawyer. I don't specialize in divorce cases, but I'll take care of this for you at no extra charge."

Paul was suddenly offended. "I can pay you. I have the money."

"No, you don't," Roth said. "The retainer is almost gone. Your business is on the brink of insolvency. And with a divorce on the horizon, a judge may freeze your personal assets until both you and your wife reach a settlement."

"What are you saying?" Paul asked.

"If this case goes to trial, you might not be able to afford me."

SIXTY-FOUR

Callaway walked up the metal stairs to his office when he saw Fisher was waiting for him by the front door.

"Okay, what did I do now?" he asked, raising his hands in mock surrender. "Is Holt waiting in a squad car around the corner?"

"Very funny, Lee," she said. "If I came to arrest you, I wouldn't need Holt. I could haul your ass to the station all by myself."

Callaway shrugged. "I can't argue with that. So is this a professional visit, or a personal one?"

"A little bit of both."

"Okay."

"I came to tell you that we have enough evidence to seek the death penalty in Paul Gardener's case."

Callaway grimaced. "I bet it was Holt's idea."

"It was, but I can't find any reason to disagree with him."

"Why are you telling me this?"

"I'm telling you because Gardener is your client."

"He used to be my client. He's not anymore. We had this discussion before, remember?"

"So, you don't care what happens to him?"

"I don't," he said.

He moved past her and unlocked the door to his office.

"In that case," she said. "Sorry to have wasted your time, Lee."

She started to move down the stairs.
Callaway sighed.
"Stop," he said. "I do care."
Fisher walked back up.
"I don't know," he said. "But my gut is saying it's all too convenient."
"Convenient?"
"The body in the house, the knife in his car, his prints on the knife, the fight he had with his daughter on the morning of her death. It smells like it was staged."
She raised her eyebrow. "Staged?"
"Yeah, like someone wanted Paul charged for the crime."
"You're beginning to sound like his defense," she said. "You might not have heard this on the news yet, but on top of everything you just said, Kyla was also pregnant, and she's not Gardener's biological child."
"Whoa," Callaway said in disbelief.
"Whoa indeed." After Fisher let her words sink in, she said, "The case is overwhelmingly against your client."
"But you don't believe he did it."
Her eyes narrowed. "What makes you say that?"
"Why else would you drive all the way here to tell me?"
She sighed and looked away. "I don't know about the whole 'staged' angle, but I do know something doesn't feel right about this. Holt's got his man, but I don't feel I do."
"I was there that night," Callaway said.
"We all know that."

"But what you don't know is that I was there long before Paul or even Sharon showed up."

"Okay."

"When you are following a target, you have to be at a spot early, and you have to be willing to stay late. I watched that house like a hawk. I saw Sharon drive up to the house. She had grocery bags with her, so I assumed she had gone out shopping. I saw Paul pull up into the driveway. He was dressed in a suit, so I assumed he was returning from work."

"Where're you going with this? I don't have all day."

"But I never saw Kyla come home."

Fisher shrugged. "Were you there *all* day?"

"Of course not."

"Then how do you know she wasn't home already?"

"When I arrived at the house, the sun had started to come down. While I waited in my car, I watched as the streetlights were turned on. But you know what's odd? No lights inside the house came on during that time. Only when Sharon showed up and went inside did the house become illuminated."

"So, what are you saying?"

"What if Kyla was never at home that night?"

"How's that possible? She was found by her mother in her bedroom the next morning."

"I don't know, but I'm telling you, no one was home when I got to the house."

SIXTY-FIVE

A tearful Luiz Catano stood outside his apartment building, facing a battery of cameras and a throng of reporters. He was flanked on one side by his wife and two daughters, and on the other by Senator Barron Lester.

Senator Lester spoke first. "I never imagined I would have to stop my campaign yet again to speak on another tragedy that has struck my family. The death of Pedro Catano has affected us deeply. Luiz has been a loyal employee of ours for decades. He was there before I became a senator of this great State. He was even there before I started my private hedge fund, which made me a very successful man. Luiz's loss is our loss, and so, I will be covering all funeral expenses. I will also set up a trust fund so that Luiz's remaining children have the opportunity for higher education."

Senator Lester moved aside to let Luiz speak, "I would like to thank Senator Lester for coming to my home and for telling me how sorry he is about Pedro. I have worked for the Lester family for almost thirty years. When I came to this country, I had no money in my pockets. Mr. Lester gave me a job, and I was able to raise my family. Pedro was…" He suddenly choked up in tears. "Pedro was going to work for the Lester family too, but now he is gone."

Senator Lester put a hand on Luiz's shoulder to comfort him.

"I can tell you the Lester family are good people. They care about people like me. But I don't think Mr. Paul Gardener is a good man. I think he hurt Pedro and I think he hurt his daughter."

Senator Lester quickly took over. "I apologize for Luiz's outburst. He is suffering like any father would be under the circumstances." Senator Lester held up a newspaper. "What's written here has caused us a great deal of stress. The facts speak for themselves. The evidence against my son-in-law is irrefutable, I'm afraid. That's why I am imploring him to do the right thing so we can put this tragedy behind us. I yet again thank the Milton Police Department for the excellent job they have done. I yet again ask the media for some privacy. The Catano family has lost a son. We have lost a granddaughter. Let us grieve in peace. Thank you."

SIXTY-SIX

Callaway was back at Paul's mother's house. Instead of taking the back route, he decided to go through the front. The press had doubled from the last time he was here. They had not only clogged the street leading up to the house but also taken over the house's front lawn.

He parked two blocks away—there was no parking any closer—and made his way toward the house.

The press came alive the moment they saw him approach. Cameras turned in his direction. Reporters jumped out of their cars and vans. Photographers began snapping photos.

He almost wished he had hopped the neighbors' fence, but he knew the chance of not getting seen this time was slim to none.

The press converged around him like a mob, but they did not impede his path. They yelled questions. They took photos. They rolled their cameras.

He merely smiled and walked straight up to the house. He rang the doorbell. He could feel the press crowding in behind him. They wanted a photo of Paul Gardener.

The front door opened an inch, and Callaway slid inside. Paul was behind the door. Callaway had called before coming. Paul was not in the mood to see anyone, but Callaway was persistent.

Paul stood motionless in the dark hall as if he feared coming out into the light would burn him. Callaway did not blame him. If he were in his place, he too would want to hide from the world.

"How're you holding up, Paul?" Callaway asked.

Without replying, he moved to the living room. Callaway followed him. Paul stopped at the fireplace and turned to him. He had aged significantly from the last time Callaway had seen him. His shoulders were slumped, his eyes were dead, and his lips were curled in a frown. He looked like a man who was defeated.

"Did you see the news?" he asked.

Callaway knew he was referring to the press conference outside Luiz Catano's apartment building. "I did."

"It's a charade by Sharon's family to push me further into the corner," Paul said. "They would rather I disappear than affect the family negatively in any way."

"Or affect Senator Lester's campaign for re-election."

Paul considered this. He nodded. "I'm thinking of pleading guilty. Roth has advised me to consider it."

"He has?"

"He doesn't think I can afford a lengthy trial."

"And can you?"

"No," he said slowly. "Ever since this nightmare started, I haven't gone back to work. I have no idea how much worse things have gotten. You may not know this, but my software company is underwater."

Callaway was aware before he took Paul as a client. He liked to conduct a background check on each client to find out more about them. But he always assumed Paul was good financially because of the Lester family name. He never imagined they would cast him aside like a leper.

"But if you confess to the crime," Callaway said, "you could be looking at a long sentence, even life."

"What choice do I have? I don't have the money to fight them." Paul put his face in his hands. "What if they are right? What if I did kill my daughter in a fit of drunken rage?"

SIXTY-SEVEN

"Did you kill your daughter?" Callaway asked.

"I don't know," Paul said. "I don't remember much from that night."

"What if you had?" Callaway asked.

"It's something I've agonized about over and over in my head."

"She wasn't your biological daughter," Callaway said.

"I loved her and adored her," Paul said firmly. "I didn't know the truth until now, so why would I hurt the little girl I raised as my own?"

There's that conviction again, Callaway thought.

"Before you do anything that could change your life forever, let me look into this," Callaway said.

Paul stared at Callaway. "You want me to hire you?"

"Yes, I'm much cheaper than a high-priced lawyer."

"I don't have much money left over. Whatever I had, it went to retain Roth's services."

"Whatever you do have will help in my investigation."

Paul walked over to the window. He did not dare open the drapes. The mob outside would descend on the front porch like a horde just to snap a photo of him. He said, "If this is your attempt at squeezing money out of someone who is desperate, then I loathe what you are doing."

"I can squeeze far more money out of cheaters and philanderers. They will pay up on the spot just to make me go away, so this is not about money. But I do need it for out-of-pocket expenses. And I will waive my own fee."

Paul turned to him. "Why are you doing it if not for the money?"

"I don't know who killed your daughter, but I don't think it's you."

"What makes you so sure?"

"What makes *you* so sure you did it?"

He was met with silence.

Callaway asked, "Tell me what happened that night."

Paul rubbed his temples. "It's all foggy. Whenever I try to think about it, I come up blank."

"Okay, then tell me what you *do* remember."

He took a deep breath. "I came home straight from work. I wasn't drunk like they wrote in the papers, I'm sure of that."

"How do you know?"

"I know, or else I wouldn't have been able to drive home. I did have a drink once I was inside, though," he said. "I grabbed a bottle from the liquor cabinet and headed straight for the guesthouse."

"Was your daughter home?" Callaway asked.

"I'm not sure. She's twenty. She doesn't need or want me to watch over her like I did when she was younger."

"What about your wife?"

"She was at home. I saw her car parked in the driveway, but I never spoke to her. We've been estranged for some time. Usually, when I get home, she's up in her room. We don't talk. I'll warm up whatever food is in the fridge, or I'll pick up takeout on my way home. I'll have my dinner in the guesthouse, sitting in front of the TV.

"Is that what you did that night?"

"I'm not sure. I don't think I had any dinner that night."

"Okay, then what happened?"

He took a deep breath and shook his head. "I don't remember. I really don't."

"Think hard, Paul. Your freedom depends on it."

He shut his eyes tight. "I think I passed out on the sofa. Wait! I remember a noise. I don't know what it was… it was like a hissing noise… like someone was releasing air… but I do remember it tasting… *sweet*."

Callaway was confused. "Sweet?"

"Yeah, I know it sounds weird," he said. "Everything about that night was weird."

Callaway rubbed his chin. He said. "I want to see everything Roth has on your case. The detectives' notes, the lab reports, the autopsy findings, everything. I want to review it."

"Okay."

"Also, have you had a drug test?"

Paul was confounded. "Why? I don't do drugs."

SIXTY-EIGHT

Holt and Fisher were in the DA's office.

Barrows said, "I had a lengthy discussion with Evan Roth."

"About what?" Holt asked.

"About the possibility of a plea deal."

"Gardener is willing to plead guilty?" Holt said, not the least bit surprised by this.

"Not yet, but I get the feeling his defense may go in that direction."

Fisher said, "How many years are we looking at?"

"If he goes in front of a judge and confesses to the crime, then I don't mind asking for life with a chance of parole after twenty."

"What did Roth think of that?" Fisher asked.

"He wants fifteen years with a chance of parole after eight."

"Bullshit!" Holt howled. "No deal."

"Calm down!" Barrows said, putting her hand up. "I haven't agreed to anything."

"You shouldn't either," Holt said. "And what about Pedro Catano?"

"What about him?" Barrows replied.

"We can also charge Gardener with his murder and ask for a double life sentence."

"Do you have concrete evidence that Gardener was responsible for Pedro Catano's death?"

"We have…"

Again, Barrows put her hand up. "The evidence linking Gardener to Catano is all circumstantial. The call to Kyla from Pedro on the day of her death, the assertion by Pedro's ex-girlfriend that Kyla and Pedro were romantically involved, the assumption that Kyla was pregnant with Pedro's child—that will not hold up in court. Did you conduct a gun residue test on Gardener when you arrested him?"

Holt stared at her. "No, we had no reason to. Kyla Gardener had been stabbed."

"Exactly. We don't have any proof that Gardener pulled the trigger of the gun that killed Pedro. Unless you find the gun with his prints on it, I'm not going to go in front of the judge and ask that those additional charges be laid on Mr. Gardener."

Fisher could see Holt was steaming.

Holt said, "We have him by the balls. He is cornered and he knows it. He wants to find a way out, and we shouldn't give it to him. No deal."

Barrows sighed. "We also have to see what can be gained from this by the DA's office."

Holt shook his head. "Politics."

"Without state funding, we don't exist, so we have to see how each case impacts us. We have to ask ourselves what the public benefit in this is."

Holt said, "The public is devouring this story by the mouthful. Each day, something new and sensational shows up. We have a father who murdered his only child. We later find out the child was pregnant, and that she was not even his child. You don't get any more sensational than this."

"We also have the family of a sitting senator involved."

Holt pointed a finger at Barrows. "I knew it was politics!"

"Senator Lester has connections, including with the state governor. He wants this to end as soon as possible. I don't blame him. He is up for re-election. He doesn't want his name or his family's name splattered across the headlines much longer."

"He's probably afraid of what else might pop up if it goes to trial," Fisher said.

"You are probably right," Barrows agreed.

Holt said, "Did you see the Luiz Catano press conference?"

"I did."

"Then you know Senator Lester also wants us to go after Gardener for Pedro's death."

"I'm sure that's what it came across as, but from what I heard from my sources, Senator Lester wants to see a quick end to this mess. The only way for that to happen is for Gardener to confess to the crime. The press conference was a way to pressure him to do just that. If he does, I will work out a deal with Roth."

"No deal!" Holt said for the umpteenth time.

"I have superiors I have to report to," Barrows said. "I do what I am asked."

"You do what is right," Holt said.

He stormed out.

SIXTY-NINE

Outside the DA's office, Fisher said to Holt, "What's bothering you? Ever since we took on this case, you've wanted to nail Gardener even when not all the evidence was there."'

"I just don't like parents murdering their children," he replied in a low voice.

Fisher now understood.

Holt was a devout Catholic. He did not believe in abortion, and he most certainly was against infanticide. Holt and his wife, Nancy, were unable to have children of their own. They decided to adopt, and they were fortunate to bring a child over from Ukraine. The boy was malnourished and they later discovered he had been suffering from neglect. They loved the child like he was their own blood. With a lot of care and attention, they were able to get the child back to good health.

But on the seventh month after the boy's arrival in the United States, he was diagnosed with a rare form of cancer. The doctors were not sure how he got it, but they were certain the birth parents had known and had done nothing about it. Holt was furious. He wanted to sue the birth parents and have them charged for child abuse. But he had more important things to worry about. He had to find a cure for his adopted son. He paid for the best health care money could buy. He and Nancy took the boy to the best specialists they could find. They devoted all their time and energy to help him get better. But before the year was up, the boy died. Holt held him in his arms as life left his tiny body.

Holt was devastated and heartbroken. Nancy went into a deep depression she still had not been able to fully come out of.

Holt was angry. He did end up suing the adoption agency, but before the case could proceed further, the agency closed its doors, and the people involved disappeared. Holt flew to Ukraine to pursue them, but he had no jurisdiction, and the local police were no help. He tried to find the boy's birth parents, but that was a futile attempt. He felt lonely and lost. It was as if no one cared what happened to the little boy who was his adopted son.

"You know," Fisher said to him, "Kyla was not four years old. She was turning twenty-one in a few months."

Holt stared at her.

"She was old enough to take care of herself."

"Maybe she never thought someone who was supposed to protect her would end up harming her," he said.

"You have to let it go," she said. "We have done our job. We have to let the DA's office do theirs."

Holt's shoulders slumped, and then he nodded.

SEVENTY

The place was tucked between a Laundromat and a barbershop. The front windows were covered by heavy blinds, and if you went inside, you would see tables, chairs, and a TV in the corner. But if you went up the side stairs to the second floor, you would enter the safe injection clinic for addicts.

It was created by a group of concerned medical practitioners who were fed up with the opioid crisis in the city. There were too many deaths due to overdoses. The elected government officials were not willing to make drug addiction a priority, so the practitioners took action. Funds were privately raised, and a makeshift clinic was established.

Whenever Callaway dropped by, which was not very often, he was always shocked to see the people who visited the clinic. Their eyes were vacant, their faces shrunken, their skin a pale gray or yellow. They were in the deep clutches of their addiction. Their lives revolved around when they got their next hit. Nothing else mattered, not even their lives.

The clinic provided them with a safe and monitored site to inject themselves with their drug of choice. Critics would argue the clinic was enabling them to become even more dependent on drugs. The practitioners countered if the addicts were left to take drugs on their own, they would share dirty needles with each other, administer more of the drug than the body could handle, and they would engage in dangerous and illegal activities. By going to the clinic, they did not have to steal, pimp, or do anything else in order to get their next high.

Callaway took the stairs up to where he got in line with about half a dozen people who were lined up in front of an enclosed booth. As they got to the front, they spoke to a woman behind the glass. She then slid a small tray with the desired drug and paraphernalia across the counter. The users then walked over to a smaller booth in the corner and administered the drug under the watchful eye of a medical professional.

Callaway spotted him standing in the corner.

He smiled as Callaway approached. "To what do I owe the pleasure?"

"I need something tested," Callaway said. After meeting with Paul, Callaway had gone out and purchased a drug kit from the local pharmacy, which he used to take a sample of Paul's blood. His movements had caused a big commotion when the press caught him leaving and returning to the house. He did not care.

Callaway held up the vial with the dark red liquid.

"I'll put it with the other samples," the man said. The clinic sent samples to the lab to see if addicts were making progress. The clinic's aim was to wean the addicts off the drugs by slowly reducing their dosage.

"What name do you want me to use?"

"The same one I use all the time."

"Gator Peckerwood, it is."

Callaway smiled. He had done a few favors for the people at the clinic, so they were willing to reciprocate. He blackmailed a city official who was opposed to the creation of the clinic. Callaway followed this official until he caught him acting boorishly outside a pub. The official agreed to back off if Callaway destroyed the evidence. Callaway agreed to do so, but he still kept a copy in his DVD box in case the official decided to change his mind.

"And what should we be looking for?" the man asked.

"My client doesn't remember anything from the night before. In fact, he pretty much blacked out the entire night."

"Memory loss and loss of consciousness," the man said, taking notes. "Got it. We'll see if anything was in his system that might have caused this."

SEVENTY-ONE

Paul sat in the living room with his head in his hands. If the press was not bad enough, a group of protestors had gathered outside his mother's house. They held signs. They chanted slogans. They were loud, and they would not stop.

He had turned off all the lights in the house. He wanted the darkness to envelop him and take him away from here.

They called him a child killer when his daughter was a grown woman. They called him a monster, even though he did not remember doing what he was accused of doing. They called him entitled when he had always earned everything he got in his life.

His mother was in the kitchen. She had gone to make tea, but he knew she wanted to be as far away from the noise as possible.

His mother had warned him to stay away from Sharon and her family. They were not like them. He came from a humble beginning. His grandfather worked at a factory during the Depression, building trains and railway equipment. His father sold insurance door to door and would be away for weeks or months. They were not poor, but they were always struggling. They never had enough of anything: not enough food, not enough clothing, not enough money, not even enough happiness. Their situation had made them a miserable lot. Before Paul's eighteenth birthday, his father jumped in front of a subway train. It was ironic. His grandfather had spent his entire life building trains, and his father committed suicide by one.

Paul had big plans. He would not end up like his father or grandfather. He would not spend his entire life making ends meet. He would be the master of his fate. He would build a company from the ground up, and it would make him enough money to take care of his family for generations.

He did just that.

His software company, at one point, was recording sales of over one million dollars a month. There was hope they could double or triple their earnings the next year. But then, everything started to go in the wrong direction. The mobile company which heavily pushed their apps started to lose market share and soon was struggling to keep a foothold in the industry. Other mobile makers suddenly adopted new operating systems. His company's biggest mistake was not making their apps compatible with all platforms. By the time they made the changes, it was too late. Consumers had moved on to other apps that were far more advanced than theirs. His company began to spend more than they were bringing in. Whatever cash flow reserves they had were used to update the apps, they became a casualty of the ever-changing technology industry.

Against his mother's advice, he had gone ahead and married Sharon. In hindsight, he should have been skeptical of the unexpected pregnancy, but there was a reason beyond having a baby that made him do it. Sharon's father had offered to pay for their wedding, and he had also agreed to extend him a loan to fund his new business. He needed a leg up to make his dreams come true. And with no bank willing to give him the money he desperately needed, he accepted his father-in-law's help.

He sighed. *I was supposed to have the perfect family and the perfect life. How did it all fall apart?* he thought.

The chants started again. They were even louder than before.

He closed his eyes and tried to drown out the noise, even though he knew it was a futile gesture.

SEVENTY-TWO

Callaway was at Evan Roth's office. Roth was not pleased he had to hand over materials on a case to a third party, but on his client's instructions, he was forced to oblige.

He pushed a file across his desk. "I had my secretary make a copy for you," he said. "It contains everything the prosecution had on the case so we could prepare our rebuttal."

Callaway lifted the file. It was thick and heavy.

"I'm not sure if you'll find anything useful in there," Roth said.

"Probably not, but I still want to take a look." He moved his fingers across the file as if by doing so, he might conjure up something vital inside.

"You know they want to charge Paul with the death penalty," Roth said.

"I know," Callaway replied. "But what I don't understand is, why are you abandoning him at this time?"

Roth looked offended. "I'm not abandoning him. I'm trying to help him."

"By advising him to plead guilty?" Callaway asked.

"Each day that goes by, new evidence surfaces that has, so far, not helped Paul. When I took on the case, the prosecution had a plea deal on the table. It was for fifteen years with a chance of parole at eight, which is what I'm still trying to get for Paul. As time has passed, the prosecution's case has gotten stronger, and they are now less inclined to an offer that would be favorable to him. I'd be lucky if I can get him twenty-five years with a chance of parole at fifteen. I'll keep at it, but I doubt they'll budge much now."

Roth paused a moment. "You have spoken to Paul. Do you know if he is going to plead guilty?"

"He hasn't said anything to me." Callaway did not want to tell Roth that that was what Paul was considering at this point.

Roth said, "When I take on a new case, I never ask my client whether he did it or not. All I ask are the facts. Based on those facts, I see whether I can win the case or not. In Paul's case, I didn't. It doesn't help me when my client has no memory of what happened on the night of the murder. I can't argue he was not at the scene of the crime when he clearly was. I can't argue the blood on him was not the victim's when, in fact, it was. I can't even argue he did not commit the crime when the murder weapon was found in his vehicle and his fingerprints were all over it. I can try to build a case around the fact he may have suffered a psychotic episode that propelled him to act in a violent manner, but that requires Paul to be analyzed by psychiatrists and other medical professionals. It is a long, drawn-out process to identify what his mental state was at the time of the crime. I don't know if he is prepared for that, or if he has the financial resources to go down that route."

"If you knew the case was unwinnable from the beginning, then why did you take it on?" Callaway asked.

Roth shook his head. "I did it for the Lester family. I've known them for years. Barron and Richard are my firm's best and oldest clients. When Paul was taken into custody, I received a call from Barron to get his son-in-law out. At that time, the Lester family thought it was all a mistake. They believed Paul was innocent and there was no way he could have hurt Kyla."

"But now they have changed their view on that," Callaway said.

"In light of the recent evidence, yes, they have."

"Are they pushing you to convince Paul to plead?"

"Yes and no. They want this matter behind them as soon as possible. They have made this known through the media as well. But *I* also think it's a smart decision now for Paul to take a deal if it's on the table. He's still relatively young. By the time he gets out on parole, he can still rebuild his life."

"What if he is innocent?" Callaway asked.

Roth's head fell to his chest. "If he went to prison for a crime he didn't commit. Then I have failed him as his lawyer."

SEVENTY-THREE

Callaway took the file Roth had given him and headed straight for the nearest diner. He found a seat in the back of the restaurant. He ordered coffee—extra strong—and he told the waitress to top up the cup whenever it was almost empty. He would need the caffeine to help him get through the file because there was a lot of material. Photos from the crime scene, statements from witnesses and the accused, notes from the detectives, lab reports, and even the medical examiner's analysis.

After two hours and six cups of coffee, a couple of things stood out to him. The first was the position Kyla was found in the bedroom. She lay on the bed with her arms resting next to her body on either side. Her head faced the ceiling with her eyes closed. If one were to ignore the blood, they would assume she was sleeping.

Then there were the clothes she was wearing. They were not sleeping attire. She was dressed as if she was ready to go out. Was she preparing to run away? Perhaps with Pedro? But Callaway could not find anything in the file to indicate she had packed her bags for such a trip. So that theory did not hold.

Next was the autopsy report. It stated Kyla had died of asphyxiation, not from the stabbing. If it was the other way around, blood would be everywhere.

Another thing that caught his attention was the knife found in the glove compartment of Paul's car. The knife's tip was clean while the rest of the blade was covered in blood. It did not make sense because Kyla's body was full of puncture wounds, which could only have come from the knife being thrust directly into her body.

The last thing that made him pause was the bloodstain on Paul's golf shirt. It was a long, smooth streak, not drops splattered all over. It was also on the back of the shirt, not the front. It would make more sense during an altercation for the blood to spray on the front of the shirt, but there was not a single drop there.

Callaway's eyes narrowed. A theory began to form in his head. It seemed farfetched, and if he told someone what it was, they would laugh him out of the room. But it was all he had to go on right now.

The waitress came over to top up his cup for the seventh time. He put his hand over the cup. "I'm done," he said.

She looked relieved. "I was kind of worried you would keep going. You sure you don't want anything to eat? It would help with all that coffee in your system."

He thought a moment. "You know what? I am kind of hungry."

She smiled. "We have the cheeseburger special today. It comes with fries and your choice of drink. I would recommend anything but another cup of coffee."

"Yeah, that's sounds good. And I'll get plain water with it."

"Coming right up."

He pulled out his cell phone and sent a quick email.

SEVENTY-FOUR

Callaway returned to his office. The first thing he did was turn on his laptop. Back at the diner, he had taken his time with the special the waitress brought for him. The cheeseburger was the best he had tasted in a long time. Maybe it had a lot to do with the amount of coffee he had consumed. Once the caffeine wore off, he was famished. He savored each bite of the burger, and the fries were just right: not too crispy and not too soggy.

He checked his watch as the laptop booted up. He hoped enough time had passed for the recipient of the email to check her messages. When he signed into his browser, he smiled.

There was a reply from Echo Rose. Callaway had met her in Fairview when he had gone there to follow up on a lead for another case. She had wanted to hire him for a job. He turned it down because the information was decades old. He did not think he would be able to complete the job. But then he found himself in a bind, and it was only when she put her life on the line that he was able to solve his case. He then gave his full attention to solving her problem. Last he heard from Echo. She was grateful for his help. He now needed her help.

Echo was not only resourceful but also had a way with computers. One could say she was an amateur hacker.

He clicked open the email. Echo's message contained the usernames and passwords to various online accounts and social media sites. They all belonged to Kyla Gardener.

Callaway was not sure how Echo managed to find them on such short notice. He was just thankful she did.

He punched in the address of a social media website and signed into Kyla's account. The first thing he noticed were the heartfelt messages of sadness from friends, classmates, and even strangers. He assumed they were strangers because next to their names were icons to request friendship. They were not clicked, so Kyla most likely did not know them or did not want to befriend them.

He scrolled past the individual messages, tributes, and poems that pretty much summed up that she was loved and would be missed forever.

He scrolled all the way back to the day she had died. He then slowly went through each of her posts. There were dozens.

Why do young people think anyone would be interested in what they did each and every minute of the day? he wondered.

While working as a private investigator, Callaway had become aware of the dangers online. If you posted anything, no matter how mundane or obscure, it was forever available to those who wanted to find it.

Callaway found copious amounts of dirt on the client's spouses just by conducting a simple online search. And if he had Echo's skills, it would cut his work by half. He would not even have to leave the office in some cases. He could do all his work with his fingers.

The naiveté people displayed when they assumed their lives were hidden to strangers online was baffling. Anyone with even the most basic computer knowledge could find out whatever they wanted about you. And it had become even easier now that everything contained a computer chip. You did not even have to hack a cell phone or computer. You could hack the computer system of a vehicle and find out where the individual commuted to each day. You could hack into the thermostat of a home and find out where someone lived. The possibilities were endless.

He was scrolling through the lists of posts when his eyes fell on one.

On the day of her death, Kyla had teased that she was going to be making a big announcement.

Callaway believed the announcement was either about her pregnancy or that she was getting married soon. The post had a dozen *thumbs-up* responses. He clicked on the post to see who had liked it. He spotted Pedro's name in the list. No surprise there.

He was about to move to the next post when he saw there was one *thumbs-down*. He clicked the image, and a profile photo appeared on the screen. The man's eyes were hidden behind dark sunglasses, and his face was tilted to the side as if he was looking away from the camera.

Callaway jotted down his name.

The social media site also had a feature where users could tag all the places they had visited on a particular day. The user's visits showed up on a map with tiny red dots. If you clicked on the dot, a post or photo would appear, depending on what the user chose to provide.

Callaway began to make notes of all the places Kyla had visited. He was going to retrace her steps on that fatal day.

SEVENTY-FIVE

Callaway was back at the safe injection clinic. "That was quick," Callaway said to the medical professional.

"I requested a fast turnaround," the man said. "I figured you needed it for a job."

"I did."

The man handed him the test results. "Whoever your client was, they had some serious stuff in their system."

Callaway suspected the medical professional might have guessed the client was Paul Gardener, but he was not worried the test results would leak to the press. Whoever came to the clinic, addict or not, their privacy was strictly protected. If the authorities suddenly decided to raid the clinic, they would find nothing. The clinic never asked the addicts their real name.

Callaway scanned the test results.

His mouth dropped.

He looked up at the medical professional in disbelief.

"Rohypnol?" Callaway asked.

"That's what they found in the blood sample you left."

Rohypnol, AKA "the date rape drug," was initially created to treat insomnia, but it began to show up as a recreational drug at clubs, raves, and music festivals. Callaway knew that when this drug was administered for sinister purposes, it could render a person not only unconscious but also cloud a victim's memory. *Is this why Paul's memory about that night is foggy?* Callaway wondered. *That would explain a lot.*

According to Holt and Fisher's notes, Paul showed signs of confusion, sluggishness, and looked hungover. They attributed this to the bottle of scotch found in the guesthouse. What they failed to realize was that these were all signs of Rohypnol poisoning.

Callaway resumed reading the test results.

His eyes widened. "Chloroform?" he said.

The medical professional nodded. "When you said your client had blacked out and did not remember anything, I requested that the tests focus on certain chemicals. As you can see, there is a high chloroform concentration in the blood."

"All I know is it knocks people out, but I'm not too familiar with it as a drug."

"Throughout history, chloroform was used for its anesthetic purposes. But because of its high volatility, its use was discontinued. It's colorless, and it's sweet-smelling."

"Did you say *sweet*?" Callaway asked.

"Yeah. People have said it smelled sweet."

"And you're sure it was in his system?" Callaway asked.

"If the sample you brought us belonged to your client, then yes, your client came into contact with those chemical agents."

SEVENTY-SIX

When Callaway explained the results of the drug test over the phone, Paul had no idea how any of them could have gotten in his body. He was horrified at the mere thought of it. Callaway was certain Paul had not taken them on his own volition. He did not come across as the type of guy who partied hard at night or consumed recreational drugs. But he was under a lot of stress. His marriage was falling apart, and his business was struggling, so he could have consumed Rohypnol to ease the tension. But there was no explanation for why he would have chloroform in his body. It just did not make any sense.

But one thing was for sure. Paul was telling the truth when he said he did not remember anything from that night.

In order to solve how Paul might have gotten these drugs in him, Callaway had to go back to the scene of the crime.

As he drove up, he was surprised to see no press outside the Gardener residence. He was sure some reporter would have camped out on the front lawn, just in case something turned up.

The front door was covered with yellow police tape, but Callaway was not interested in the house. He was interested in what was behind it.

He took the side path until he was confronted by a wooden gate. It was locked. He peeked through the side opening. He could see the bolt.

He searched his surroundings and found a tree branch on the ground. He stripped it of leaves and protruding twigs and stuck it between the gate's openings. He then gently lifted the bolt.

The gate swung open.

He entered the backyard. He headed straight for the guesthouse. Fortunately, there was no police tape on the door. That still did not mean what he was doing was lawful, however. He was breaking and entering.

Callaway did not care. An innocent man's life was on the line.

He pulled on a pair of gloves and turned the door handle. He smiled. Whoever was here last had not bothered to lock the door. Maybe they did not think anything useful was left in the guesthouse. *Big mistake*, Callaway thought. *The guesthouse is the key to this mystery.*

He entered and took in the space. He spotted the futon in the corner that Paul had slept on. There was an empty spot next to it. The recliner had been tagged and taken away as evidence. Kyla's blood was on the recliner. It could have gotten on it from Paul's shirt. Across from the empty spot was a coffee table. It, too, was empty. The bottle of scotch and glass would be used to prove that Paul was drunk that night when he attacked and killed Kyla.

Callaway looked around. He was not sure what he was hoping to find, but it had to be here. He then noticed a window next to the spot where the recliner used to sit. He walked up to the window and moved his hand around it. He felt something at the bottom. He leaned down and saw the window was slightly open. Air was seeping through the crack.

No wonder the room feels so cool, he thought.

He left the guesthouse and walked around the structure. There was a narrow path between the guesthouse and the next-door neighbor's property. Callaway was easily able to squeeze through it and make it to the window. He pulled out a flashlight and shined the light on the ground.

He spotted a partial footprint hidden by leaves and broken twigs.

Someone had accessed the guesthouse window from the outside.

Who did that? he thought.

SEVENTY-SEVEN

Callaway left the guesthouse and walked back to his car.

He spotted a man standing in the driveway. He was wearing a light jacket, jeans, and a baseball cap.

There was something odd about the way he stood there. He did not come across as someone who was curious to check out the house where a father had allegedly murdered his daughter. It looked as if the man was paying his condolences.

The moment he spotted Callaway, he turned and began walking in the other direction. Callaway decided to follow him.

The man turned and saw Callaway behind him. He quickened his steps. Callaway did the same.

The man crossed the road and hurried toward a green vehicle parked on the side of the street. Callaway did not want to lose him. He went into a full jog.

The man bolted. He must have realized he did not have enough time to get inside the car and drive away.

Damn, Callaway thought, and ran after him.

The man raced down the street and disappeared around the corner.

Callaway made it to the end. He saw the man was already making his way up the steep incline of the adjacent street.

Callaway's legs burned as he kept up the chase.

He was panting as he made it to the end of the street. He looked around, but the man was nowhere to be seen.

He thought about turning back. He could always get the license plate number of the green vehicle and locate the name of the owner, but a part of him was angry that he had lost the man.

He was about to double back when he spotted the man at the far end of the street. He was cutting through a park, making his way toward a tunnel that went underneath a road.

From his vantage point, Callaway estimated the man was thirty yards away. He suddenly had an idea. If the tunnel had an entrance, it must have an exit.

He had to find where this exit was.

He hurried down another street. This one traversed an even steeper incline, but it went downhill.

Callaway made it to the end and cut right. He narrowly missed running into an old woman with a walker. He apologized and kept going.

He was nearly out of breath and sweating profusely when he reached the other side of the tunnel. He looked around. The man was not there.

Damn. Am I late? Did I miss him?

His mouth was dry, his throat was parched, and it felt like his lungs were on fire.

He should have just gone back to the green vehicle and waited for the man to return.

Callaway heard a noise coming from the tunnel. He could not see who it was because of the darkness, but he could tell the sound was feet hitting the pavement.

He moved to the side of the entrance and waited as the footsteps became louder and more distinct.

The man emerged from the tunnel, not seeing Callaway as he hurried by.

Callaway took three long strides and tackled the man from behind. The man fell forward and hit the ground. The baseball cap flew off his head.

Callaway turned the man over so he was facing him and cocked his fist.

The man put his hands over his face. "Please don't hurt me," he pleaded.

"What were you doing outside the Gardener residence?"

"I didn't do anything."

"Answer my question, or else I'll take you down to the police," Callaway said.

"I am Kyla's father," the man replied.

"What?" Callaway asked, confused.

"I am Kyla's real father."

SEVENTY-EIGHT

The man's baseball cap had hidden a bald pate. His hands were big and calloused, and there was dirt underneath his fingernails. His eyes were blue, and they darted from one spot to another as if looking out for any sign of danger.

His name was Gus Holden, and he lived a hundred miles from Milton.

Callaway had felt bad for scaring Holden, so he offered to buy him a drink. They could not find a bar nearby, so they grabbed a seat at a café's patio.

"Why did you run away when you saw me?" Callaway asked.

Holden took a sip of his drink. "I don't know. I wasn't expecting anyone to catch me."

"And why were you worried about anyone catching you?"

Holden looked away. He looked like he did not want to say too much. Callaway needed answers, and he was not about to let this man go without getting some.

"I'm trying to find out what happened to Kyla," Callaway said. "So whatever you tell me might help me do just that."

"I saw you on TV," Holden said instead.

"TV?"

"Yeah, you were leaving Paul Gardener's house. I know you're helping my daughter's killer."

"He didn't kill your daughter."

Holden's eyes gleamed with surprise. "He didn't?"

"No, and I'm going to prove it."

Holden suddenly looked relieved. "I never believed the news when I heard it."

"Have you met Paul?"

"Once."

"And?"

Holden was silent again.

Callaway leaned closer. "Listen. Right now, I have no idea what's going on, but what I do know is that a man may get the death penalty for a crime he never committed. So, let's start with a few simple questions, okay?"

Holden nodded.

"Why haven't you come forward and told everyone Kyla's your real daughter?"

"I can't."

"Why not?"

He sighed. "I was paid never to tell anyone she was my child."

Callaway blinked. "What?"

"Yes."

"Who paid you?"

Holden hesitated a moment. "Barron Lester," he whispered.

"Senator Lester?"

"Yes."

"Why would he do that?"

"It was a long time ago," he said. "Sharon and I were young. I met her at a rock concert. I was there with my friends, and she was there with hers. We started talking during the sets, and I was immediately attracted to her. At the end of the concert, I asked her out for drinks. I was surprised when she agreed. I could tell she came from a wealthy family. She drove a nice car, and she had on expensive jewelry. My dad owned an automotive garage, and I worked there as a mechanic, so money was always tight. Anyway, we went to a bar and drank. We then went to my apartment, where we did pot. And then one thing led to another. When I woke up the next morning, she was gone. I didn't pay too much attention to it, but a couple of days later—or maybe it was week, I don't remember—Sharon showed up at my dad's garage. I think she saw a business card in my apartment, and she knew I was a mechanic, so it wasn't hard for her to find me. She told me she was pregnant. She said she came from a conservative family, and when they found out, they'd kill her. She said I had to marry her. I was scared. I didn't know what to do. But I told her I would speak to my father and it'd all be all right." He paused and took a sip from his cup. "Before I could get the courage to tell my dad, I got a visit from Sharon's father. He wasn't a senator at the time, but I could tell he liked being in control. Sharon told him what had happened, and he wasn't pleased with it. In fact, he looked so agitated that I thought he would hit me. Instead, he said he had an offer for me. If I agreed to never see Sharon again and tell no one I was the child's father, he would pay me a large sum."

"How much?" Callaway asked.

Holden lowered his head. "One hundred thousand dollars."

"And I bet you took it."

"I didn't see any other choice. I didn't want to be a father, and I didn't want to get married either. I was still young. Plus, I needed the money. My dad's garage had a lot of loans on it, and I wanted to help him out. I met a lawyer. I don't remember his name. I signed a document, and I walked away with a check for a lot of money. I'm not sure what they told Sharon, but I know she felt abandoned. So, she married Paul Gardener, and they told him Kyla was his child."

"Then what happened?" Callaway asked.

"I regretted what I did the moment I took the money, but it was too late. If I went back on the agreement, the lawyer would have sued me and taken my dad's garage away. So instead, I kept my distance, but every once in a while, I would check up on her."

"You mean Kyla?"

He nodded. "I followed her a few times. I know it sounds creepy, but I needed to be sure she was being taken care of. And by the looks of it, she was."

"You said you had met Paul once," Callaway said. "When was this?"

"It was maybe when Kyla was ten. I faked car trouble by the side of the road. I knew Paul would be driving by around that time. I wanted to see what kind of man he was. To my surprise, he stopped and tried to assist me. He had no idea I knew more about cars than he did. He then called a tow truck and waited with me for it to show up. During this time, I got to talk to him. I asked about his family—my real motive was to know about Kyla. I could see the pride and joy in his eyes whenever he spoke of her. That's when I knew I had nothing to worry about. But when I heard about her death, I was devastated. I wanted to go see her, but I knew I couldn't. Senator Lester is not the man you see on TV. The man I met was cold and calculating. He would not only use our agreement against me, but he would also make sure I was completely destroyed."

"I don't see how he would be able to do that."

"He could go to the media and tell them I had sold my right as a parent for money. Plus, I have a family of my own now. I am married with two boys, so Kyla was my only girl. They have no idea of my past, and I don't want to drag them into this mess. It would devastate them, and it could destroy my marriage and my relationship with my sons."

Holden choked up. "I always hoped one day, when Senator Lester was gone, I would get an opportunity to tell Kyla the truth. Now that she is dead, that hope died with her."

Callaway could not help but feel sorry for Holden. He had made a decision he would regret for the rest of his life.

After a brief pause, Callaway asked, "Before Kyla's death, who knew you were her real father?"

Holden thought a moment. "Sharon, her father, and her brother."

SEVENTY-NINE

Fisher drove back to the station. She was able to catch up on her sleep, and she even managed to run some errands. Overall, it was a productive day. The Gardener investigation had come to its conclusion. Barrows would work out a deal with Roth, and the case would be closed.

Holt was still miffed about this. After leaving Barrows' office, he had refused to answer Fisher's calls. He fervently believed they had a case to send Gardener away for life. Even the death penalty was a possibility if Barrows pushed for it.

Holt was laying blame on the DA's office for not doing their job. They had an open-and-shut case, and they were caving in to the defense's demands when the prosecution had the upper hand.

Fisher understood Barrows was in a tight spot. She had to please her bosses who were being pressured by Senator Lester to make this go away.

In all the cases Fisher had worked on, she was certain of the guilt of the accused. In Paul Gardener's case, she was not so sure. All the evidence pointed in his direction, which made her suspicious. She could smell a setup from a mile away. But she had no proof to confirm her hunch. Plus, it was not her job to do so. The defense should have been on this from the beginning. They were not, which probably meant they knew Gardener was guilty.

She made her way to her desk. Holt was waiting for her with a wide smile on his face.

"Don't tell me," she said, shaking her head. "You found new evidence in the Gardener case."

"I did, indeed."

"Really?" she asked, surprised.

Holt waved a document in the air. "The ballistics report came back."

"And?"

"The bullet found in Pedro Catano came from a 9mm Glock."

"Okay."

"Guess who else had a 9mm Glock registered to his name?"

Fisher sighed. "Paul Gardener."

"Bingo."

"But we searched the entire house, and we didn't find any weapons."

"And you know why?" he said. "About a month ago, Gardener had reported the Glock missing. I'm guessing he had it on him the entire time."

"Then why didn't he just shoot Kyla with it? It would have been cleaner than stabbing her, and he would have avoided getting evidence on his clothes."

"I don't know. Maybe he's just dumb."

Fisher frowned. "This doesn't feel right."

"We don't base a case on feelings. We base them on the evidence we get."

She crossed her arms over her chest. "And that's coming from you?"

"I know you think this is personal to me, and maybe it is, but I know when to follow my gut. And my gut tells me Gardener murdered his daughter and her lover. This report further confirms this."

Fisher was silent.

"Listen," Holt said. "Even if you don't agree with me, how do you explain Gardener owning a 9mm Glock and that the bullet found in Pedro was from a similar weapon?"

"I can't."

"Exactly," Holt said. He clenched his fist. "I'll be damned if Gardener gets a deal now."

EIGHTY

Callaway rang the doorbell and waited. A Filipino woman answered.

"Yes?" she asked.

"Is Mrs. Sharon Gardener home?"

The woman hesitated.

"Tell her it's Lee Callaway. I work with her husband, Paul."

"Please wait."

She closed the door behind her.

Callaway turned and stared at the water fountain.

On his drive over, he had spotted a couple of news vans parked on the side of the road. They did not dare enter the house's gates lest they be charged with trespassing. He hoped that wouldn't end up happening to him. He came here for a reason, and he did not want to leave without it.

The door opened, and the Filipino woman said, "Please come in."

He found Sharon waiting for him in the living room. She looked like she had not slept in weeks. Her eyes were red and puffy. Her skin was pale, and gray strands were visible in her hair. Both she and Paul had aged substantially from the time their daughter was found dead.

Callaway did not know how he would go on if something were to happen to Nina. He was fully aware he had not given her enough of his time. He always figured he would make it up to her later. But if he was robbed of that opportunity, he was not sure how he would go on with his life.

"I'm not supposed to talk to anyone," Sharon said. She did not offer Callaway a seat, nor did she sit.

"I'm sorry for your loss," he said.

She stared at him. "Thank you."

"This must be a difficult time for you, so I'll keep it brief," he said. "I don't believe Paul killed your daughter."

Her eyes became moist, and she bit down on her bottom lip.

"Paul loved Kyla and he would never harm her."

"Is that what he told you?" she asked.

"He did."

She fell on the sofa and covered her face with her hands. For a second, Callaway thought Sharon would break down and cry.

"Mrs. Gardener, I know this must be weighing heavily on you," he said. "So, I'm giving you a chance to clear your conscience."

She looked up. He could see it in her eyes. She desperately wanted to talk, but her family was preventing her from doing so. "What do you want to know?"

"Did you know Kyla was pregnant?"

"No."

"Did anyone else in your family know she was?"

"I don't think so."

"Did you see anything between Kyla and Pedro?"

"Like what?"

"Like if they were romantically involved."

She thought for a moment. "I didn't pay too much attention to what was going on in her life. I was too busy with mine."

She shook her head.

"When you came home from shopping that night," he said, "did you see Kyla?"

"No. I didn't bother to check her room. I was preoccupied with something else."

"Your late-night visit with Mr. Kenny Goldman?"

She shot daggers at him, but then her eyes softened. "You know, ever since Kyla's death, both of our lives have fallen apart. Kenny's wife has left him, and he's now living in a motel. I am alone, and I'm living in my brother's house."

Callaway did not want this interview to be about her tryst. He wanted to confirm some things, and he knew he did not have much time before she asked him to leave.

"After your visit with Mr. Goldman, you came home, and then what did you do?"

"It was very late at night. I took some sleeping pills, and I went to bed."

"Did you see if Kyla's bedroom lights were on?"

She thought for a moment. "I don't think they were, or else I would have spoken to her about it."

"And during the night, did you hear any commotion coming from your daughter's room?"

"Even if there was anything, I wouldn't know because of the medication."

"So you have no idea if your daughter was home when you came back from your shopping, or when you returned from meeting Mr. Goldman?"

She sighed. "I don't."

Callaway pinched the bridge of his nose. Then he plunged into deep thought.

"How is Paul doing?" Sharon asked.

He was surprised she was concerned about him. All this time, she and her family were going in front of the cameras and playing the victim while he was left to hide in his mother's house like a monster.

"I mean, how is he after he found out that Kyla isn't his?" Sharon said.

"He's devastated."

She lowered her head. "I didn't mean to hurt him, but I know I did. There were other men, but he still stuck with me. I think he did it because of Kyla. He loved her so much, and he couldn't bear the thought of not being a part of her life."

Callaway grimaced. *Nina's my child for sure, and yet I barely see her*, he thought.

"One last question," he said. "After you found Kyla in the bedroom, you went to the guesthouse to wake Paul up. Did you notice a smell?"

She looked baffled by his question. "Smell?"

"Yes, perhaps something sweet."

Her brow furrowed. "I'm not sure if it was sweet—my mind was all over the place at that moment—but now that I think about it, I did smell something odd."

EIGHTY-ONE

Callaway was on his way back to his office when he received the call from Fisher. She explained the findings of the ballistics report.

"Thanks, Dana," he said and hung up. *Not good*, he thought. Not only would they charge Paul with Kyla's death, but they would also tack on Pedro's as well. Whatever plea deal Paul was hoping to get was now out the window. Callaway could not see the prosecutor showing any leniency when it was a double homicide.

He called Paul, but his phone went straight to voicemail. Callaway had a bad feeling in the pit of his stomach. He turned the car around and drove straight to Paul's mother's house.

Callaway was not sure if the news had reached the press camped outside the house. It would soon enough. Something like that could only stay a secret for so long. An ambitious reporter would have to make one call to his contact in the Milton PD, and after sweetening their agreement, the contact would be more than willing to part with that information.

Callaway parked behind a news van and got out. He did not bother trying to be low-key. He had more urgent matters to be concerned about. As expected, the press sensed something was up when they saw him rush toward the house. They descended on him, but with his head down, he pushed past them and moved up to the front porch.

He banged his fist on the door and yelled, "It's Lee Callaway!"

The door opened slightly.

"I need to speak to Paul," Callaway said.

Paul's mother held the door for him.

He went inside and said, "Where is he?"

"He's upstairs in his room. His lawyer called, and after that, I don't know what happened. I'm worried. He won't come out."

Callaway raced up the stairs and knocked on the door, "Paul, it's Lee. Can I come in?"

There was no response.

Callaway placed his ear to the door. He could hear movement inside. He knocked again. "Paul, we need to talk. I know you didn't kill Kyla. I even spoke to Sharon, and she doesn't think you did either."

The handle turned and the door opened a crack. Callaway saw Paul peering out. "You met Sharon?" Paul asked.

"I did, yes."

"And she believes I didn't do it?"

"She knows you loved Kyla like your own and that you would never harm her. Now, can I come inside and talk to you?"

The door swung open. The room was a mess. Clothes were on the floor, items were scattered all over, a lamp was on its side, and the furniture was in disorder.

"Do you have any weapons at home?" Callaway asked.

Paul looked at him, confused.

"Do you have any guns?"

Paul shook his head.

Callaway spotted a knife on the nightstand.

"You thinking about hurting yourself?" he asked.

Paul lowered his head and sat on the bed. After a brief pause, he said, "I didn't kill Pedro."

"I know you didn't, but I need to know about the gun. It was registered to you."

"It was stolen."

"When?"

"About a month ago."

"Where did you keep it?"

"In a locked box."

"And what happened?"

"I came home one day, and I couldn't find the box."

"Did you ask Sharon?"

"She had no idea."

"You believed her?"

"Yes, she had no reason to take it."

"Who else knew about the gun?"

"My father-in-law, Barron."

"Why did you tell him?"

"He was the one who encouraged me to get one."

"Why?"

"Barron supported a bill that would restrict the average person from owning military-grade firearms. Once he did, he started getting death threats."

"Does he own a gun?" Callaway asked.

Paul shook his head. "No, because of the optics. The gun-loving public would call him a hypocrite. If he could buy a gun to protect himself, then why couldn't they?"

Callaway frowned. "But he was against owning military weapons, not regular weapons."

"It doesn't matter. You were either pro-gun or anti-gun. You were never in the middle, according to some people."

"When the Glock went missing, did you ask your father-in-law?" Callaway asked.

"Of course," Paul replied. "He told me to file a police report, which I did." Paul's face contorted into a mask of dread. "The DA's office is ready to lay additional charges on me. Even if I manage to avoid the death penalty, I'll spend the rest of my life in prison. So what's the point of all of this?"

Callaway looked him straight in the eye. "If you hold tight and don't do anything stupid, I just might be able to get you out of this mess."

EIGHTY-TWO

Jay Buchwald worked at a cell phone kiosk in a shopping mall. He was tall with curly blond hair, stubble on his chin, and studs in his ears. He was dressed in a dark blue uniform, and he was showing a smartphone to a middle-aged woman.

Callaway had found Buchwald's name through Kyla's social media web page. Buchwald had clicked *thumbs-down* on her announcement post. When Callaway had reached out to him, Buchwald was more than willing to meet him.

Callaway walked around the kiosk. The glass case had several cell phone models on display, along with their respective covers. A colleague of Buchwald's approached him to help. Callaway pointed to Buchwald, and the colleague understood and moved to the next customer.

The middle-aged woman smiled whenever Buchwald showed her a feature on the phone. She agreed to purchase it. Buchwald quickly rang up the sale. He also managed to sell her a cell phone screen protector and cover.

Buchwald turned to Callaway. "You're the PI, right?"

"I am."

Callaway looked around the mall. "Is there someplace we can talk in private?"

"I have to grab lunch. The restaurants are on the first floor. You can join me, but I can't talk long. We get really busy at this time."

"We'll talk on the way there."

As they walked through the mall, Callaway said, "When we spoke, you mentioned you had dated Kyla. How long ago was that?"

"We dated for over a year, but she broke it off abruptly. It was at least three months ago."

Callaway's brow furrowed. "Kyla was nine weeks pregnant, so the baby couldn't have been yours."

Buchwald stopped. "When I saw it on the news, that's the first thing I thought of. I had no idea that she was even pregnant. But then, when I did the math, I knew I couldn't be the father, you know."

"Did Kyla ever talk about Pedro?" Callaway asked.

"Sure. She talked about him a lot. They were good friends."

"Were they ever involved?"

He shook his head almost violently. "Are you kidding me? That entire thing on the news about Kyla being pregnant with Pedro's child is all bullshit."

"So, it wasn't true?"

"Of course not. Kyla was an only child. She had no siblings of her own, so Pedro was like a brother to her. And he watched over her like she was his sister. When Kyla and I started dating, Kyla insisted I meet Pedro. She actually wanted to see what *he* thought of me."

"If the baby is not Pedro's, then whose could it be?" Callaway asked.

"It's not mine, that's all I care about."

Callaway rubbed his chin. "Did Kyla give you a reason for your breakup?"

"No. She just called me one day and said she had been doing a lot of thinking, and that it was time we saw other people. I was floored. I thought we had something special between us."

Buchwald's twenty-one. Everything feels special or important at that age, Callaway thought.

"Did you know about the money she was going to get when she turned your age?" Callaway wanted to push Buchwald's buttons to see if he said something he should not.

"Kyla never mentioned it to me," he replied. "She didn't like talking about money anyway. I think she saw herself as an average kid."

"But you knew she came from wealth, right?" Callaway said.

Buchwald scoffed. "Hey, listen, I had no idea she was pregnant or that she was gonna get a ton of money, and I most certainly did not hurt her, if that's what you're trying to get at. I just liked her a lot. She was a lot of fun to be with."

"What was her relationship with her parents like?" Callaway asked.

He shrugged. "She got along well with both of them."

"What about her father?"

"From what I could tell, she had a great relationship with him."

"Did you ever meet him?"

"Sure, once. A friend of mine was having a party, and her father dropped her off. We spoke briefly. I thought he was a cool guy. I just never thought he would kill her, you know."

"He didn't."

"Okay," Buchwald replied as if not believing him. "Hey, I better go. I'm kind of late."

"Is there anything you can tell me about her that's not on the news?" Callaway asked.

Buchwald thought a moment. "They never mentioned that Kyla was a little insecure."

"Insecure? What do you mean?"

"She was always complaining about how she looked. She thought she was overweight. I didn't think she was. She didn't like the shape of her nose. It was a little flat."

Much like Gus Holden's, Callaway thought.

"I thought it was cute," Buchwald said. "She wanted fuller lips. I thought they were fine. She always joked she would get her uncle to fix her up."

Callaway was confused. "Fix her up?"

"Yeah, her uncle is a doctor. I think he has his own clinic."

Dr. Richard Lester, Callaway thought.

EIGHTY-THREE

The Lester Center for Cosmetic Surgery was located in an affluent area of Milton. There were luxury clothing stores, designer shoe and handbag outlets, and a couple of high-end car dealerships.

A secretary greeted Callaway when he entered the clinic. From afar, the secretary looked like she was in her late twenties, but after a closer look, Callaway saw she was really in her mid-forties. Her eyes gave her real age away. They had a story to tell, and that could only happen for someone who had lived a long life.

Callaway introduced himself. He was told Dr. Lester was with a patient. Callaway said he would wait. He was then told the doctor had a busy schedule and to make an appointment. He asked the secretary to let the doctor know who was waiting for him. If the doctor wanted him to come back at a later time, he would.

Callaway knew it would not come to that.

He grabbed a magazine and took a seat. The secretary returned and told him the doctor would be with him shortly. He gave her a smile.

Twenty minutes later, Dr. Lester came out. "Mr. Callaway, I'm surprised to see you here. Why don't you come to my office?"

They went through a door and headed down a hall that led to a small room. In Dr. Lester's office, certificates and degrees covered the wall behind an expensive oak desk. Artifacts from all over the world were displayed in the room. Callaway saw an African headdress, a Native American carving, and a religious statue from Thailand.

"I'm glad you've changed your mind, Mr. Callaway," Dr. Lester said.

"Changed my mind?"

"About the photos you took of my sister that night," he said with a smile. "Name your price, and I will write you a check."

"No, I'm not here about that."

His smile faded. "Then why are you here?"

"It's about Kyla."

Anger flashed in his eyes. "I know you work for my brother-in-law, and while I commend your loyalty to him, I don't appreciate you showing up at my clinic or my home asking questions about my niece. Your visit to Sharon really shook her up. You can't imagine what it's like losing your only child. She is fragile, and what happened has really put her close to the edge."

"Close to the edge?"

"She has contemplated suicide, Mr. Callaway," he snapped. "I'm seriously concerned for her mental state."

Paul's also on the brink of a mental meltdown, Callaway thought. *Not that you would care, though.*

"And when you show up asking questions, it doesn't help her to move on to the next stage of the grieving process."

Dr. Lester took a deep breath to calm himself. "What my brother-in-law did has destroyed our family. The way he brutally murdered my niece…"

"*Alleged* to have brutally murdered your niece," Callaway corrected him. "He hasn't been found guilty yet."

"I hear the evidence is overwhelming against him."

Callaway was quiet.

Dr. Lester looked at his watch. "I am already running behind on another appointment. Now, if you'll excuse me…"

"Please, Dr. Lester, I drove all the way here. I will bill Paul for hours I put on his case, even if they lead nowhere."

Dr. Lester seemed amused by that. "Okay, fine. What would you like to know?"

"Did Kyla come to you about getting plastic surgery?"

Dr. Lester's eyes narrowed. "It's a personal matter. I'm not sure what this has to do with anything."

"I'm just curious."

He sighed. "Yes, she came to me. She complained about the way she looked. She wanted me to remove fat around her waist. She wanted me to make her lips plumper. She wanted me to thin her nose. She wanted stuff that most women her age are sensitive about. They are insecure, and they think having a certain look will help them overcome it. As a surgeon who makes his living on women's insecurities, I will tell you that no amount of cosmetic surgery will make you confident. If you were not happy with yourself before surgery, you will never be happy after it. And so I talked Kyla out of it. I knew Sharon would not have approved of it. Kyla was still young, and she would eventually grow into the woman she hoped to be."

"Did you know she was pregnant?" Callaway asked.

He blinked. "Why would I know that?"

"I figured as a doctor, she would have confided in you."

He shook his head. "From what I heard, she confided in no one. Our family was blindsided when we heard it."

"Sorry to have wasted your time, Dr. Lester," Callaway said.

Dr. Lester stared at him. His face relaxed. "I understand what you are trying to do for Paul, but my family just wants this ordeal behind us."

"I can see that from the press conferences your family keeps holding."

"They are my father's idea, I'm afraid. He has a re-election to consider." Dr. Lester got up to open the door for Callaway, signaling the end of the interview. Dr. Lester offered his hand, which Callaway shook. "Good luck in your investigation, Mr. Callaway. I wish you the best."

When he removed his hand from the doctor's, Callaway noticed something.

"Didn't you have a bandage on your hand?" he asked.

Dr. Lester looked confused. "Sorry?"

"I clearly remember that when you came to my office, your hand was covered."

"I might have gotten my hand caught in the door or something foolish like that. I can be clumsy sometimes."

EIGHTY-FOUR

Callaway returned to his office, feeling deflated. So far, he had not come up with anything that could help Paul. He should not have made any promises to him. Callaway was used to catching cheaters in the act, not getting people off a murder-one charge. Only once had he captured a killer, and that was with the help of Echo Rose. He was in way over his head. If Roth could not do anything for Paul, what made him so sure he could do something?

He rubbed his temples. He felt a headache coming on. He could use a drink about now.

He turned on the TV and froze in his chair.

Judy Barrows was standing on the courthouse steps. Flanked on either side of her were Holt and Fisher. Holt had a grin on his face while Fisher looked like she would rather not be there.

Callaway turned up the volume.

Barrows said, "In light of new evidence, the District Attorney's Office has laid additional charges against Paul Gardener. These charges are on top of the first-degree murder of Kyla Gardener. They relate to the death of Pedro Catano. I would like to add that neither Mr. Gardener nor his lawyer, Evan Roth, were in court. However, a representative from Mr. Roth's office was there to hear the charges on his behalf. A written copy has been sent from my office to Mr. Roth's firm. A court date has been set for Thursday."

Only two days away, Callaway thought. *Damn.*

"Mr. Gardener is required to enter a plea of guilty or not guilty to these additional charges. Failure to do so may result in the judge taking actions at his or her disposal."

Callaway shut the TV off and closed his eyes.

The rope around Paul's neck had tightened even further. He had two days to make a decision, whether he liked it or not. Roth would encourage him to plead guilty. He had no interest in this case going to trial. Paul could not afford one, and Roth did not want to lose one.

At this stage of the investigation, Callaway doubted very much that a deal was still on the table. Holt would make sure it was not.

There was no incentive for the prosecution to agree to one anyway. The cards were stacked in the prosecution's favor.

It was not a matter of *if* Paul would spend time in prison. It was a matter of *how long* he would be there.

If, for some strange reason, Paul did not cave in to the pressures and still went to trial, he would be looking at the death penalty.

Callaway could feel the pressure. It was suffocating. He no longer wanted a drink. He just wanted to get far away from Milton.

EIGHTY-FIVE

Time was running out, and Callaway knew he had not a minute to spare. He had gotten himself into this, and he had to find a way out.

He left the office, but instead of going to a bar, he headed to a convenience store and bought a cup of coffee from the vending machine. The coffee was old and stale, but he needed the caffeine to jolt his senses.

He came back to his office and sat down behind his desk. He opened the file Roth had given him. He took a sip from the cup and nearly spat the coffee out. The beverage tasted bitter. He threw the cup in the garbage.

He turned his attention to the file and started from the beginning. He wanted to make sure he had not missed anything.

An hour later, he dropped his head into his palms and closed his eyes. He had found nothing that could help him in his cause. He had gone over everything twice and still had come up empty.

The entire file was strewn across the office floor. He wanted to grab the papers and toss them out the window.

He felt defeated. He had lost, and the real killer had won.

Callaway was certain of Paul's innocence, and he wanted to prove it not only to Paul but also himself.

He sighed. *How am I going to break this to him?* he thought. *I don't want to push him over the edge and make him kill himself.*

He opened his eyes and saw a photo lying at the foot of his desk. He leaned down and picked it up.

It was a close-up photo of Kyla's face, taken when she was found in her bedroom.

A light went on in his head.

He rushed out of the office and walked down the block to a payphone. He did not want his telephone number displayed on the other end. He dialed a number, and after a short conversation, he hung up.

In his mind, the pieces began to fall into place. He could not believe he had missed this detail when he first saw it. If he had put it together earlier, he could have solved Kyla's case by now. But he still needed to confirm what he felt to be true.

He remembered the places Kyla had visited from her social media page. He decided to go check out the last place she had gone on the day of her death.

The restaurant was upscale but not snobbish. An eclectic range of clientele was already seated inside when Callaway approached a waiter and asked to speak to the owner.

After explaining what he wanted, the owner shook his head. "We don't let just anyone see footage from our security cameras."

"But it's a matter of life and death," Callaway said.

"I'm sorry. If you want to see it, then you'll need to come back with a warrant."

"I'm a private investigator."

"Exactly. You're not a cop."

Callaway could tell the man was not going to budge.

He left the restaurant, feeling deeply frustrated.

EIGHTY-SIX

Callaway waited outside the restaurant, watching as a car pulled up to the curb.

Fisher got out. Callaway had seen no other option, so he called her. She was reluctant at first, but after he begged her, she agreed.

"This better be important," she said.

"It is," he said.

They went inside the restaurant. The waiter recognized Callaway and flagged down the owner.

"She's a cop," Callaway said to him.

"I hope she has a warrant," the owner replied.

"I don't need one," Fisher said. "I just saw that your liquor license expired a week ago."

"I'm going to get it renewed."

"But it's not renewed today. I'm sure I can contact the Alcohol Beverage Control Agency and have them come and shut down this place until you get a new license."

"You won't do that," the owner said, hoping she was bluffing.

"Just watch me."

Fisher pulled out her cell phone.

The owner put his hands up. "Okay, okay, what do you want?"

"Show us the security footage, and I'll ignore ever seeing your expired license. But you have to get a new license as soon as possible, and by that, I mean tomorrow."

"Got it. No problem."

He took them to his office in the basement. The room was small, and with a desk and chair, the room looked even more congested. The owner pointed to a computer monitor. "All the cameras get relayed to this screen. What do you want to see?"

Callaway gave him the time and date.

The owner punched it in, and the image changed. They watched as customers and waiters moved around the dining area. Callaway kept an eye on the clock at the bottom of the screen.

Whenever a woman entered the restaurant, his heart would swell with hope. When he saw it was not Kyla, his hope would vaporize in an instant.

After almost half an hour, he realized Kyla had never come into the restaurant.

Fisher turned to him, "You got any other bright ideas?"

He was shocked. Kyla had not only tagged herself being at this location, but she had also taken a photo of herself in front of the restaurant and had posted it on her page.

"Wait," he said. "Can you show me the footage from the camera on the front of the restaurant?"

"Sure, whatever," the owner replied.

The image on the screen switched. They watched as customers moved in and out of the restaurant. Cars drove by on the road, and people walked past.

Callaway's back arched when a woman appeared on the screen. It was Kyla! She was on the other side of the road, across from the restaurant. She stopped in front of a bar and then proceeded to take a photo of herself. Her back was to the restaurant, which explained why her phone had caught the restaurant's name.

She went inside the bar.

"We need to go check out their security footage," Callaway said to Fisher.

"They are closed right now," the owner said. "They don't open until after 4 P.M. But they stay open 'til early in the morning."

Callaway rubbed his chin. He was contemplating his next step. "Can we see more of the footage?"

"Sure," the owner said with a slight shrug.

Callaway watched the screen with intense focus. If his hunch was right, he would see someone soon. Close to ten minutes later, a man walked up to the bar. Callaway recognized him. The man looked around and then went inside the bar.

Almost half an hour later, Kyla came through the front doors again. The man was right behind her as she stormed away.

They both disappeared from view.

Callaway could only imagine what happened next because a few hours later, she was found dead.

EIGHTY-SEVEN

"It's Dr. Richard Lester," Callaway said. "He killed Kyla Gardener."

They were in an interview room at the Milton Police Department. Callaway sat across from Holt. Fisher was standing by the wall. She refused to betray her partner. If they were going to do anything, she was not going to do it alone.

They had shown Holt the footage from the bar. In it, Kyla entered the bar and took a seat in the corner. She waited until Lester showed up. He ordered a bottle for himself and a glass of water for her.

For close to half an hour, Kyla and Lester got into a heated argument. There was no audio in the footage, but they could tell whenever she raised her voice. Her arms would flail wildly, and he would try to calm her down by holding her hand. It would work for a little bit until she would go off on him again. Finally, she got up and stormed out of the bar. He followed right behind her.

"Outrageous!" Holt bellowed, shaking his head. "If this is your way of trying to save your client, then you're too late. Paul Gardener is going to trial, and he's going to die in prison."

"Paul's a good man," Callaway countered. "Probably the only innocent person in this entire mess."

"I don't buy it. Plus, that video doesn't prove anything."

"It shows Kyla was last seen with her uncle."

"So what?" Holt snapped. "Do you have a video of her getting in the same car as him?"

Callaway opened his mouth but then shut it.

"Exactly," Holt said. "We don't know what happened after the end of the video. What if she went home right after that, and her father saw her and attacked her?"

"Look at the time stamp on the video," Callaway said. "It's almost an hour before Paul got home. I should know. I was at the Gardener residence on a stakeout. I can tell you that no one was home at that time. Not Kyla. Not Sharon. Not even Paul."

"Okay, how long is the drive from the bar to the Gardeners' home?" Holt asked.

Callaway looked at Fisher. She pulled out her cell phone and did a search. She frowned. "It's about a twenty-minute drive."

Holt smiled. "That's enough time to get there before Gardener and his wife made it home."

It was Callaway's turn to smile. "I was there *way* before that, and I can tell you the house was empty. I have photos to prove this."

"Your photos have done enough damage, so no thanks," Holt grumbled. "You're wasting my time. I'm not interested in conjectures and theories. All evidence points to Gardener, and that's who I'm going after."

He stood up to leave.

Fisher said, "Greg."

He stopped. Fisher only called him by his first name when it was important. "Just hear him out. Please," she said.

He stared at her and sat back down.

EIGHTY-EIGHT

Callaway said, "There is a reason why Paul doesn't remember anything from that night." He slid the toxicology report across the table.

Holt read it and looked up. "Rohypnol and chloroform?"

"Yes."

Holt's face creased. "Who's Gator Peckerwood?"

"Ignore that," Callaway said. "But I guarantee the test results are from Paul's blood."

Holt waved the report in the air. "This is inadmissible in court. It doesn't even have your client's name on it."

"You can go right now and get a blood sample from Paul. There are still traces of the drugs in his body. It will confirm what that report says."

Holt paused, thinking. "Okay, let's say I believe you. How did Rohypnol and chloroform get in him?"

"I made a phone call to Lester's clinic and I acted like I was calling from the medical supply company. I asked them to confirm if they had ordered a bottle of chloroform. It's nearly impossible to get it on the market, but it's still accessible to doctors, and some still carry it in their office. His secretary was surprised when I asked her, but when she checked her records, it showed Lester had put in a request for a bottle the day *after* Kyla's murder."

Holt's brow furrowed. "So, what does that prove?"

"It proves he had taken a bottle from his clinic for personal use and then ordered another the next day to replenish the inventory."

"He could have used it on a patient and run out."

"Why not have his secretary order more? She does it on a regular basis. I believe Lester didn't want her knowing he had taken a bottle."

Holt leaned back in his chair and crossed his massive arms over his chest. "Still doesn't answer my question as to how Gardener got these drugs in his system."

"Let me explain. Most doctors prefer to use ether for anesthesia, but it takes longer to knock out a person. Chloroform is volatile, but it's quicker to put someone under. So, I believe it became the go-to choice for Lester. If you go to his clinic, in his office, you'll see artifacts from all the trips he has taken abroad, most predominately to African countries. I did a quick internet search and found out Lester has been to Uganda multiple times on humanitarian missions. In war-ravaged areas, his services as a plastic surgeon are invaluable. Women are raped and disfigured. He can make them look normal again."

"What's your point?" Holt asked impatiently.

"In Uganda, it is very easy to buy chloroform on the streets. Criminals spray chloroform through windows and ventilators in order to sedate the occupants inside a house. They then break into the house and rob them, or worse, rape them in some cases."

Holt's face was hard. Callaway was not sure if he believed him or not.

Callaway added, "I visited the Gardner residence, and I took a photo of the window in the guesthouse where Paul was found asleep." Callaway pulled out his cell phone and showed it to Holt. "You can see the window is slightly open. I only noticed it because of a cool breeze that was coming through it. If you scroll to the next photo, you'll see a boot print next to the window. It's not enough to get a shoe size, but it confirms someone was at that window. I believe it belongs to Lester, from when he released chloroform into the room, knocking Paul unconscious."

Holt frowned. "I assume you broke into the guesthouse?"

"Well, I don't have a warrant like you guys, do I?"

"Again, inadmissible in court."

Callaway ignored the last comment and continued. "And as far as Rohypnol is concerned, Lester's a doctor. He has access to a variety of drugs. It was used so Paul did not remember anything from that night."

"Why?"

"So, he could set him up for Kyla's murder."

"I still don't buy it."

Callaway pulled out a photo and laid it on the table. It was a close-up of Kyla's face. "This is what triggered it for me. In the photo, you can see clearly that Kyla's lips are swollen. There's even a cut on the upper lip. They could have only ended up like that from being struck by something, most presumably, a hand. When I initially met Lester at my office, I noticed a bandage on his hand, but later, when I asked him about it, he said he must have *clumsily* cut his hand." Callaway paused. "It's an odd thing to say for a plastic surgeon. Their entire career relies on what they can do with their hands. For that reason, they take extra care of them. And if you check the photos of the arrest, Paul has no cuts or bruises anywhere on his body, specifically his hands."

Callaway could see Holt was mulling this over. He saw his chance to win him over.

EIGHTY-NINE

"Dr. Richard Lester is the father of Kyla's unborn child," Callaway said.

"What?" Holt was beside himself. "Do you have conclusive evidence of this, or are you merely making false accusations to prove your point?"

"I don't have any evidence, but just look at the footage from the bar. You can see Lester ordered a bottle of alcohol for himself but only ordered a glass of water for Kyla. He lied to me when I asked him if he knew Kyla was pregnant. He always knew because she had told him."

Holt still did not look convinced.

"Listen," Callaway said. "In the video, you can see them arguing. I bet she was telling him her intention to keep the baby and also that she wanted him to marry her. It was the reason she'd had the fight with Paul on the morning of her death. Paul had no idea she was pregnant, but he was against her getting married because he thought she was too young. On her social media page, she had mentioned she would be making a big announcement soon. I think she meant telling the world of the baby and her desire to get married. She was going to do that after she had spoken to Lester. His reaction, although muted when compared to hers, explained that he was against this. She then stormed out, and he followed her.

"I think later, it could even be right after that video, he hit her in a fit of rage. The bandage on his hand and the cut on her lip confirms this. She might have even lashed out at him at this point, and fearing what he had done, he strangled her. This was supported by the medical examiner's report. He then had to get rid of the body, but he couldn't dump her just anywhere. The patrons at the bar had seen him arguing with her. He needed a scapegoat, and it was Paul. He drove her body back to her house and then he proceeded to sedate Paul with chloroform and Rohypnol. He then placed her body in the bedroom and proceeded to stab her, even after she was already dead."

"Why would he do that?" Holt asked.

"He needed to link Paul to the crime. He then wiped the blood on Paul's golf shirt—you remember that there was only a streak of red and not a splatter. It could have only come from a knife being wiped clean on a piece of cloth. He placed the knife in Paul's hand to get his fingerprints on it, and then he placed it in the glove compartment of the Audi. If you also remember, the tip of the knife was clean while the rest of the blade was covered in blood. I believe Lester held the knife from the tip so as to retain Kyla's blood and Paul's fingerprints on it."

Holt held up his hand to stop him. "If what you say is true, how did he manage to do all this without Sharon Gardener finding out?"

"She was not at home at that time, remember?" Callaway said. "She was having a tryst with Kenny Goldman."

Holt saw the connection. "But how did he know she would not be home?"

"The apartment she met Goldman at is registered to Lester."

Holt's eyes widened. "It is?"

"Yes."

"Go on," Holt said.

"Also, when Lester came to my office to buy the photos from that night, he wasn't doing it to protect his sister, he was doing it to protect *himself*. He did not expect that Paul had hired a private investigator, and he feared he might show up in the photos. He had nothing to worry about because I was in another part of the city, tailing his sister."

Callaway could see he had Holt. He was analyzing all the information Callaway had presented to him. As a detective, he could not ignore how things were now falling into place. The narrative made more sense than the one Holt had created.

He finally said, "Even if I believed everything you just said, you still broke a lot of rules in getting this information, Callaway."

"I did," Callaway agreed.

"It means I can't take this to the DA. The evidence won't hold up in court."

Callaway held out his cell phone for him. It had a photo of Kyla. "This was taken by her outside the bar. That's how we knew where she was when we saw the restaurant in the background. If you look at the photo carefully, you'll notice Kyla is wearing a heart-shaped pendant. Her ex-boyfriend, Jay Buchwald, had given it to her, and for some reason, she continued to wear it."

Callaway then slid to Holt a Polaroid of Kyla lying in her bed. "This was taken when she was found dead. You'll notice she is wearing the same clothes, but the pendant is missing."

Fisher chimed in, "I went through the box of evidence and saw our guys tagged no pendant from the victim."

Callaway said, "We find the pendant. We find the killer."

Holt stared at him. "And how are you going to do that?"

"I have an idea," Callaway replied.

NINETY

Dr. Richard Lester examined the patient closely. The woman was the wife of a media magnate. She was in her late forties, and he could see that she already had too much work done on her. The dozens of injections over the years to fade the wrinkles had frozen her face into a permanent scowl. She looked more like a hideous wax doll than a living, breathing human being.

She should stop and let nature take its course, he thought, but the quest for youth was beyond rationale. People got old, and their bodies aged with it as part of the cycle of life.

But Lester would not reason with her, nor would he talk her out of it. She did not need additional procedures, but she was worth a lot of money, and he would bill her accordingly.

"I would recommend we inject the lips, soften the wrinkles, and tighten the skin under the chin," he said.

She tried to smile, but it was futile. "I like the sound of that."

"Great," he replied. "Why don't you talk to my secretary at the front desk, and let's see if we can't squeeze you in as soon as possible." In reality, his schedule was empty. His clinic was hemorrhaging money. It once thrived to the point where he had to turn people away. Even working twelve-hour days was not enough to meet the demand. But after the Great Recession of 2008, people had begun to reign in their spending.

There was a misconception that only the rich and wealthy got work done on their bodies. If that was the case, most plastic surgeons would be out of business. There were only so many affluent people in the city, and not all were shallow enough to spend thousands of dollars to be young again. It was the average person—the people off the street—who were his best clients—a mother looking to get rid of extra flab around her waist after her second or third child. A teenage girl who wants her nose to look like a certain pop singer's convinces her parents that she needs the procedure. A young man who thinks all men should be hairless, thanks to TV ads, and comes in for laser hair removal. All these services, even if he personally was not involved in them, helped bring money into the clinic. This allowed him to focus on well-off clients. He would cater to all their needs. He would visit their homes at all times of the day. He would drive to a party in the middle of the night if they needed a quick touch-up. He had even flown across the country so they could look good for a presentation. He would charge a bundle for these personal calls.

Now things were a little different. He had to cut his staff by half, and those who were still employed worked part-time.

The woman thanked him and left his office.

He was reaching for his cell phone, in case there was an urgent call, when his secretary knocked on the door. "Dr. Lester, there are some people here to see you," she said.

"Tell them to make an appointment," he said, annoyed. Even if his schedule was free, he never took walk-ins. They were only interested in finding out his fee, and when they did, they almost never came back. He preferred appointments only after his secretary had gone over their pricing structure with them. Also, he wanted to give off the impression that he was an in-demand surgeon. He once was, and he believed he would be again. The economy went up and down, and at the moment, it was in a downturn. But the moment it moved back up, clients would come flocking in.

"They are not here for a procedure," the secretary said. "They are detectives from the Milton Police Department."

Lester was silent a moment.

"Okay, I'll see them," he said.

He went out and found a man and a woman waiting for him. They flashed their badges and introduced themselves. He knew who they were. He had seen them on TV at the press conference. Detectives Holt and Fisher.

"Is this about my niece?" he asked.

They looked at him.

"I mean, you are assigned to her case, are you not?"

"Yes, we are," Detective Holt replied.

"How can I help you?"

"We are trying to contact your sister, Sharon Gardener, but we've not had any success. Do you know where we can find her?"

Lester's brow furrowed. "She's still living at my residence, but I thought she had already given her statement to the police. So what's this about?"

Detective Holt pulled out a Polaroid and held it up for him to see. "Your niece was wearing this pendant. It is evidence that we believe can help us solve this investigation. We were hoping to speak to your sister in case she may have it."

Lester frowned. "I thought my brother-in-law killed my niece?"

"I can't go into any details, but we have information to the contrary. Can you please have your sister contact us?"

"Yes, of course." Lester took Holt's card. He said, "As you know, my sister is under a lot of stress, so she's not taking any calls. But the moment I see her, I will have her contact you."

NINETY-ONE

Lester watched the detectives leave the clinic. He went back into his office and shut the door.

He pulled off his white coat and grabbed the cell phone on his desk. There were several missed calls. He never answered his phone when he was with a patient. The calls did not look urgent, so he stuffed the phone in his pocket.

He went back to the front desk and told his secretary he was going out for lunch. She reminded him of an appointment later in the day, but he was already out the door.

He got in his Mercedes-Benz and drove out of the clinic's parking lot.

He took the highway. He knew the route by heart.

Twenty-five minutes later, he pulled in front of an apartment building. He drove around to the back and parked in a tenant parking spot.

He rushed into the building and took the elevator up to the sixth floor. He entered the unit and headed straight for the bedroom. He looked underneath the bed, the mattress, the side table, and inside the closet. He then moved to the bathroom. He was certain it would not be here, but he had to make sure. After he checked the floor and the area around the toilet, he turned to the living room. He pushed the sofa aside, looked behind the TV stand, and pulled aside the drapes.

He frowned and went to the kitchen. He pulled open the cupboards and the fridge. He cursed and slammed the fridge door shut.

He went back to the living room and sat down on the sofa.

He shut his eyes and tried to retrace his steps that night. He was at his clinic when he had received Kyla's call. She wanted to speak to him. Her voice sounded urgent but also excited. He rushed over, and they met at a bar.

He already knew she was pregnant. She had told him several weeks before. It was a mistake he regretted the moment it had happened. She was young and beautiful; he was divorced and not seeing anyone.

She had come to his clinic, wanting to get work done. He had always managed to talk her out of it. He was surprised one day when she asked about the apartment. She knew of her mother's affairs. Unlike her father, she was not naïve about what was going on in the family. She wanted to see the apartment where her mother took the men.

He saw no harm in it. She already knew about it, so why not take her there? She was an adult, after all. She was capable of making her own decisions. He was also concerned that she would tell others about the apartment if he did not comply.

The apartment was used by him, his sister, and even their father on some occasions. It was a family secret, one they did not want the public to find out about.

He would take his female patients to the apartment for a few hours when the opportunity arose. It was the main reason for his two divorces. His ex-wives had found out about his affairs, and he paid them handsomely to keep them from telling anyone.

At the bar, Kyla had informed him of her decision to keep the baby. She also wanted him to marry her, as she did not want to raise the child on her own. "There is no way I can do that," he had said to her. Then he expounded on how his sister would be livid and his reputation would be ruined, not to mention the impact it would have on his father's bid for re-election. If word of their family drama got out, his father's political career would be over.

They argued until she stormed out of the bar. He followed her, and he was able to calm her down. He drove her back to the apartment. He wanted to have a long conversation with her in private. Maybe he could talk some sense into her, and this matter would be behind them. But it did not turn out that way.

She was incensed that he would even consider making her get an abortion. She called him nasty names. She threatened to tell her mother the truth and expose him to the world. He got angry, and he hit her across the face, splitting her lip and gashing his hand.

She was shocked at what he had done. So was he. He did not believe in violence.

She screamed at the top of her lungs. She tried to lunge at him, and that was when he grabbed her by the throat. She was still screaming and calling him names when he pushed her to the wall. He squeezed tight. He wanted her to quiet down. Her eyes suddenly bulged, and when he let go, she was dead.

Tears flowed down his cheeks as he remembered that moment. He never meant to hurt her.

He opened his eyes when something occurred to him. He rushed out of the apartment and took the elevators down to the main lobby. He raced to the Mercedes-Benz and opened the trunk.

He pushed aside a gym bag and a trunk organizer. He spotted it in the corner. He leaned in and picked up the heart-shaped pendant. It must have fallen off when he had placed Kyla's body in the trunk.

A shadow fell over him.

He turned and saw Detectives Holt and Fisher.

"Keep your hands where we can see them," Fisher ordered. Her hand was on her gun holster.

He complied.

Holt came over, and with a gloved hand, he grabbed the pendant from Dr. Lester. "Look at what we have here," he said as he placed the pendant in a clear plastic bag.

Fisher cuffed him and said, "Dr. Richard Lester, you are under arrest for the murder of Kyla Gardener."

Lester lowered his head. He knew it was over.

NINETY-TWO

Callaway leaned on the hood of his car. He was parked in front of the Milton PD. He checked his watch and looked around.

He spotted Fisher coming out of the main doors. She had a smile on her face. "Lester confessed to the whole thing," she said.

"I knew he would," he replied.

"Your theory of how it went down was pretty accurate. Lester filled us in on anything we were not sure of."

"Where's Holt?"

"He's booking Lester as we speak."

Callaway could not help but smile himself.

"How were you so certain that Gardener didn't do it?" Fisher asked. "I mean, the odds were stacked against him."

"There was something I did not tell you."

"What?"

"On the day Kyla was murdered, Paul was at my office. He had come to pay me the first installment for the job. He didn't look like a man who was going to murder his daughter later that night. He was tired, but he was calm. He was more preoccupied with what was going on with his business, which I knew was struggling."

"That still is not enough to think he couldn't have done it."

"I can't explain it, but when I looked into his eyes, I didn't see a murderer. What I saw was an honest man who, even though he was under financial pressures, wanted to make sure I was paid before I started the job. It was something I could never shake off."

"Well, I'm glad you pursued this until the end, or else we would have sent a man to prison for a crime he never committed."

Holt approached Callaway. "I guess I owe you an apology."

"I think you owe Paul Gardener an apology."

He stared at Callaway for a second. Then he nodded and held out his hand. "Thanks," he said.

Callaway shook Holt's hand.

Fisher's phone buzzed. She answered it. When she hung up, she said, "You won't believe this."

"What?" Holt and Callaway asked in unison.

"I'll explain on the way there," she replied.

They drove straight to the house. After parking next to the water fountain, they raced up the stairs to the second floor. They spotted a Filipino lady weeping by the bedroom door. They entered the bathroom and found a body submerged in the bathtub. There was a bottle of alcohol on the floor, and next to it was an empty bottle of sleeping pills.

Sharon Gardener's eyes were closed, but it was obvious she was dead.

"I guess the guilt got the better of her," Fisher said.

"Why?" Holt replied. "She didn't kill her daughter, and I doubt she knew her brother was the baby's father."

Callaway said, "Maybe she blamed herself for not being home the night her daughter was murdered."

Holt sighed and shook his head. "This is one weird family."

NINETY-THREE

Outside the house, Callaway said, "So, I guess all the charges against Paul are dropped, right?"

"Not quite," Holt said. "Lester only confessed to murdering Kyla Gardener, not Pedro Catano."

"What?" Callaway was incredulous. "Did you push him on it?"

"Sure we did," Holt replied. "He said he has no idea what happened to Pedro. He was too busy with staging Kyla's murder to look like Gardener had done it."

Fisher added, "Lester wouldn't budge in his statement. And I have to admit, the evidence against him killing Pedro isn't strong enough. The timeline just doesn't add up."

"So, what are you saying?"

"The gun registered to Gardener was used to shoot and kill Pedro," Fisher said. "Until we solve that, the charges against Gardener stay."

Callaway shook his head, thinking. "If Lester didn't kill Pedro, and Paul didn't either, then who could it be?"

"Your guess is as good as ours," Fisher said.

Callaway's eyes widened. "Why didn't I see it before?" he said, more to himself than to Holt and Fisher.

"What?" Fisher asked. "You solved Pedro's murder too?"

"I think I just might have."

"Okay, so who is it?"

Callaway began walking away from them. "I need to do something first."

NINETY-FOUR

Callaway pulled up to the Gardener residence and parked in the driveway. Instead of going through the front, where the yellow police tape was still visible, he went around to the back. The gate had been unlocked after his last visit.

He saw the guesthouse up ahead. He turned left and headed straight for the sliding doors at the back of the house. He checked and found the doors were unlocked. He entered.

The house was dark. He went through the kitchen and entered the living room. He spotted a figure standing in the shadow by the windows.

"You're not Mike Grabonsky," the man said.

"You're right, Mr. Senator," Callaway said. "I'm not."

Senator Barron Lester came into the light. His face was hard, and his steely eyes were focused directly at him.

Callaway had gone to Mike's house, and when he explained what he wanted him to do, Mike was more than willing to help. Mike had called Senator Lester and told him he had seen a car driving away from the strip mall on the night Pedro Catano's body was found. Mike even provided a license plate number, which Callaway was able to get from an online search.

A witness who worked at a diner across from the strip mall had stated in the newspapers that he had seen a black sedan driving away from the scene. It was easy to mistake it for a black Audi. What most people did not know was that Senator Lester drove a black Lincoln Town Car.

Once Mike had Senator Lester's attention, he told him he wanted twenty-five thousand dollars, or else he would go to the media and the police.

Callaway knew Senator Lester would agree to meet. He had, after all, paid Gus Holden to stay away from his daughter and granddaughter. Senator Lester was known to buy his way out of a bad situation.

"You are the private investigator my son-in-law hired, aren't you?" Senator Lester said.

"I am."

"I'm not sure what game you're playing, but I'm leaving."

Callaway pulled out his cell phone and played a recording. It was the conversation between Mike and Senator Lester.

"I'm sure the voters of this fine state would be troubled by this."

"How much do *you* want?" Senator Lester asked through gritted teeth.

"I don't want money, sir," Callaway replied. "I just don't want an innocent man to go to jail for something he didn't do, that's all."

"I'm not sure what you're talking about."

"I know you killed Pedro. I just want to know why."

Senator Lester smiled. "You expect me to confess so that you can record it?"

"No, I expect you to tell the truth, sir."

"Why would I do that?"

"The guilt must be eating away at your soul."

Senator Lester stared at him.

"At the press conference with Pedro's father, you said you would cover his son's funeral expenses. That was your way of making amends for killing his son," Callaway said. "But you did kill him, sir."

Senator Lester's shoulders slumped. He grabbed a chair and sat down. He lowered his head. "It wasn't supposed to happen like that. I didn't want to hurt Pedro. I really didn't. Luiz has worked for me for decades. Pedro grew up right before my eyes. When he was young, I used to give Luiz a bonus for Christmas so that he could buy the boy a nice gift. I can't believe I did that to him."

Senator Lester choked up in tears.

"What happened, sir?" Callaway asked a minute later.

Senator Lester sighed. "Richard told me what had happened between him and Kyla. I was beyond furious. Sharon would never forgive Richard for what he had done. It would tear the family apart. I told Richard to do everything to convince Kyla to abort the baby. It was the only way for us to move on as a family. Richard was able to convince Kyla, but then she abruptly changed her mind.

"The night Kyla was found dead, Richard had called me. He said he and Kyla had gotten into an argument and he was taking her to the apartment to discuss the matter in private. I waited patiently for him to call me and tell me she had agreed. When I didn't hear from him, I decided to go to the apartment. I figured maybe I could help him reason with her. When I got there, the place was empty. I had no idea what had happened. I left when I saw Sharon enter the parking lot."

Callaway did not remember seeing Senator Lester that night.

"I knew why Sharon was there. Richard and I were aware of the men in her life. I should have gone straight home, but I decided to go to Sharon's house. I wanted to make sure everything was okay. By this time, Richard was not answering his phone. I was concerned. When I reached the house, I caught sight of Richard carrying something heavy from his car to the house. I had no idea what it was, but it didn't look normal. Why was Richard at Sharon's house at that time of night? And where was Kyla or Paul, for that matter?

"When I saw Richard leave, I went inside. I headed straight for Kyla's bedroom, and what I saw made me sick to my stomach. I couldn't believe what Richard had done. Horrified, I raced out of the house, and that's when I ran into Pedro by the front door."

Callaway remembered how Kyla had spoken to Pedro that day. He must have tried to get in touch with her, and when she did not respond, he came to check up on her.

"When I saw him, I knew how the situation looked," Senator Lester said. "There was a dead body inside, and I was seen running out of the house. I then pulled out my gun, and I ordered Pedro to get in the trunk of my Lincoln."

Callaway stopped him. "How did you manage to get Paul's gun? I know you had convinced him to purchase one."

Senator Lester nodded. "I supported a bill to make it illegal to purchase military-grade weapons by civilians, but the outcry was more than I expected. I was constantly getting death threats. I feared some gun-toting nutjob would show up at one of my rallies and do me harm. But I was in a difficult position. I couldn't go out and purchase a weapon, and I couldn't have armed bodyguards with me at all times. So, I came up with the idea to get Paul to buy a firearm. I had him show me the gun, and when he did, I knew where he kept it. The next time I was at Sharon's house, I stole it. I then paid someone to break into the box for me."

"It seems like you pay your way out of any trouble," Callaway said. "Then what did you do with Pedro?"

Senator Lester shook his head at what happened next. "I drove him to the back of the strip mall. I had campaigned there a few weeks earlier, so I knew the mall did not have adequate security. I shot Pedro in the trunk of the Lincoln and then I dumped his body in the dumpster. I hoped no one had seen me, but I guess I was wrong."

"You weren't. The call from Mike Grabonsky was only a ruse to get you here. No one caught you leaving the mall that night."

"Now, what happens?" Senator Lester asked.

"Now, you go to jail for the murder of Pedro Catano."

Senator Lester stood up and pulled out the Glock from his pocket. He aimed it at Callaway. "I don't think so. I doubt very much that you also recorded this conversation of ours."

"I didn't have to," Callaway replied. "There are two detectives sitting in a parked car outside the house. They know I am not carrying a weapon. This means you can't shoot me and argue self-defense. Plus, I bet that gun you are holding is registered to Paul, which means there's no way he could have shot Pedro, and there is definitely no way for you to pin my death on him when he is at his mother's house right now, surrounded by a press mob."

Senator Lester contemplated Callaway's words.

"There is no way out, sir. Drop the weapon and give yourself up."

A wan smile crossed Senator Lester's face. "There's always a way out," he said bitterly.

He aimed the gun squarely at Callaway's head.

Callaway stood frozen.

Senator Lester turned the gun around and placed it in his mouth.

Before Callaway could stop him, he pulled the trigger.

His skull exploded, and he dropped to the floor like a rag doll.

Senator Barron Lester was dead before he hit the floor.

NINETY-FIVE

Callaway was in his office when there was a knock at the door. He got up to check and found Paul standing by the door with a smile on his face. Paul looked better than the last time he had seen him at his mother's house. The past week or so had taken a toll on him, but now, a tremendous weight was off his shoulders, and his relief showed on his face. He no longer looked like a man who was contemplating suicide.

All charges had been dropped against him. Dr. Richard Lester would go on trial for the murder of Kyla Gardener, and Senator Lester had already paid the ultimate price for Pedro Catano's murder.

"What are you doing here?" Callaway asked.

"I thought I should come and thank you in person."

Callaway shrugged. "You thanked me enough on the phone already."

"I know, but it still wasn't enough," Paul said. "Without your help, I would probably be in prison or dead."

Callaway did not know how to reply.

Paul said, "Detective Holt dropped by to see me this morning."

Callaway was surprised. "He did?"

"He apologized for the way he pursued me in Kyla's death."

"And what was your reply?"

"I accepted it. I mean, it's not every day a lead investigator comes to your door to say he's sorry."

"If I were in your place, I would have squeezed every drop of the apology out of Holt."

Paul was silent. He then lowered his head. "I never imagined my life would turn out this way."

"I think it turned out for the better," Callaway said.

Paul looked at him. "How?"

"Your wife, your brother-in-law, and your father-in-law are out of the picture. The Lester family tried to destroy you, but they ended up destroying themselves. You are free to do whatever you want with your life. If you choose, you can travel on that boat of yours now. Plus, with your wife dead, you're Kyla's next of kin, which means all the money she was going to inherit will come to you."

"I would rather have my daughter than the money," Paul said. "Even if she wasn't my blood, I still loved her."

"You're a good man, Paul. I thought that the moment I met you."

Paul pulled out an envelope and held it out for Callaway.

"What is this?" Callaway asked.

"Your fee for the job you did to prove my innocence."

"I told you I was going to waive my fee."

"I know, but I'm still paying it."

Callaway peeked inside the envelope. There was a stack of hundred-dollar bills. "That's a lot of money, Paul."

"It's the money I would have paid Roth for the trial anyway. I figured you should have it instead."

"But…"

"Take it. I would have had to pay Roth three times what I'm giving you now, so it's a bargain, in my opinion."

"In that case, I'll keep it," Callaway said.

Paul held out his hand. "Thanks again for what you did for me. I will never forget it."

Callaway shook Paul's hand. "You take care of yourself, Paul."

NINETY-SIX

When Paul was gone, Callaway went inside and counted the money. It was indeed a lot. He suddenly began to feel lucky. Maybe he should go to the racetrack, the casino, or a bookie's. He could double or triple his money.

He got in his car and drove away. But instead of going to any of those places, he decided to go someplace far more important.

"You're back," Patti said, looking surprised.

"Is Nina home?"

"Yeah, why? Everything okay?"

"I got three tickets to the baseball game, and I was wondering if you and Nina would like to go with me."

"You mean as a family?"

"Yeah, I guess."

"I don't know if it's a good idea, Lee."

He held out an envelope for her.

"What's this?" she said.

"It's for you and Nina."

Her eyes went wide at the stack of bills. "That's a lot of money."

"If I kept it, I'd end up burning it. I know you can do a lot of good with it."

"Is this from the Paul Gardener case?" she asked.

"It is."

"I read about it in the newspapers. I'm proud of you, Lee. Even Nina was excited to tell her friends about it."

Nina appeared from behind her mother. "Daddy!" she said.

"Hey, baby." Callaway hugged her. He did not want to let go of her, ever. He said, "So, Mommy, what do you say?"

Patti turned to Nina. "Darling, do you think we should go to a baseball game with Daddy?"

Nina jumped up in the air. "Yes! I want to go to a baseball game."

Patti smiled. "Why don't you come in and sit down? It'll take us a couple of minutes to get ready."

Callaway smiled and went inside the house.

Visit the author's website:
www.finchambooks.com

Contact:
finchambooks@gmail.com

Join my Facebook page:
https://www.facebook.com/finchambooks/

LEE CALLAWAY SERIES

1) The Cold Daughter
2) The Gone Sister
3) The Falling Girl
4) The Invisible Wife
5) The Missing Mistress
6) The Broken Mother
7) The Guilty Spouse
8) The Unknown Woman
9) The Lost Twins
10) The Lonely Widow

THOMAS FINCHAM holds a graduate degree in Economics. His travels throughout the world have given him an appreciation for other cultures and beliefs. He has lived in Africa, Asia, and North America. An avid reader of mysteries and thrillers, he decided to give writing a try. Several novels later, he can honestly say he has found his calling. He is married and lives in a hundred-year-old house. He is the author of the Lee Callaway Series, the Echo Rose Series, the Martin Rhodes Series, and the Hyder Ali Series.